LAK

Loose lips sink ships, or they can confess a love that has never died through the heartbreaking years.

Shannyn Leah's **Lakeshore Love** *has just the right amount of swoon-worthy moments, passionate moments, moments that would try the patience of a saint and finally, the high tension moments just as the conflicts come to a dangerous head.*
~Dii, Tometender

This is my third McAdams Sisters book and I just connected with Jake and Sydney in such a positive manner. ~ **Vicki, The Page Turner**

Ms. Leah is a genius with coming up with characters that you will fall in love with. Lakeshore Love has steamy parts you will love, a loving and meddling family, as well as fear and uncertainty. ~ **Cathy, Rochelle's Reviews**

"Jake" just become my favorite character. (Sorry Marc.) Sentimental without being wimpy, considerate without being cocky, all-around good guy with so many troubles and issues of his own. ~ **Lori, Wee Bit O' Whiskey**

SHANNYN LEAH

LAKESHORE LOVE

Colleen

Lakeshore Love

Friends to Lovers
Syd & Jake

Shannyn Leah

SHANNYN LEAH

Cheers

Friends to lovers

Syd & Jake

Shanny
Leah

Lakeshore Love
The McAdams Sisters
Book Three, Sydney McAdams
By The Lake Series
Shannyn Leah

SHANNYN LEAH

Copyright © 2015 by Shannyn Leah
All rights reserved
No part of this book may be reproduced in any form or transmitted by any electronic or mechanical means including information, storage and retrieval systems, without the permission in writing from the author. The only exception is by a reviewer, who may quote short excerpts in a review.

This book is a work of fiction. Names, characters, places and incidents either are products of the author's imagination or are used fictitiously. Any resemblance to actual persons, living or dead, events or locales is entirely coincidental.

Shannyn Leah
www.ShannynLeah.com

LAKESHORE LOVE

For the person in my life, who always has the answer to all of my questions, my Papa!

SHANNYN LEAH

LAKESHORE LOVE

Chapter One

WATERPROOF MASCARA...CHECK. Tissue...check. Sunglasses...check. Camera...

Sydney McAdams paused from adding the contents from her mental list into her black satin clutch. She didn't have a camera. In fact she hadn't had a camera in years. Where was she going to get a camera last minute when they were practically walking out the door?

"Mom, are you ready?"

At the sound of her daughter's soft voice, Sydney turned from her current dilemma and found Haylee standing under the kitchen archway looking all grown-up and absolutely gorgeous in her knee-length, rhinestone-embellished, teal green formal dress.

Get the tissue. Get the tissue!

She could feel the tears working their way to her eyes as her heart swelled with pride. Her daughter was graduating middle school with honors. If that wasn't enough to be proud of Haylee was also giving a speech, which she'd been working on for weeks, at the ceremony. Haylee was book smart brilliance. What mother wouldn't be overwhelmingly proud, bringing on tears? Sydney's sensitive, emotional self was getting the best of her. She was prepared for the knowing looks from her family for her continual stream of tears during today's events too. The same kind of look Haylee was sending her right now.

"Seriously, Mom if you start crying now, what are you going to be like at the ceremony?"

A waterfall guaranteed. A thunderstorm like no other. The crashing waves hitting the shoreline during a severe rainstorm.

Sydney pulled a tissue back out of her purse and dabbed the edges of her eyes. *Waterproof mascara...what a wonderful invention.*

When she felt her voice could produce words without choking on her emotions, she told her daughter how beautiful she looked. In Sydney's eyes her daughter was beautiful, inside and out with a pure heart of innocence, sweetness and true kindness. Today that aura especially radiated around her, an exciting anticipation in her smile.

Haylee did a little spin and her long blonde curls, identical to Sydney's, soared around her shoulders as the dress soared around her legs.

"Thanks, Mom." Haylee looked Sydney over approvingly and flashed her pearly whites. "You look beautiful too, Mom. So..." She paused, tweaking her nose, seemingly looking for the right word. "...sophisticated." She smiled, pleased with the definition that clearly wasn't part of Sydney's down-to-earth wardrobe of lace, pearls, and soft pastels. Today Sydney wore a gorgeous open-lace, grey, knee-length dress that had stylish class instead of the bohemian dresses lining her closet. She barely registered her daughter's compliment as the tears threatened to return.

"I can't even take a picture of you because I don't have a camera." *Her dilemma.*

Haylee shook her head, but a smirk tugged her lips as

she crossed the room and grabbed Sydney's cell phone off the antique pine harvest table. She waved it in front of her mother. "Your cell phone has a camera."

Sydney frowned. *Of course it did.* She was losing her mind under the stress of her daughter growing up way too fast. While Sydney was the proudest a mother could ever be with the accomplishments of her daughter, she was scared at the same time of all the hills of life her daughter was about to journey up and down—good times and bad, easy and hard.

"You take pictures on your cell all the time," Haylee reminded her in a teasing tone making a clicking action with her hands and adding a know-it-all wink.

Sydney snatched her cell. "Don't be smart with me," she said, capturing the sides of her daughter's face in her hands, mostly just to have a moment to reflect at her beauty. Haylee was the spitting image of a younger Sydney with her porcelain skin and long blonde hair. Haylee's fell naturally straight while Sydney's naturally curled and waved like beach-hair after a day tanning under the sun, but they both possessed a quiet, polite demeanor.

"My baby is graduating." Sydney kissed her cheek. "I have a mother's right to be a bit frazzled." She kissed her other cheek.

Sydney could still remember Haylee's first day of kindergarten. Her daughter's tiny hands wouldn't part with hers as she hid behind Sydney's legs, shy and unsure, peeking around at the new scary surrounding. Now in the fall, Haylee would be walking through the high school doors with goals of becoming her own person, finding her own dreams and preparing for her own life. That was all terrifying enough on its own, but add boys to the equation, plus everything else that put a parent on the edge of sanity during those years, and Sydney's sanity was unfolding before her eyes.

Sydney was grateful her daughter was focused on her grades and determined to graduate with a veterinarian degree. She hoped Haylee would by-passed most of the high school drama...not getting pregnant at sixteen, like herself, would be a huge step in the right direction.

Haylee cringed with each kiss, trying to pull away. "Mom, my hair! My make-up!"

Reluctantly, Sydney dropped her hands and Haylee flew to the mirror behind her, examining her appearance to make sure no strands of hair were astray or makeup smudged.

Haylee had been pampered all morning by one of Sydney's older twin sisters, Peyton, a retired hair and make-up stylist. Peyton had transformed Haylee into a runway model, styling a half up/half down hairstyle, applying the perfect amount of make-up for her age, painting a French manicure on her fingers and a silver glitter pedicure on her toes. All the while Peyton was five months pregnant...with twins!

When Haylee was satisfied with her appearance, she posed as Sydney took a few pictures...with her cell phone.

"Grandma should be here any minute. Let's wait outside." Sydney looked down at the cell phone burning with embarrassment...*camera...check*...and dropped it in her purse.

As they stepped into the breezy summer sunshine, they found a limousine parked along the street in front of the house waiting for them. A tall, gorgeous man dressed in a designer charcoal-colored suit was leaning against the black limousine. His thick muscular arms were folded across his wide torso and his legs were crossed at the ankles showing off a pair of leather loafers. *Leather loafers! When did he get those? And that suit was rare on him, but stunning.*

He was a vision of a woman's deepest fantasy...definitely one of Sydney's fantasies...even more so the last few months.

A whirling heat of excitement spun a web throughout her body and her breath caught in her throat. She didn't even notice her tongue was running across her lips with a longing desire to make contact with *his* lips. *This* was the reaction her body was generating lately, whenever *he* was around...or simply visions of him popped into her head.

How was it even possible that Jake Stow could look even more handsome now then on any regular day She supposed taking away the denim and t-shirts that he was accustomed to wearing and replacing them with the suit tailored to fit his gym-ripped body to perfection was a start. Not to mention his regularly tousled hair was trimmed and he'd shaved away his daily five o'clock shadow...but she loved his daily five o'clock shadow. That smooth chin was certainly making her heart flutter though too.

He was gorgeous. It was wonderful torture.

"Don't be weird with Uncle Jake," Haylee said, slashing into the very sensual thoughts that were becoming a standard fixture in Sydney's mind.

Weird? Why would she be weird? Oh, you know why. Did staring at him like he was a bike she wanted to get on and ride count as weird? *Yup, that was weird...but wonderful.*

"I don't act weird with your uncle." Sydney casually waved at Jake to prove her point, wondering how and when Haylee had noticed they were acting strange with each other.

Probably the day after you woke up naked next to him.

When he waved back, it was accompanied with his melt-your-toes grin, that had never made her toes liquefy into her black heels like they were in that instant. She was sure that accounted for some of the *weirdness* her daughter was referring to.

Oh, great.

Did Jake see that she was acting weird around him? At least if he did he would know why. If he only knew the underlying thoughts that followed the weirdness...*wishing for the memory past the kisses, wishing her fingers could run along his magnificent torso, and worst of all, regretting running off so quickly the morning after!*

Yes, she regretted running away, but how could she tell him that revelation now after she'd made it clear a relationship between them was not on the table. Although if he laid her on the table, that would definitely persuade her to rethink that decision.

Sydney had to get out of this zone and back to reality where she had to work harder at *not* being weird.

Haylee sent her an adolescent look that meant *"Whatever"* before saying, "You *both* have been acting weird lately."

Oh, thank goodness! I'm not the only one. That was only half comforting.

She'd been so busy trying hard not to act weird around Jake that she hadn't even noticed that he was matching the weirdness. She almost laughed at the notion of them acting like young foolish teenagers wanting to make-out and trying their darndest not to show it. *Make-out? What was she back in high school?* Maybe, cause making out sounded heavenly.

"We have not," Sydney denied at the same time pondering the possibility that everyone saw the strain between them. It was quite possible if Haylee was getting the vibes, then Joan was and so was everyone else around them. How embarrassing.

Sydney wasn't exactly good at hiding her emotions which commonly played across her face during situations. *Shoot.* And she'd been trying so hard ever since that night...more like that morning. *Aw, that morning.* It was a sweet horror. Waking up with her cheek against his warm chest and feeling his strong arm wrapped around her shoulder like a shield of protection, while their legs were tangled in a web of nakedness. She remembered the silky warmth of his naked upper body against her naked chest and how she had been ready to jump up and mount that bike again for another ride of her life. Only her common sense had rushed in and slammed reality into her and she was forced not to indulge in spontaneous acts that would not only affect them, but also Joan and Haylee.

He was Haylee's uncle! There could be no quickies or one-night stands or another mistake like *that* night.

Would his naked torso ever leave her mind?

"Yes, you do." Having the final word, Haylee skipped down the porch stairs as Joan, her grandmother, emerged from the limo wearing a white pencil-line dress under a matching blazer, professionally tailored for her petite body. Her wavy blonde hair was styled, her nails groomed and her poise proper as always. She fit the profile of the well-off lady she was.

It was a pleasant shock to find she'd accompanied

Jake since the two didn't get along all that well. For a stepson and step-mother who had shared the ownership at the Cliff House, a bar and grill, for the last ten years, it was surprising they didn't get along better...or hadn't strangled each other by now.

I guess, Sydney thought, making her way down the porch stairs trying to calm the butterflies fluttering around in her stomach. She felt like she was going to talk to her teenage crush for the first time. *I can accomplish* not *being weird with Jake today if the two of* them *can manage to be civil to each other.*

When Sydney stopped in front of them, Jake's outdoorsy pine soap scent swept over her, reminding Sydney of his bedroom where the smell was deliciously overwhelming. She could see herself packing a bag and pitching a tent with this man in a wooded bush.

Joan's attention was solely on Haylee. She doted over how lovely her granddaughter looked in the dress they'd gone shopping for and chosen together. Joan touched Haylee's hair, commented on her nails, admired the diamond stud earrings, a graduation present from Joan, and couldn't hug Haylee enough.

Sydney and Haylee were lucky to have Joan in their lives. After Joan's son (Haylee's dad), Kyle died in the car crash that also took Joan's husband, the widow, the pregnant sixteen-year-old and the baby on-the-way had been united together under unfortunate circumstances and had been the beginning of a treasured life together.

Jake swooped in for his turn to hug Haylee and to congratulate her, but she was more ecstatic about the *awesome ride. Awesome ride.* More like overpriced and absolutely sweet of Jake who normally didn't flaunt his money. But, today, for his niece, Sydney understood why. Jake loved Haylee from the moment he was introduced to the little one, who shied away and tucked her head in Sydney's shoulder, but never took her eyes off Jake. Sydney would never forget that afternoon he walked through the Cliff House doors looking exhausted and like he'd aged ten years but hadn't even been gone for two. It had been a day of relief, a day of wonder, and a day to start new beginnings.

Joan and Haylee jumped inside the limousine for a better look leaving Jake and Sydney alone for the first time since that night.

Jake slid the black sunglasses from his face and his lake-blue eyes bore into her deepest awareness of him like a shovel digging out all the events of *that* night she could remember, even as she was trying so hard to forget them...just for this one afternoon to avoid any more weirdness.

Stand straight. Square your shoulders. Smile. Not too much. She could see how this was going to get weird really fast.

"Syd, you look amazing." His appreciative eyes matched his words as they traveled over her body, obviously checking out her lace-covered curves. She'd done the same to him, maybe even twice while he had been distracted by Haylee.

How were they not going to be weird when he was looking at her like *that* and she was looking at him like *that* and they had agreed not to mention what had opened their eyes to each other in the first place? *Oh Lord!*

"Thank you." She pretended not to notice the way his

eyes were lingering or to let the giddiness that was bubbling up in her chest show...at least she *hoped* it wasn't showing.

"And, you don't look so bad yourself." *Good, try to stick to casual. Oh my gosh Jake, you're drop dead gorgeous. Don't say that.* "You clean up nicely." Did he ever, like a stainless steel sink after a good baking soda and vinegar rinse: shiny, shimmery and giving you the desire to want to stare at the reflection.

Jake pulled the front of his suit and, with a low husky tone, said, "This old thing?" Haylee's slang word, *whatever* crossed her mind. That suit was brand new and he couldn't fool her. She knew he'd purchased it just for this occasion.

Sydney grabbed the purple tie in a teasing manner, regretting it the second the back of her hand felt the heat of his body through the shirt.

Before that night if she had touched his tie like this it wouldn't have set off fireworks in her body. They were close friends and the joking, teasing, and touching was always platonic and never sexual. Until they'd actually ended up sexual and the embarrassment had kept her avoiding Jake now for four months. Four long, lonely months without her best friend. Staring into his familiar, comforting eyes she discovered she missed him more than she knew, like wanting the sun to peek through the clouds on a long winter day but not realizing how fantastic it really was until the clouds parted and the sun graced your face. She wanted to share all the exciting stories from the soap shop with him and regretted not finding him sooner to talk.

Sydney decided today was the day she was going to force herself to quit hiding from him and make an effort to resume their platonic relationship so she could see him on a regular basis again. They had slept together and it was a mistake...wasn't it? What difference did it make now? It was in the past and many aspects of her life were results of the past, so she wasn't adding their relationship to that pile.

Taking a deep breath she felt confident she could tone down her thoughts and be his friend again. She forced past the exciting flutter from their contact, no doubt plastered all over her face, to continue with her wit.

"You randomly have purple ties hanging in your closet?" That was good, a joke, teasing...keep it up. Platonic, not sexual. Platonic, platonic, platonic!

Jake bent down closer to her and she felt their casual interaction being engulfed by sexual tension.

Oh man, this closeness sent her thoughts right back to his king-size bed!

"You'd be surprised what you can find in my closet." His low husky tone was a staple the corresponded with the mysterious persona he retained and it swooped into her stomach and slammed every inch of her body into hotness overload.

Double oh man!

She forced a friendly chuckle, accepting his firm hand and climbed into the limo. She collapsed on the leather wrap-around seat like it was forty plus degrees out there. She waved her purse across her warmed face creating a breeze and doing the same with the edge of her skirt to generate a cool breeze for the throbbing below.

She was grateful when Haylee and Joan were too busy in their own limo world to notice how flustered she was.

Darn it. How was she going to focus on her new plan when she found herself wondering exactly what surprises she would find in that mans closet?

Chapter Two

YOU'D BE SURPRISED what you can find in my closet? You'd be surprised what you can find in my closet! What did that even mean?

Jake Stow had the urge to slam his fists against the top of the limousine after allowing such a lewd remark to pass by his lips. Especially with the shy, reserved woman he respected enough to know would not enjoy such suggestive risqué play of words...or would she? He couldn't say he knew for certain she wouldn't enjoy the playful and intimate banter. He was certain it wasn't her type of teasing, but then again, he wasn't her type either and he could remember her really enjoying him.

Instead he opted for pausing at the door and resting his arms on the rim. His hands were still hot from her touch. He'd noticed when he took her small, smooth, delicate hand in his that the sun had given her light skin a little color, but not nearly as dark as his own. Sydney burnt under the sun like a roasted marshmallow over a fire and she slathered on the sun protection all year round. He also noted his hands didn't want to let go of hers, giving him the distinct knowledge that he was in dire need of a moment to himself in order to regroup his thoughts.

The gathering clouds coming from above the lake were invading the clear sky. There was a storm on its way and he wasn't talking about the one brewing in his pants: hot, wild and out of control for the blonde beauty, trying to be cool yet doing such a poor job he almost laughed. He didn't dare in fear of embarrassing her even further. Jake found it adorable how easily embarrassed Sydney became and the way color blushed her skin. How her face framed every emotion and she would sometimes lose her words behind those luscious lips.

Why hadn't lightening just shot from the sky and struck him down before he'd said, *You'd be surprised what you can find in my closet.*

He groaned.

It would seem as though his tongue had missed the memo regarding subtly. Why had he felt the time was right to bring it to Sydney's attention that he was interested in perusing more with her than just the solid friendship already between them?

He wasn't looking for friends with benefits either. Hell no, he would never look at Sydney like that...no man should. Sydney was a woman worth giving it your all or getting the hell out of her life altogether.

That thought terrified him, he couldn't imagine a life without Sydney in it, but he could sure envision a future with this woman. Smiling, laughing, touching, and being together...always. Not like the last four months, since *that* night, and she'd been avoiding him like he was a contagious disease.

After confessing her love one night, then running away the next morning, she'd left him stumped...did she love him or not? Did she want to spend the rest of her life with him or not? Had the extreme amounts of alcohol she'd consumed been responsible for everything she confessed or had they been the tools she needed to say the true words she meant?

He needed to know!

From the way she'd checked him out on her walk to the limousine in her ever-so-indirectly kind of way, he assumed that her drunken mouth had spout off the truth buried deep down...he hoped anyway.

When he finished scolding himself with a warning and reissuing the original plan...tastefully and slow, Jake climbed into the limousine beside Sydney.

She smiled at him and pulled the lace edge of her dress over her knees as far as it would stretch. That only made his thoughts turn to her legs...and he loved her legs. Porcelain pillars of smoothness with a tiny dip behind each knee and a long scar along her outer thigh that was only visible when she wore one of her dresses that swayed, clung, dipped and stretched just right, especially when she used to reach for beer glasses above the bar. *Ah, the good old days.*

"Uncle Jake have you seen what this thing does!" Haylee called from the far end of the limo where she and Joan were seated.

Jake hadn't looked into the extras when he'd rented the limousine. He simply requested top-of-the-line for up to fifteen people and the driver had picked him up in this stretch Expedition SUV. He would have been more interested in the extras if the anticipation of seeing Sydney hadn't occupied his every thought. He swore if they didn't talk soon he would end up accidently ordering another four cases of flowery scented Gewürztraminer wine for the restaurant instead of the chardonnay the tourists preferred.

When Jake shook his head, Haylee proceeded to demonstrate the lights above them before pouring each of them a drink, non-alcoholic, which he'd requested because they were picking up Sydney's dad who was a recovering alcoholic. He couldn't even give away the excess gewürztraminer wine.

"Jake we didn't need anything this elaborate," Sydney said, her voice rising and lowering with Haylee's turn of the volume button. "We didn't need a limo at all."

"My niece is graduating...with honors," he announced loudly enough that Haylee would hear him and he winked at the young version of Sydney. Haylee possessed the brains of everyone in the limo combined. "This is a huge deal." He lowered his voice to Sydney. "Besides we're picking everybody up."

"Everybody?" she asked surprised.

"Your family. We can't let them to show up in their vehicles when we all arrive in style." He slid his arm across the back of the seat, and crossed one leg.

Sydney didn't hide her surprise or delight at including all her family. "Way too much."

"Can I take this to the dance?" Haylee asked.

As Jake said, "Yes," Sydney said, "No."

Haylee smirked at the two to see who was going to bow down first. It was usually Jake, but he had the feeling he could persuade Sydney just this one time and hopefully he could get some alone time with Sydney out of the deal.

"It's rented for the whole night," he said.

"Jake!" Sydney cried. "It's too much." Her reaction didn't surprise him given that Sydney wasn't a materialistic woman. That was one of the things that he found attractive about her...one of the many, many things. Right now, he was finding the way the hollow lace was teasing the flesh along her neckline and playing peek-a-boo, dipping low before the silk lining hid the mounds that rose with each inhaled breath, *very* attractive.

He saw Sydney's hands searching the back seat for a buckle, which distracted his mind from going any further into what was under her dress. There were no seat belts and once she realized it, a tiny frown found her neutral painted lips. Ever since the accident, Sydney had a fear about vehicles. He almost regretted renting the limo as he watched her eyes dart around, with panic slowly rising, as they pulled away from the curb and onto the road.

"I hired a photographer for family photos at the beach after the ceremony, since everyone will be dressed up," Joan said, establishing a motive for the transportation. "Then back to the Cliff House for supper. Renting the limousine was the logical thing to do, Sydney. We needed transportation for all of us."

Joan made up for Sydney's lack of material items, being materialistic in all sense of the word. Her daily attire, weekend visits to the spa and professionally decorated mansion on the cliff illustrated it. However, she wasn't a lazy woman and five days a week she showed up for the lunch crowd at the Cliff House and managed into the late afternoon.

Jake suspected she did so to feel closer to his dad. Jake always felt closer to his dad when he was working in his father's last investment. Spending a life of buying, selling and renting out properties across the country, the Cliff House had been Henry Stow's final investment. After a long and highly demanding career, he'd been ready to settle down, retire and spend the rest of his life at the Cliff House with his family. Henry died just as his dream had begun and Jake hadn't been there.

Guilt devoured Jake's insides instantly. Remorse and blame were always on the edge of his emotional avalanche whenever it came to his dad's death. His attempts to ignore it usually went unnoticed, ready to consume his whole body at the thought of his father's death.

"It only makes sense that Haylee take it to the dance with a guaranteed safe drive home," Joan continued, brushing her hair from her shoulders and sending Haylee an encouraging smile.

While Jake was dragged into his past, so was Sydney. He watched her face shift, obviously thinking about the accident she didn't talk about. Her worry was creating pull lines above her gorgeous blue eyes. Eyes that were now glazing over and luscious lips that were drawn in a thin tight line.

"Is that yes...?" Haylee asked, her eyes darting between him and her mother. Haylee was oblivious to the flicker of fear that Jake saw so clearly. "Mom?"

"It would seem like Jake's got this all figured out." Sydney rushed the words out with a forced smile.

"Yes!" Haylee's fists went into the air excited. "I'm texting all my friends. They will so want to come with me and arrive at the dance in a limo." Haylee flopped back in the seat, crossing her legs while her fingers moved like lightning as she texted away on the tiny device.

Joan also had her cell phone pulled out occupy her time. Jake didn't see the need to have a cell phone at every moment of every day with access to friends, family and people you don't really like twenty-four seven. Although his cell phone currently resided in his pocket it was in case of emergencies at the Cliff House. He wasn't about to pull it out while they were enjoying the luxury of travelling together in an extravagant limousine.

Jake slid closer to Sydney until their bodies almost touched. He ignored the memory of how their flesh felt pressed together and, instead, took her hand in his, giving it a gentle squeeze. He was still upset about the frown lines on her smooth face.

"We aren't leaving town," he told her reassuringly. "The driver is not going to speed. He will not run stop signs, and it's not snowing or icy outside." He tugged at her to sit back and unwind beside him.

These were all factors in the accident that Jake had only heard about after he had returned home. Jake had been coming home to tell his dad he'd been right about his mother only to find a grave instead of the man. Henry had been driving Kyle and Sydney out of town, speeding on an icy road in the middle of a winter storm, when they ran a stop sign, crashing into another car.

"Relax."

Sydney sent him a frown. "Is it that obvious?"

"Not to those two." He nodded in the direction of Joan and Haylee, lost in their own world of online social media. They were deaf and blind to Sydney and Jake, who were still holding hands. He liked the feel of his hand cupped around hers and relished even more the gentle squeeze she gave back.

Sydney shifted toward him so her knee rested across his leg and she could face him. "This was really sweet of you. I still believe it's too much, but..." She glanced over her shoulder at her daughter. "...Haylee will never forget it. Thank you."

He liked that...big gestures...never forget.

"My pleasure." He let go of her hand. He didn't want to but the lines across her face lifted and he knew it was time before the other two noticed. "So, how's the store doing?"

Her smile widened at the mention of the Old Town & Soap Co., the store she and her sisters had opened the first day of March. It was also the day she had stopped working at the Cliff House full time. The day he really began to miss her.

"Wonderful. We are so busy. We already have a steady clientele of locals and the tourists are adding to our busy days and it's only the end of May. July and August are going to be crazy. But wonderful."

"That's good."

Sydney leaned her head on the back seat, right against his arm, looking directly at him. "But I miss the Cliff House. I miss the staff and the regulars."

Sydney had worked there since she was in her teens, so it made sense that she missed everyone.

"There is a position for you anytime you want," he offered, but knew how important her business was.

She smiled. "I miss you." This woman had no idea how much he missed her.

"You miss free food."

Her eyes flew wide open at his teasing. "I do miss the delicious, and free, food your cooks whipped up for us for lunch. But, I am right beside Mrs. Calvert's and, no lie, her maple sugar muffins are the best home-baked breakfast a girl can ask for." She closed her eyes and took a deep breath as though she was smelling one of those muffins right in the limo with them. "Every single morning I sneak over there and dip into one of those warm, melt-in-your-mouth, pieces of heaven."

"Speaking of food and heaven, don't forget to pick up a few bags of those roasted peanuts from Hastings Port for me."

Every first long weekend of the summer, Sydney, Haylee and Joan took Joan's sixty-six foot princess yacht to Hastings Port. They would be leaving the next morning bright and early, before the sun rose.

"Mentally noted," she promised.

"Possibly more than one bag this time?"

"I will consider it, since you went all out and rented Haylee a limo."

He laughed. "That's awfully considerate of you."

When they reached Kent's house, the McAdams' family were waiting on the front lawn in their best apparel, waiting for the limousine they'd all known was arriving. Jake had only wanted to surprise Sydney and Haylee and he'd enjoyed the looks on their faces when they saw him waiting out front. *Mission accomplished.* He had really enjoyed when Sydney's tongue ran across her lips. It made him want to dip into her mouth and taste *that* heaven.

When the limousine pulled to the curb, Joan and Haylee managed out the door first and Jake helped Sydney out before himself. Only for the sole purpose of being a gentleman and having nothing to do with watching her dress rise up her derriere as she climbed out of the limo. Really, it was because he was a gentleman.

Chapter Three

SYDNEY'S FAMILY WERE obviously all aware of Jake's plan. They hooted and hollered and took turns congratulating Haylee with hugs, kisses, flowers and cards.

Her dad, Kent, and his new wife, Elaine, were at the end of the lineup and stole their granddaughter from the rest of the group for some private time. Kent wasn't used to sharing Haylee with so many family members now that Sydney's older twin sisters, Kate and Peyton, had moved back home.

Even Elaine was new to the family and Sydney was glad that her dad had found such an amazing person to live with the rest of his life. She was the same Elaine Patterson who also happened to be Peyton's mother-in-law. It had been an interesting February. Elaine had the biggest heart and bonded with everyone, including Haylee, without much effort. Her presence was natural, like she'd always been a part of their lives.

Sydney walked to her sisters. Kate and Peyton were tall brunettes, while the youngest Abby, had dyed her dark locks a dirty blonde. All three contained a sass and bluntness about them and never shied away from anyone or any situation. Very opposite of Sydney.

Even the way they stood now in their gorgeous

dresses depicted an attitude that Sydney didn't posses and usually ended with her mouth hitting the floor in shock. Although she shouldn't be shocked, since they had always been that way.

"It's the mother of the graduate," Kate said, reaching for a hug. Kate was stunning, as always, in a black skirt/blazer combo that fit her curvy frame to a t. Sydney liked the way Kate gathered her hair to the side in a loose braid-wrapped, low bun grazing her neck. She made a note to try that in the future.

"I don't think that's actually a title," Sydney said, relishing in the sound of it anyway.

"Still, it's worth acknowledging, especially when your daughter is top of her class," Marc Caliendo, Kate's husband, and owner of the Caliendo Resort at the edge of town, pointed out. Marc had attended private school and although he had been around since their mother died when Sydney was fifteen, he was raised proper with expectations and appreciated high grades. The tailored suit he wore now was part of his regular attire, unlike Jake, who was sporting it just for this special occasion. Suit, jeans, t-shirt, birthday suit...Sydney appreciated Jake in anything he wore. Although if he had pulled that suit out of his closet...what else was in there?

At the thought of his deep, dark, secretive closet, Sydney's eyes immediately found Jake who had now made his way over to observe Rosemary, Kate and Marc's five-year-old daughter, who was an adorable bundle of sweetness. In her lovely pink lace dress she was managing to play a round of ball hockey with Colt, who was a retired hockey-pro.

Rosemary paused mid-swing, caught sight of Sydney and waved. "Hi Aunt Sydney!"

Sydney smiled and waved back. "Hello Rosemary. You look beautiful in your dress."

Rosemary smiled wider. "Thank you." Then a mischievous grin, reminding Sydney of the very one Kate had adorned most of their childhood and teenage years, crossed her little face. "Wanna see me shoot a goal? I'm real good. Colt's been giving me lessons." Rosemary, the next pro-hockey star.

"Yes, I sure do sweetie!"

The fire in her eyes doubled as she concentrated on hitting the ball between the two trees Colt was using as a net. She lifted the stick and with a quick swing, the ball did exactly as she planned.

Sydney clapped. "Way to go Rosemary!"

"Yay!"

Colt also cheered, running across the yard and swooped the girl into his arms, flying her in circles in the sky.

"Colt, don't ruin her hair!" Peyton called, shaking her head. Peyton was chic, modern and her baby-bump pressed out against her fitted black sleeveless dress. "I'm going to skin him," she said, but the look of love crossing her face contradicted her words.

"Wait until you have your own," Abby said slowly as she reached for Peyton's stomach and rubbed in a circular motion. Peyton wasn't a fan of people touching her stomach, she put up with it, but didn't like it. If you weren't part of the family, look out cause more than likely she was going to swing at you.

Peyton swatted her hand away and frowned at Abby.

She put up with family...sometimes. "Why do you always rub my belly like that?" she demanded, smoothing out her dress then hugging the bottom of her belly and sending Abby a deep frown.

Abby laughed, enjoying the rise she often got out of her pregnant, and sometimes cranky, sister. Her own floor-length black, studded dress stopped just above her heeled boots, as she straightened. "Like what?" Abby asked innocently.

Peyton's glare didn't waver. "Like it's some big surprise that there are babies in there. We all know there are babies in my stomach. We can all see the weight I've gained." Peyton circled her hand around her stomach.

"Two of them," Abby added. She grinned at everyone else. "Sydney was not this big with Haylee at five months." There was Abby's little inappropriate teasing that usually got her into trouble.

Sydney grinned against her better judgement not wanting to encourage their youngest sibling and waited for Peyton's retort. Peyton and Abby bantered more than any of them.

"Sydney had one baby." Peyton held one finger up to make the point clear. "In her stomach, Abby. I have two." Another finger bounced up. "That's double the space."

"Oh yikes," Abby said. "If you're stomach doubles Sydney's at nine months you're not going to be moving."

Peyton's mouth dropped open.

"That's my cue to leave," Marc said, kissing the side of Kate's grinning face before joining the hockey crowd.

"Stop it." Kate swatted at Abby. "Leave her alone."

"I think we should make Abby drive herself," Peyton

said.

"Hey! That's not fair," she pouted. "I'm the only sister who doesn't have a rich man doting on her."

"You have Riley," Peyton said.

Abby rolled her eyes. "He's not rich, and he's not mine."

"Technically, Sydney doesn't *have* Jake either," Peyton said and Sydney felt the same old conversation coming on. It didn't matter how many times Peyton went down this road, nothing changed between her and Jake. She wasn't sure why Peyton continued to pester. *Turn your pestering back to Abby, she deserves it.*

"I mean she has him wrapped around her little finger, but she doesn't *have* him. Like in her bed or his bed or wherever."

His bed. What a nice thought. There was that pine smell again, tangled in the sheets where she woke up, snuggled around and sent her tingling through her body. She felt a smile coming on and her eyes wanting to steal another look at Jake.

Then Haylee's word popped into her head: weird. Weird was not the accurate word for what was conspiring between her and Jake. Sydney would replace the word "weird" with "lust". Plain old basic yearning...desire...lust. But, if Haylee mentioned her observation in front of her sisters, she would only be throwing timber onto the fire. She had to keep the Jake topic on the down low as she saw Haylee make her way over to the group.

"Why haven't you two hooked up yet? I think I missed something while I was away," Peyton said. "What happened?" she asked Sydney, suddenly serious. "What went wrong to deter the two of you from getting involved? Is he not good in the sack?" Peyton gasped. "Are you not good in the sack? Because let's face it, look at him." Sydney retrained herself while her sisters found Jake. "Whoa! Look at him!" Peyton said.

Sydney couldn't help it, she followed her sisters' eyes. Jake was so handsome. He was ruggedly handsome in all sense of the word, but with an edge of danger, even while wearing a designer suit and loafers. The way his tanned skin moved with his chiseled features, even today while he was missing his peppered stubble...he was the guy whose permanent five-o-clock shadow suited him to perfection...his sinister looks were too breathtaking for a woman not to notice...or want to touch...kiss...*No, no touching. No kissing. No anything Jake Stow.*

His bottomless mysterious eyes caused women to look at him and see a rough-around-the-edges broken man they wanted to fix. Jake Stow needed fixing too. Oh, how this mystifying man held secrets he didn't dare to share. But, again, Sydney couldn't hold that against him when she had secrets of her own tucked away.

"I miss the leather jacket," Abby said.

Everyone laughed. Abby had it bad for tattooed, leather jacket-wearing men.

Sydney was beginning to wonder if deep down she had the same dark side for this one particular tattooed, leather jacket-wearing man. From the very first time she laid eyes on him back in high school when he walked his new city-boy screw-you attitude down the halls, standing tall behind that leather jacket, Sydney had been hook, line and sinker for the dramatic mysterious man. Jake had then cut the line and let the reserved girl sink, until he realized she floated and planned on bobbing in and out of his life forever. They'd bonded a strange friendship of an angry boy and shy girl that had lasted all these years. A friendship...until recently. Sydney let his good looks and soft spot for her create a mass of feelings that were so far from a friendship that it was like summer versus winter.

As they continued to admire Jake's new attire Haylee joined them. *Please, don't say anything Haylee. Please!*

"Look how handsome your Uncle Jake is," Peyton said to Haylee.

Sydney held her breath.

No more Jake talk. Finished, done, the end and move along to a different topic. Any other topic. Go back to Peyton's belly!

Haylee rolled her eyes. "Are you going to get all weird with him too?"

Sydney could have crawled into a hole.

"Weird?" Peyton questioned, sending Sydney a knowing look. You can take that look back Peyton, because I'm not giving you an inch.

"It's nothing," Sydney said, hoping to put an end to this conversation. She didn't want Haylee to start naming dates because Peyton and Colt had attended the family day dance where Sydney's drunken night began and had ended naked in Jake's bed. *Jake's bed.* She hadn't told her sisters and didn't plan on it either.

Haylee continued anyway and Sydney wondered how she was not catching the *no more* looks she was sending her. But Peyton caught them and was all smiles. She was getting a kick out of the whole thing.

"Uncle Jake and Mom have been acting all weird around each other. Haven't any of you noticed?"

It was clear by the surprised looks her sisters passed around that they hadn't noticed. *Bravo, Sydney, keep up the good work.* She was actually rather proud of herself, because Jake's naked torso was in her head every day.

"We haven't been acting weird," Sydney said, trying her best to be casual and dismiss her daughter's observations even if she knew better.

Haylee's smarts were Sydney's disadvantage because her sisters all respected Haylee and were not so quick to brush off the *weird* comments.

Haylee turned to her. "You have."

Sydney turned to her sisters. "We haven't."

Haylee turned to her aunts. "They have," she said, before slipping away, again with the last word. What was that all about?

The sister circle enclosed tighter around Sydney with curious eyes and folded arms. Sydney couldn't do this with them right now, not when she was trying her hardest to pretend nothing happened.

"Well, well, well," Peyton said first, with her wicked little smile returning.

Sydney's insides cringed.

It was no surprise Peyton spoke up first. She loved to voice her opinion about Jake and Sydney's relationship, whether wanted or not...usually not wanted.

"What any other reason would you have for acting weird with Jake besides realizing you love him?"

Making out on his couch then making love in his big king-size bed.

Wait a minute, back up the limo...*love him?* What was her sister talking about? They had only had sex and she lacked the pleasure of remembering the details.

Suddenly a thought flashed in her mind...had they been in his closet? Had there been something special she didn't know about...something in there that they had...used?

Sydney felt light-headed.

Had his little comment about his closet been referring to something that happened between them that night and she didn't catch it because she couldn't remember what happened? Did Jake remember? Of course he did, he could actually hold his alcohol. Sydney on the other now so much.

Peyton gasped. "You had sex with him." She elbowed Kate and whispered to her. "She had sex with him."

Sydney grabbed Peyton's other arm. "Shush." She glanced over Peyton's head, watching her family begin to load into the limousine and Jake helping them inside. Perfect gentleman.

They were all oblivious to the conversation at hand. *Thank the stars!*

"Where do come up with this stuff? I'm not like you Peyton; I don't randomly have sex with men in the shower!"

Peyton's eyes flared at her sister's reaction. "Listen to the defense wall build up." She almost sounded proud.

"It's not a defense wall." It was totally a defense wall. It was the Great Wall of China. "It's the plain truth." Jake wasn't some random guy, so that part was definitely the truth.

"That random man turned out to be the best thing I didn't know I was looking for." Peyton's loving eyes fell to Colt and Sydney felt a sting of jealousy. She had a wonderful relationship with Jake...when it wasn't weird...and yet, if she let the truth surface, she longed for more between them. She always had.

"That wasn't how you announced your shower rendezvous over dinner," Abby reminded Peyton.

The sisters shared a round of amused smiles remembering Peyton and Colt's first fight, Sydney was glad her baby sister had shifted the topic away from her and Jake. Peyton and Colt's announcement had been a family affair, done right around the dinner table. They simply had let the cat out of the bag that they'd had sex in the shower and neither was happy about it...but they had been only fooling themselves.

Abby continued, "After the two of you had a forever make-out session that Elaine walked in on while you were naked in his childhood bed..."

Peyton held her hand up. "We...I was not naked Abby and we have gone over this and I wasn't in his bed..." A mischievous look took over Peyton's face. "...but the make-out session was hot. That man can lift me up against a wall in one swift motion and his other hands know exactly where to go and what to do and..."

"Whoa!" The sisters all held their hands up. "Way too much detail!"

Peyton laughed, enjoying them squirm.

Sydney would never be able to talk about her personal life so openly like Peyton or any of her sisters. She was having a difficult time just dealing with it inside her head.

"Like I was saying, we are supposed to be having a conversation about Sydney and Jake," Peyton said.

"We really aren't," Sydney said. "There is nothing to

talk about."

They grinned at her like they knew something she didn't. Defending herself would be a waste of a breath since they had their minds already made up. Either that she'd had sex with Jake or she loved Jake and she didn't care for any of them to clarify.

"Quit it you three. You're going to make it weird," Sydney said, although she was doing a bang-up job all on her own.

"Because we know?" Peyton asked.

"No. Because you're jumping to conclusions." There was no way she was telling them that Peyton was smack on.

"We are waiting on you four!" Jake called out.

"He's waiting on you," Peyton said, pinching Sydney's arm on her way past. If Peyton wasn't pregnant Sydney might have very well slapped her arm.

"I've been around you and Jake forever. Way longer than these two," Abby said, stopping on her way past. "And if you guys are shacking up..." she shrugged, "Well, it's not surprising and nothing you should be ashamed about Sydney or feel the need to hide from us." She smiled...sincerely. "It is about time you guys hooked up. You both have always had eyes for each other for as long as I can remember. It's sweet you two finally realized it." Abby hugged Sydney before leaving her stunned at her youngest wild sister's serious and gentle, comforting words.

"*That* was weird." Kate looped her arm around Sydney's on their way to the vehicle.

Sydney agreed. "Where did that even come from?"

Kate shrugged. "I don't know."

They laughed.

Chapter Four

THREE TABLES WERE pushed together to accommodate the McAdams family at the Cliff House for supper. Jake naturally found his seat beside Sydney and Abby naturally found hers across from them, smack dab in the center of the table so she could dip into everyone's conversation.

Abby was sending Jake weird looks that he'd noticed all the sisters seemed to have acquired this afternoon. Looks he wasn't understanding.

During the photo shoot at the beach he'd caught them all staring at him at least half a dozen times, watching him, then smiling when busted. In the limo, he'd seen them exchange looks before landing on him. It was all a little odd. He wasn't sure what was going on, but he was starting to wonder if Sydney had told them about the Family Day after party at his house.

The new favorite topic around the table was about the Old Town & Soap Co. He liked hearing about the success of the shop. He hadn't heard all that much with Sydney ignoring him since they opened. However at the current moment, he was relieved that it was distracting the McAdams sisters from not staring at him. He was beginning to get a complex.

After everyone ordered, which was entertaining all in itself, Haylee brought up the annual boat trip to Hastings

Port.

"It's only for the weekend," Haylee said. "Because of the soap shop, but we will still get all the festivities, so that will be fun."

"Sydney, you can take more time off," Kate said before sipping her glass of water. "The three of us can work around the days you're gone."

Sydney shook her head. "Four days are plenty." She sent Haylee her motherly, no more, complaining look.

"I said it was still going to be fun," Haylee argued.

Joan waved her hand in the air. "Oh, three nights, four days will be perfect. There are lots we can do, Kate. As a business owner, I understand the importance of supporting your business, especially when you've just launched. Now is your prime important time."

Jake couldn't help remember the memory of a time when Joan had been the younger live-in nanny watching over him and his sister, Adalyn. That was before she became his father's mistress and drove his mother away, putting a wedge between all his family members.

Let it go, Jake. That was a long time ago.

Kate smiled at Joan. "Thank you. It has been an amazing experience opening the shop." They went right back into shop-talk, until Abby became bored with that topic.

"I am taking a week off for a summer vacation," Abby announced. "I don't know what I am doing or where I am going, but damn it is going to be the laziest week I've had in months!"

There was a round of chuckles then Peyton sent him another smirk and he was convinced Sydney spilled their evening adventure.

LAKESHORE LOVE

He leaned over to her and whispered, "Your sisters have seen looking at me strange all afternoon."

She turned slightly so she could see his eyes. "They think you're very handsome in your new suit. I think it's because you shaved." Sydney's fingers touched his chin claiming warmth around them. The softness of her touch in that very spot made him decide he was going to shave his chin for the rest of his life.

"Except Abby, but don't take offense, she is missing the flashy tattoos and leather jacket."

He was missing his leather jacket which was hanging up in his office.

"No, I saw those looks at your dad's house. These looks are different." *Come on, Sydney spill the beans woman...did you tell your sisters about that night?*

Sydney laughed under her breath.

What was so funny? She had! "What did I miss?"

She shook her head.

"Syd?"

"Okay." She sent him a look to lower his tone. "Haylee may have mentioned that you and I..." *Oh Lord, she told Haylee!* "...act a little weird around one another lately."

They needed to correct that statement, all of them. He knew how to maintain a straight face and proper composure. Sydney on the other hand, wouldn't be able to hide her true feelings if her life depended on it and therefore she was the one acting weird.

Remembering the reason behind her weirdness he almost smiled, quite possibly even did smile, envisioning her naked little self running around his room searching and scooping up her clothes with his sheet wrapped around her like a cape. It was like he'd had his own personal superhero that morning.

"That look right there," Sydney said. "That's the one that's getting us into trouble."

Oh crap. So he wasn't as good at hiding his thoughts as he assumed he was. *Well done Stow.* He didn't even dare look around the table to see who caught that look.

"That's the one they're looking for," she teased.

"I think I'm going to use the little girl's room." Abby said standing. "Anyone else need to go?"

Kate stood. "I think I will come with you."

Sydney stood. "Me too."

Jake grinned and before Peyton even said anything he knew what was going on.

Peyton rolled her eyes. "I don't see a point for me to go," she grumbled.

"I think I have to go," Colt said standing.

Peyton gasped and pulled at his arm. "Sit down."

He claimed his arm. "I have to release my bladder Woman!"

"Bull." Peyton picked up her water and sipped on the straw, glaring at her husband, as he took off from the table.

The four, apparently needing to have a bathroom break together, quickly made their way down the hall. Their lack of subtlety was unbelievable. Instead of going in the direction of the bathroom, they turned the other direction toward the kitchen.

Kent chuckled at Peyton. Sitting next to her, he rubbed her arm. "Oh quit you're pouting. In four months you can go right back to sneaking away from me to rot your gut."

"Not if I'm breast feeding." Then she gasped realizing

what her dad had said. "You know?"

Elaine and Kent laughed and Jake grinned. Did she really think they were that good at hiding it?

"I'm not a blind fool and my smell is one hundred percent in working condition." He leaned toward his daughter as if he had a secret. "I can smell the alcohol every time you return."

Peyton sent him a remorseful look. "Oh, Dad I'm sorry."

He chuckled again, leaning back. "Don't apologize. You kids handle your liquor better than I ever have. That is nothing to apologize about."

"Except we flaunt it. I just feel so terrible."

"You're not flaunting it, darlin'. Besides..." He turned to Elaine. "...I have this wonderful woman to keep me on track."

Elaine sent him a loving smile followed by a kiss.

Envy stirred inside of Jake as he watched the happy couple. His wonderful woman was sneaking away to share a bottle of wine with her siblings and he had the sudden desire to be able to kiss her whenever he felt, hold her hand, wrap his arm around his waist.

He wanted Sydney McAdams.

Joan's chair scraped the floor. "Excuse me, I have to use the powder room, and I actually do," she confirmed, but Jake knew better.

He watched her turn left toward the kitchen just as he had suspected and he shook his head unable to hide the smirk. They better be sneaking that gewürztraminer if they weren't paying for it.

***

"THERE WAS NO code given that you sneaky kids were sneaking back to sneak wine," Joan scolded, catching them all red-handed passing around a bottle of wine Sydney had charmed Devon, the manager, when Joan or Jake were away, into giving her.

Sydney had been about to take a swig of the sweet red deliciousness that would calm her wild heartbeat that had grown from the heat radiating off Jake's body. She stopped and wondered if Joan realized how many times she used the word sneaky in one sentence and pondered the possibility she'd already dipped into the liquor today.

Sydney looked around the guilty circle. "I was just taking it away," she lied, shaking her head at everyone. "Shame on you all, sneaking back here behind Dad's back for a sip of this." She shook the bottle at them.

Kate crossed her arms.

Abby rolled her eyes.

Colt tried to grab the bottle away, but Sydney moved it too quickly and Joan snatched it right out of Sydney's hand and took a swig herself.

That figured.

A long swig.

The woman had an office full of her favorite wine, why was she honing in on theirs? It didn't bother Sydney and actually made her grin along with everyone in the circle. When she was finished, she read the label and looked appalled at what she'd just swallowed. "Who chose gewürztraminer wine?"

Sydney wasn't a fan either. "Devon," she blamed.

Joan didn't look impressed. "It's dry." Sydney agreed. "By the way, you're dad just educated everyone at the table that he knows exactly why his kids are always sneaking away," Joan informed them, passing the bottle to Abby, who'd just had her turn before Joan showed up.

Abby took a sip and it continued around the circle again until it finally reached Sydney.

"You better take him some garlic bread with you to quench his thirst," Joan instructed before taking another sip and leaving.

Sydney was pretty sure that wasn't how addictions worked, but what did she know, so she brought a couple plates full of garlic bread to start.

"Did Joan find you?" Jake asked, as she sat down.

"Mm-hmm. No fooling that lady."

Jake chuckled. "You got that right. Is there any left in my wine cooler?"

"I can't guarantee it."

He chuckled.

"Soon Haylee will be old enough to drive the boat and can give Joan a break," Elaine said.

Sydney did not like the sound of that.

"I can't wait!" Haylee squealed, tearing into her garlic bread.

"Three year countdown to your license," Abby said to Haylee.

Sydney's stomach knotted like sailor's rope at the thought. She dreaded that day even more than her boating license.

"I can't wait." Those comments out of her daughter's mouth did not help ease her fears.

Sydney dropped the bread she had been about to enjoy and folded her hands on her lap.

The crash still woke her up in the middle of the night. The rollover shook her body into panic. Seeing Kyle and Henry's lifeless bodies smashed through the front window...unmoving, bleeding, and dead, paralyzed her thoughts.

If those fears hadn't been enough to scare her away from vehicles, this past March she'd been in another crash with Peyton, who had been in the early stages of her pregnancy. This crash had sent Sydney into another jolt of fresh fear that she was having a hard time overcoming.

"Take a breath Sydney."

Sydney looked up from her lap, where her hands were squeezing her dress, into Jake's concerned and knowing eyes. She would have felt embarrassed if it wasn't Jake catching her going down this road twice in one day. It had to be the extra stress of Haylee's graduation adding to her fear because she'd moved past this two times a day worry many years ago.

He leaned sideways and whispered so only she would hear, "They weren't buckled up." It was the same line every time, knowing there was a good chance they would have survived if they'd strapped their seatbelts. It was logical, but it didn't really help Sydney when she went into this mode.

Jake didn't comprehend the fears whenever Sydney's thoughts travelled down this road but he understood the pain that resulted after the crash. He had lost his father and step-brother in that crash, but he didn't know the whole truth. He didn't know why they were all in the vehicle together that night, the fighting, the screaming, and the confessions...none of it. Nobody knew...except Sydney.

"It's just..." her voice trailed off into the sounds of that horrific night, the rain pelting the vehicle, the ambulance's sirens upon arrival and the voices she didn't know asking her questions she couldn't concentrate on.

For a brief moment, she'd wanted them to leave her alone to die in that vehicle. For a brief moment, all her battles, Jake's absence, a hidden teen pregnancy, and the loss of her mother had seemed like enough reason to close her eyes and never wake up.

"I know." Jake's hand reached under the table and covered her trembling hands. All this over one comment about a license. That was three years away...how was she going to handle the day when it arrived and Haylee looked up at her with excitement?

Jake's gentle and caring touch was one she missed. Even after she had been avoiding him for months, he still went out of his way to sit beside her, comfort her and be her friend. What had she done in return? Run away and cower to forget what they had done, while he was being mature after their obvious mistake.

Sydney took a deep breath and turned her attention back to the table and the conversation she had completely missed.

She had a reason for lacking maturity in regards to their situation. Heat pulsed against her hand from his skin sending sparks through her body like sparklers the kids ran around with on the long weekend. Only these sparks were not waning.

She wanted Jake.

He was trying his hardest to be her friend and she was battling her hardest to comply with that status. But, darn it, if she didn't lace her fingers through his and hold his hand until the food came to the table.

Chapter Five

AFTER SUPPER EVERYONE climbed into the limousine. Jake instructed the driver to be on hand for Haylee if she needed to go anywhere before, after or during the dance, giving him Sydney's address.

The whole time he was worried Sydney was climbing in with them and his opportunity to talk would be lost until they returned from their weekend at Hastings Port. The disappointment dug deep discomfort.

Sydney surprised him by staying behind for a night cap. They spent the evening on the patio, laughing and catching up on the months that they'd been apart, just like old times. He didn't know how he had spent so many days without her.

When the darkness began to fall, Jake offered to walk her home, via the scenic route. They took the wood stairs down the cliff and strolled along the beach, breathing in the night's summer air off the lake.

For the first time in months, Jake felt an ambience of calm pulse through him. The days since Sydney left the bar weren't the same. Sydney had a relaxing atmosphere that followed her around like eternal sunshine. Her smile was contagious and she alone could shift the moods of his entire staff as though she concealed a magic wand. Since she left the Cliff House, the spirit was lacking as was the buffer to manage the strain between him and his step-mother...Sydney was their buffer.

Today had been a good day with his step-mother. The strain between them was becoming less on her behalf as much as his own and it seemed easier to smile and joke then the constant fighting battle that usually flared between them. Jake wondered if it was time they settled their differences and moved on. It was a nice thought but far from his mind as he walked in the company of the woman who consumed most of his free thoughts. One woman at a time, and he wanted to concentrate on the one next to him.

"This is nice," Sydney said.

Jake could see her silhouette out of the corner of his eye and even stole glances as her bare feet sunk into the sand while her heels dangled from her hand.

She was beautiful in the moonlight. She was beautiful any time of the day, but with the moon reflecting off the rippling lake...she was magnificent.

"It feels just like old times," she said.

He missed the old times. He missed what felt like years ago but was in fact only months, when he'd settled with his laptop at the bar, where she was working, to deal with other investments all the while knowing she was only feet away. She had a manner about her that no one else did. She knew when to let him delve into his work, when to set a beer in front of him, when to send him a smile, and when to shut his laptop screen. She knew him. He missed that about her and he found himself wanting Sydney like he never had before. When she'd worked at the Cliff House, showing up almost every day, it was like a crutch having her around, but not really having her at all. Now, he wanted her...all of her. Day and night, to wake up beside her just like that glorious morning before she ran off, when he held her in his arms and everything in his life felt perfect.

"Before I left the bar and started working with my sisters. We spent a lot more time together."

Oh, was that what she was blaming their lack of seeing each other on? After months of her being embarrassed and avoiding him it was about time they talked about what happened. He would have done so sooner but she was keeping herself well occupied these days and with summer, creeping up it was the busiest time at the Cliff House. He found his days booked solid. This was, in fact, the first time they'd been alone since that morning and that in itself was weird after years of spending hours together every day.

He braced himself for her reaction as he said, "Before you started avoiding me."

A tiny shocked gasp escaped her at his blunt honesty. "I have not been," she denied.

"Just like we do not act weird when we are together?" He leaned over and gently pushed her side to relax her tense shoulders.

She let out a sigh but didn't say anything, letting her gorgeous features flush and give away her mortification.

"It's alright," he said. "It has been a little awkward."

She looked up at him, relieved he had admitted it out loud, but he could still see the discomfort across her face. "It's been so uncomfortable and I left so quickly after we...you know..." She took a deep breath. "Had sex."

Had sex? Had sex!

Jake almost choked on the two little words. He

certainly wouldn't have waited four months to talk to her if they'd had sex! He knew, just the connection of their two bodies joined together would have left his mind no room for anything else and he would have sought her out so much sooner.

No wonder she'd been avoiding him for months, she thought that they had slept together. Since they hadn't it meant she didn't remember what had actually happened. In turn, it also meant she likely didn't remember confessing her love. There was humor in the situation, but there was also a deep feeling of a lost battle. How would they retouch on the shared confessions if she didn't even remember sharing them?

He wasn't about to jump right into that, but he did feel the responsibility to clear up the events of that night...maybe with a little ice-breaking teaser to ease her distress, going against everything he had been trying to maintain earlier that morning. Maybe it was because they were back into routine that he didn't feel like he had to tiptoe around her or maybe it was the few beers he'd had to relax him. Either way, he wanted to tease her...a little.

"Yeah," he agreed. "And I saw your naked body, and I mean it is beautiful, it's gorgeous and..."

"Jake!" she gasped, giving the rise he had intended.

"What?" He lifted his shoulders in a shrug, acting as though he didn't know she was referring to his candour. "It *is* beautiful."

She covered her face with her hands and groaned. "Stop, please."

He laughed. "I'm just digging."

She peeked above her hands still covering her mouth.

"Digging for what?" she asked through her hands.

He grinned. "Jake, your naked body was gorgeous and hot—"

She laughed then and hit his shoulder. "Shut up!"

He continued. "All those mornings at the gym are turning your biceps into glorious mountains."

"No," she laughed. "Enough."

"No?" he asked, pretending to check his biceps. "You don't think they're glorious."

She shook her head. "Yes, they are glorious."

He laughed then. "That's all I wanted to hear."

Sydney shook her head. "Yeah right. You have enough women at the bar ogling all over your glorious mountains."

"But the way you say it..." He sucked in a breath of air between his teeth. "I actually believe it."

"I'm lying," she teased.

"You're killing me Syd."

They walked in silence again, a comforting silence he'd known only with Sydney.

"We never really talked about that night," she said quietly.

"We didn't," he agreed.

"Should we now?"

"Do you want to?" They needed to clarify the events of that night.

Sydney sighed again, a soft breathless sound. "I don't know. I'm having such a nice time." She looped her arm in his and rested her head on his shoulder.

He enjoyed the feel of her warm body against his and for a long time they continued their quiet walk along the shoreline, listening to the wind push the soft waves to touch their feet every so often. He wanted these days forever with this woman, he always had, but she'd made it clear when he returned home over ten years ago that she wasn't interested in perusing anything other than a friendship. He'd accepted her wishes but he never said he liked them.

As they passed the private properties heading toward the main strip and the lights brightened he decided now was as good as time as any.

"You know the Family Day dance?"

She tensed. "So we are going to talk about it." She didn't sound pleased. Funny, because he'd always been the one who didn't want to talk, but lately, spending his days without her, he felt inclined for the truth to come out so they could get back onto their normal path or possibly start a new path together. He was hoping for the latter.

"We are," he confirmed.

"Fine." Her voice was almost pouty. "But no more details."

"I can't make any promises."

"I beg of you."

"Alright," he promised. "Syd, I'm just going to tear the bandage off here." She looked up at him with worry. "We never slept together." There he did it, ripped it right off.

She stopped walking and pulled away from him. His body instantly missed her touch and he regretted saying anything. They could have talked about this after she'd pulled away first.

She narrowed a look at him. "What are you talking about? I woke up naked in your bed. *With you*. Naked." He hadn't been technically naked. He'd been wearing shorts however his bare chest must have brought her to her conclusion.

"I thought we weren't talking details."

"Jake."

He chuckled. "In the term, I guess we *slept* together. But we never really slept together."

She stared at him confused.

"You were drunk. Very drunk."

"You were very drunk." Her statement came out in an accusing tone and he almost laughed.

He hadn't said he wasn't drunk and he'd be the first to admit he'd downed a lot of shots that night, more than he usually did. After working years behind the bar serving drinks and dealing with drunks he didn't do all that much drinking. A shot here, a beer there, but generally not enough to get drunk.

"Let's just say that I wasn't as drunk as you were."

"I was *naked*." He watched her face as she relived the morning after, going through the motions that had brought her to her conclusion, as she gazed into the darkened distance.

"I remember." Oh, Lord did he ever. No matter what he did, he couldn't forget her naked body. Cold showers had been a multiple daily occurrence for weeks after that night.

She narrowed another look at him. "Don't say it like that."

"Like what?"

"All husky while staring down at me like you're envisioning it."

He shrugged. "I am."

She gasped loudly, but a smile curved her lips. "Jake."

LAKESHORE LOVE

She hit the side of his arm, but he barely felt it.

"I'm just trying to explain what happened."

"Don't relive it so vividly."

There was no way he could ever not relive it so vividly, but he could quit grinning at her and enjoying the squirming he was causing.

"You wanted to..." He paused and she flushed. "Exactly, but I'm not the guy who makes love to a woman who doesn't remember anything in the morning." Even if her hands tore off all her clothes revealing an amazingly curvy, smooth body that every part of him wanted to touch. Then her quick, persistent hands went after his clothes while her kisses touched every inch of his skin she could reach.

If...when...I make love to Sydney McAdams you're going to damn well remember it in the morning.

"What did I say?"

Jake, I want you. I have wanted you forever. I love you. Kiss me and never let me go again. He was planning on doing just that tonight. There had been so many wonderful sentences from her that he'd had to battle the urge to not take this woman to bed, but now realized she didn't remember any of them.

"No details to remember."

She groaned, closing her eyes and rubbing her hands across her face. "That bad?" she asked between her hands.

Jake let her groan a bit more before taking her hand and continuing their walk down the beach. "You said sweet things."

"I doubt it."

They sure made his insides feel sweet with desire for her.

"Unless of course you did mean it when you requested I tie you to the bed and go look in my tickle trunk for props?"

Sydney looked absolutely horrified and she ripped her hand away from his to cover her mouth again, stopping dead in her tracks. "I did not. Did I? Your closet? Did it have something to do with your closet?"

He took her hand back. "No, you didn't."

Relief overcame her squished face and she relaxed her features. "Thank goodness."

They continued walking.

"Tickle trunk?" she asked and he was glad to hear the humor in her voice.

He grinned at her. "I told you that you'd be surprised what I have in my closet."

She laughed then with no detachment and he felt better.

"So what happened after I was...um...throwing my..." She paused and he caught her steal a glance at him. "...Naked self at you and you didn't even want me?"

Now she was putting words in his mouth, words that were so untrue to his very core. He'd been drunk too and it would have been so much easier to succumb to her touch and pleading, but he didn't. But not because he didn't want her. Damn, he wanted her. But because he respected her too much, any woman for that matter, to take advantage of her when she was drunk.

"I didn't say I didn't want you." He stopped this time, grasping both her hands and stepping toward her. They weren't the only couple on the beach but when their eyes locked it felt like they were miles away from the outside

LAKESHORE LOVE

world, lost in each other.

As the wind increased, it blew her hair behind her with lose strands finding their way across her face.

"Sydney?" His hand moved up her bare arms, across her lace-covered shoulder, savoring every stroke, then stopped on her bare throat, his fingers touching her jaw line. Her skin was soft like a rose petal and his thumb moved across her moist lips as he watched her swallow hard. He would have never braved a moment like this if she hadn't bared the truth in her drunkenness.

"I want you. I want you sober and I want you to remember." He was ready to spend his life with her. "Should we try this sober?" he asked, bending down inches from her parted lips and hoping she said yes.

SHANNYN LEAH

Chapter Six

SYDNEY'S SWIRLING INSIDES at Jake's presence were now doubled with a hungry desire for him to press his lips against hers.

Should we try this sober? Should they? Should they!

How was she ever going to make a rational decision when her raw, hot desire for this man was overriding every part of her body? *They hadn't slept together, why did that disappoint her?*

Suddenly all she could think of was sleeping with Jake.

Kiss me Jake. Are you sure? I don't know!

Why was this happening now? After all these years? She couldn't ignore the connection between them over ten years ago and somehow they'd managed to ignore it to continue a strong friendship. But why were these feelings coming up now and what were they supposed to do?

There were still things they should talk about. There was a past of secrets withheld from each other that needed to be discussed. Things that Jake never wanted to discuss before. But it was the past. But it made their future.

Damn, it was all too confusing to contemplate when his lips were practically touching hers.

"What are we doing?" she whispered searching for an answer she didn't have.

"Standing here...mulling over whether we are going to kiss or not."

A giggle pushed past her lips at his obvious statement. "You're Haylee's uncle. You're Kyle's stepbrother."

There was so much between them. Where would they even begin? They needed the truth and a fresh slate to move forward. Did he even want to move forward?

"I was *your* friend first." His lips moved to her ear. "I was *your* lover first." The seductive way he said it sent heat to every part of her body and her stomach jumped at the memory. It was such a long time ago and yet she remembered every moment of that evening like it was yesterday.

"It's complicated," she said.

He kissed her neck then right under her ear and she struggled for breath.

"It's a kiss," he murmured against her skin.

It was far from just a kiss! But she savored the five...yes she counted every single time his sizzling lips touched her skin...kisses he pressed gently against her jaw line before stopping at her lips.

She grinned at him. "That was five."

"Let's make it six."

His taunting abducted her internal debate and her lips no longer listened to reasoning, pressing themselves against his. The thunder rolled in around them as their bodies crashed together. The light mist began to fall against his arm wrapped around her waist, pulling her against him and her hands gripping the front of his shirt as she tiptoed to match his height.

His touch was everything she remembered: his taste

was even more delicious. But, every cold water droplet landing on her skin brought her more and more back to *who* was curling her toes into the sand.

What would they do after this kiss? Did he really think it was just a kiss? What did he want? A kiss...more...a relationship...sex? What did she want?

She wanted what she'd wanted all these years— him —but fear of reliving the hardest time of her life tightened her chest.

Jake wasn't shy and there was nothing holding him back as he dipped into her mouth, tasting her tongue and making her legs almost buckle.

Sydney wanted to treasure every stroke like pirate's gold, but her mind wouldn't let her. Jake had opened up about that February night, which had stunned her and even more that he'd initiated the conversation. For a man who avoided confrontation, she couldn't help but wonder if he was ready to open up now...about everything.

His lips travelled down her throat again, harder, wetter and she arched her head back, giving him further access even when she knew she needed to know what happened when he left Willow Valley.

His hand moved from her waist, travelling up to her stomach and she instinctively wrapped her arms around his neck while his hand roamed over her breasts.

Just a kiss!

She moaned and he captured it with his lips.

Sydney needed to tell him what happened in her life during the year he'd walked away from her. He hadn't been willing to talk about any of it, but there were things she needed to say and things she needed to hear before this could go any further.

Not wanting to leave the warmth of his mouth, but wanting...having...to know if there was more to this kiss than a kiss, Sydney reluctantly pulled away.

"Jake?"

The rain was starting to plunge larger, round rain drops, soaking through her dress and into her hair.

"Mmm," he said, cracking an audacious smile. "That was quite a kiss."

Sydney's pleasure was written across her face. "I enjoyed it."

His hands squeezed between them and caught her face, pulling her into a deeper kiss and she was lost again.

Everything about this man could pull her into a tornado of emotion and desire and still deep down it was there. *He left you. He left you!*

The fear of those days was pumping through her thoughts as she pulled away from Jake again. He continued kisses down across her shoulder blade that felt so good she could hardly force the words out. "Jake, we have to talk before we go too far."

"I." His lips grazed her throat, light as a feather. "Will." He nibbled the same area. "Talk." His tongue ran across the exact same spot and she felt no other part of her body. "To you about anything," he said in a rush like the exhilaration darting from her neck and filling her heart with relief at his words. He was ready to talk about those years. *He was ready!*

"Why don't we go back up to my place," he suggested. "We can talk or do this..." He kissed her slow, long and left her longing for more as he took her hand and they started walking back to the Cliff House.

"Do you think I'm that easy to get into bed?" she asked, finding the same comforting position with her hand wrapped around his arm and her head resting against his side.

"Ordinarily I would say no, but after Family Day, I think I'm going to stick with no comment."

"Jake!" He was right, but she would have never landed in just anyone's bed. It had been Jake, it had always been Jake, but a fear had kept her from allowing him access to the intimate side of them.

The rain continued to pelt harder down on them and Jake pulled them to shelter under one of the wooden huts along the beach so only the sound of the rain slapping against the roof touched them.

"We can wait this out for a bit." He moved the damp hair away from her shoulders then gathered her in his arms and rubbed her back.

That gave them the perfect chance to talk. At his house, in the privacy of his walls, who knew how much actual talking they would get done. "I want to talk about when you left."

She panicked as his hands stopped and his body stiffened. It had been hard enough for her to brave up the words and now his reaction had her second guessing whether they should discuss it. *They had to discuss it.* She couldn't live a life of secrets with him, if he even wanted to live a life with her. She wasn't exactly sure what was going on, but she had a deep, sickening feeling it was about to go the wrong direction.

"Syd." A warning. Jake had a way of talking to people that scared them into silence. He was warning her into silence.

Why was he warning her? She wanted to talk about a dark time in his life and she wanted to share a confusing time in hers...what was the big deal!

His tone made her angry and she pulled away from him, as much as his arms would allow. "I want to talk about it, Jake. We have to talk about it."

"It's in the past. Why would we talk about it?" There was the Jake she knew, the one who didn't talk. What had all this conversation been about today? Just to steal a kiss from her? Just to land her in the sack? She knew that wasn't true. Jake wasn't the man who tried to persuade women into his bed, but still she was hurt.

"Why are you even bringing this up *now*? How did that even pop into your little head while we were..."

"Because we've never talked about it."

"You picked a fine time to bring it up."

"It would never be a good time for you."

He let her go and turned away. "Any time would be better than this!"

Her body missed him instantly and she almost regretted bringing the subject up. But they had to talk about, about him, about her...about everything. But she could feel him pulling physically and emotionally. This was the only topic he wouldn't discuss.

Sydney reached for his arm but he drew away and turned to her. "I'm not having this conversation." His cold stone stare would stop anyone dead in their tracks. Not Sydney, not when she swore she could see the tiny crack of light into this doorway of truth. She didn't fear him the way others did and she wanted more from him.

She folded her arms across her chest. "I'm not doing *this*..." She waved between them. "...without *that* conversation. Whatever *this* is."

Through his rigid stare she could see her words had hurt him and thought for a moment that he would finally agree to talk.

"I'm glad you cleared that up before we went any further."

What? What did that mean? It means he's not having the conversation with you.

"You're going to throw this away Jake? Finally after all these years we finally make a move and you're going to throw it away over a conversation!"

"You're making the call here Syd. I'm not throwing away anything. You are," he accused.

"Just talk to me. It's not that hard. You were doing a great job five minutes ago about what happened in your bedroom."

"That's different. There's nothing you need to know about that time in my life." His voice was beginning to increase in volume.

"There are things you need to know about that time in my life!" she yelled at him

His hands sliced through the air in an angry motion. "I don't want to know!"

She jumped at his harsh tone and with it came a roar of thunder to back him up. There was no getting through to him. There would be no conversation. There was no future for them.

Her hands fell to her sides in defeat. "I'm glad we cleared that up too."

LAKESHORE LOVE

Tell me I'm wrong, Jake. Talk to me, please.

When his stare was all he offered, she said, "I will see you at Haylee's party next week." She walked past him and he caught her arm.

"Syd?"

"Those are my terms Jake." She pulled away from his grip even though it hurt, even though she was breaking inside. What had happened to him while he was gone that turned him cold, that shut him down, that he would throw away *her* just so he didn't have to revisit?

Was it fair to ask him to share a part of his life that clearly he had a hard time dealing with?

He left you. Why did he leave? Exactly.

Walking alone along the shoreline in the pouring rain wasn't nearly as wonderful, it was lonely and cold. Knowing he wasn't behind her, she secretly hoped he would change his mind and come after her, open up to her and start a future.

There was no other alternative. She needed to know why he left for assurance that he wouldn't walk away from her again. She needed to trust him completely before she gave him her heart…again…that he wouldn't break it. She couldn't handle another heart break from him.

The edge of the sand stopped at the boardwalk alongside the beach and Sydney found herself standing before The Old Town & Co. Soap Shop.

The two large display windows were Kate's favorite place to get in and re-decorate every week. For the long weekend one window was a nautical theme of rope swags and buoys hung from the ceiling while advertising their all-natural sunscreen. The other side had brightly cut out stars with a firework background to advertise their all-natural bug repellent. They were beautiful and Sydney let the wholeness she felt since her sisters returned home soothe her breaking heart. *Breaking heart?* It would be ridiculous to most people that one kiss could break a heart, but with Jake and Sydney there was history and a friendship that she had with no one else. So yes, her heart felt broken and even the comfort of her family couldn't soothe it better. Not right away anyway.

She sighed. Not ever.

If things weren't weird with them before, it certainly was going to be now.

Chapter Seven

JAKE STORMED UP the outer stairs attached to the side of the Cliff House, two at a time just like he had on the stairs from the beach. His shaky fingers pushed the code on his lock and he stepped into his third floor loft.

Shaky fingers? He made a sound of disbelief, squeezed them into annoyed fists and stopped in the doorway like a thief in the night.

The open loft was dark and empty. He was alone, just like he had been for over the last decade of his life. Dim light shone through the wall of windows on the far end, hitting parts of his rustic decor, the plank wood floors, leather sofa, the live-edge custom dining table. Jake's focal point was beyond the balcony, over the trees, to the beach where Sydney had decided their future based on the past. Events from over ten years ago!

Angry, frustrated and totally pissed off with the way things went down between them, he tore the wet clothes from his body and jumped in the shower. His body was stiff as ice. For the first time since she'd walked away, he let his body's frustration fall with the water. It swirled around his feet before disappearing down the drain. He freed the air he'd been holding in his lungs and waited while the water warmed.

Normally there were other reasons to jump into a cold

stream of water associated with Sydney. For example where they were had been headed with that kiss would have put him in a cold shower if they'd retreated on good terms. Right now that wasn't the case.

Glad we cleared that up? Glad we cleared that up!

Jake was furious. They damn well didn't need to clear anything up about events from over ten years ago involving his alcoholic, drug-addicted mother and sister. It was *his* past. Sydney could never fully understand the danger associated to that life and he didn't want to drag her into it.

Damn it.

He hit the tile and pain seared through his fist.

He deserved it.

He never should have initiated that kiss when deep down he knew her curiosity about those years hadn't diminished. His stupid feelings and hot desire, which he'd done a fine job of ignoring until now, had convinced him to believe that maybe, just maybe, Sydney forget those years and look forward to a future with him. Nope, that wasn't the case and he wasn't about to start spilling the events, not to Sydney...not to anyone.

Jake dressed quickly and headed back to the Cliff House.

The night party crowd was beginning to gather and, like every weekend, it would end in a ruckus. He was personally ready to straighten that ruckus out. Even if he had hired Devon and Chuck to do just that, he was feeling the need to vent some anger.

Someone cross my damn path so I can throw you out on your ass.

He stopped by his office and poured himself a drink

before facing the crowd beginning to line up around the bar. He stepped behind and started filling out the orders being hollered.

Just the simple act of pouring drinks, like he and Sydney had done many fun nights, made him think of her.

Jake shook his head, poured a shot, passed it along and nodded to the next customer for their order.

He could do this in his sleep but he didn't have to. No one in his family had to work another day in their lives after the money his dad left them. In fact him Joan and Adalyn...his insides tightened at the mere thought of his sister living the life Sydney wanted to talk about...could go on a permanent vacation around the world, stay at exotic hotels, or on cruise ships, take limousines to every event big or small. Jake chose to stay in Willow Valley, run the last business his dad invested in to make him proud and be close to Sydney. She was one of the few people that he considered family. All she wanted to do was dig into two conversations that weren't going to benefit anyone involved.

"Oh seriously?" His next customer sent him a frown. "I thought the two of you would be shacking up by now," Abby said, kneeling on the stool and leaning across the bar so she wouldn't have to yell as loudly over the crowd and music.

Abby had changed into a black lace mini dress with spider web arms and neckline and with zippers down each side. Her face wore an extra layer of make-up and her already almost black eyes popped behind the thick eyeliner and shadow that to anyone else would send a dark and menacing look. Her red painted lips softened the look, but added a boat load of seduction to her package. It barely registered with

Jake since he still saw he as Sydney's baby sister, even when she was young Abby had run around wild, like leaves caught up in a gust of wind.

"With all that sexual tension between you two at the table, I thought for sure you were taking her home...to her bed."

So did he. "What will it be?"

She sighed loudly, knowing defeat when it arose. Out of all Sydney's sisters, he would say Abby knew him the best and vise versa. Not only had she stuck around in town, unlike the twins who took off for six years. Abby had been a regular at his bar since she was legal to drink. "Two tequila shots."

He grabbed the shot glasses as the bubbly blonde, always attached to Abby's arm, Isabelle Caliendo, pushed her way through the crowd. She was loudly making a scene and squeezed between Abby and the person sitting on the stool beside her.

"What's taking you so long Abby!" It was not a question but rather a whiny complaint. "Come on Jake, pour a girl two shots. On the house would be best," she added with a flirtatious wink.

Jake poured the shots, chuckling to himself over the statement. *On the house for a Caliendo.* Her family owned resorts across the country and if memory served him correctly, this girl hadn't worked a day in her life and wasn't lacking in the money department.

"Jake was supposed to be banging Sydney right now," Abby said.

Oh Lord, this girl has no limits.

He slid the shots across the counter.

They threw them back and slid the empties back for

another.

"What are you doing here then?" Isabelle shouted over the band's music pulsing from the speakers at the other end of the bar. He was grateful for the music and crowds so everyone else wasn't listening to how frank these two were being about his love life.

"Yeah?" Abby asked. "What are you doing back here?"

Jake poured the shots and slid them across the counter hoping they'd take them and retract anywhere but here. He was not talking about Sydney with her.

They threw them back. Hard drinkers. He knew they could be since they were weekend regulars. He would never tell them, he wouldn't want to bust their egos, but in the last few years they had slowed their alcohol consumption and spent most of their time dancing into the morning.

Isabelle fluttered her large, round, thickly applied black eye-lined blue domes at him wiggling her way onto the stool with Abby. "Did she turn you down?" she asked seductively leaning across the counter even more than Abby with her chin on her hand. This move would send Chuck right over the edge, any man really, but Jake wasn't interested.

"If you're looking to blow off some steam, I'm free all night long." Yup Chuck would have latched onto this blonde bombshell quickly in her skin tight red dress matching the full red lips she was pursing at him and left the bar that very moment.

Abby grabbed her shoulder. "Down girl. He's Sydney's so off limits to you."

Thank you Abby.

Jake wasn't anyone's, not that it made a difference on whether he was going to take this Caliendo up on her offer. He wasn't.

Isabelle turned a pouty look at Abby. "Come on. You say Jake's off limits. Riley's off limits. You're keeping all the bad guys for yourself."

Bad guy? That was his image? He was good with that. It meant people left him alone. He liked being left alone, except when it came to the one woman who had walked away.

"Hey come on!" a man shouted from behind them. "Get your drinks and get out if the way!"

Jake's stare tapered in on a brawny man who was having his share of enjoyment staring at the women's rears while complaining about their speed.

Abby turned before Jake had a chance to even open his mouth. "Hold your pants on. We will be done when we're done." That mouth was going to get her in trouble, like it usually did. But nobody messed with a McAdams, and especially not in his bar.

"How about now!" The impatient jerk grabbed her wrist, causing Abby to lose her balance and she tumbled off the stool onto the floor. She stayed on her feet, he wasn't sure how with the height of the heels she was wearing, but a loud cry came from her lips as she hit the ground. Jake didn't know if it was surprise or pain. This guy better run if he hurt Abby.

"Hey!" Isabelle screamed, jumping off the stool and grabbing the thick arm like she was superwoman, because being just tiny little Isabelle wasn't going to get her anywhere against this man.

Jake's insides lit up. This was exactly what he needed. He flipped the counter walkway up throwing drinks across the platform and onto the floor. He heard the smashing and surprise of everyone around him but he didn't care. His hand grabbed the jerk's arm and twisted it behind his back with more force than Isabelle's tiny attempt and in a second he released Abby and was dropping to his knees in pain.

"You enjoy picking on women half your size?" Jake asked, putting more pressure on his arm.

"No man. Hey, I'm sorry. I will buy them a drink."

"It's a little late for that. Don't apologize to me, apologize to her." Jake lifted his head to Abby, who instead of being startled, was waiting, expecting his apology. She was quite the opposite of Sydney, who would be telling him to release the jerk and let it go.

"I'm sorry. Alright?"

Jake felt a hand on his arm. "Jake, I got this." Chuck came around and Jake let the guy's arm go with a little shove making him fall to his hands and knees.

"Get him out of my bar."

Chuck did exactly what he demanded.

He turned to Abby. "You okay?"

She smiled. "I'm glad you weren't banging my sister."

He didn't agree with her.

Chapter Eight

SYDNEY'S PHONE RANG at almost two in the morning. Panic rose as she reached to answer it. No one phoned her at this hour, unless...

"Hello."

"Hey Syd. It's me, Jake." Like he had to clarify. She would recognize this man's voice at any hour of day or night.

Why was he calling? Had he changed his mind and was ready to talk? The thought made her sit straight up. Or was it Abby...

She couldn't let the excitement get the better of her when she didn't know what this phone call was regarding.

She held her breath, hoping.

"Listen, Abby is here, at the bar and she's had her limit of alcohol."

Abby. Her heart sunk. Just like old times.

"I'm closing soon but she's hanging with a bad crowd and I'm not letting her leave with them."

Jake always protected Abby. Jake would always protect you if you didn't force him into the past. Jake will always protect you even if you only remain friends...he just won't touch you, kiss you, and love you the way you want.

"I have a feeling she's not going to listen to me tonight and likely end up having a scene when she realizes that I'm not letting her leave with any of these fellows. I thought you might want to come down and we could avoid a scene. She will listen to you."

Abby must be pretty drunk for Jake to call her. Sydney used to get these late-night calls before Abby moved in with Gran. The older woman snapped Abby out of most of her un-ladylike ways, including excessive alcohol, excessive boys, and excessive vulgar vocabulary. Gran had been an amazing inspiration for Abby and surprisingly Abby had listened without aiming her rebellion at Gran. Abby was better for it, but after Gran died the calls began again, and Abby seemed lost for a while. That had scared Sydney.

It was her new friendship with Riley that once again slowed her drinking, slowed her late nights, and slowed Abby down in general.

Sydney had been wary about Riley at first sight with his long hair, beard, tattoos and that he barely spoke a word. Sydney wasn't generally quick to judge people, but when her unpredictable sister was involved, she had to be extra cautious.

After Gran had passed last year and Abby took off up north, forcing her sisters to chase after her and make sure she was okay, they had found Riley had accompanied her. After spending a weekend with him, Sydney had learned Riley's rough exterior was similar to Jake's. He was kind on the inside once you got to know him. He was the boss of who was allowed to get to know him and who he let in...just like Jake. Riley didn't drink, at all, absolutely nothing. Sydney found it odd with no explanation, but he was good for Abby.

Until tonight. What happened, Abby?

"Alright, I'm coming."

Sydney pouted like a child being made to wake up

early and go to school as she pulled a denim dress over her head and slipped into her cowboy boots.

Why hadn't Jake said, *Sydney, I'm ready to talk.* Those five words would have brightened the sleepless night she was having.

Sydney grabbed her car keys off the hook, they very rarely moved from the location, but she wasn't about to try and walk a drunken Abby home from the Cliff House.

The garage door went up with a press of a button and the small car Joan had bought her for emergencies came into view. Not only was Jake not calling to take a step, but now she had to drive.

What a splendid night. The sarcasm didn't make her feel better.

Sydney took her time driving, as she always did, and when she walked through the Cliff House doors, she saw Jake was right about Abby's condition: wasted.

Wasted. Abby come on! How old are you? Act your age.

Dressed like a woman looking to have a good time, Abby was standing...stumbling...by the pool tables with a crowd of obnoxious drinking men, who had apparently enjoyed the tight dress and high heels. No Isabelle in sight, which was odd.

Sydney's eyes searched for Jake next and found him behind the bar staring at her. *Should I go over? Should I say thank you?* She wanted to stand in front of him, hoping he would say the five little words she yearned to hear. That hope alone almost made her turn toward Jake instead of her sister, but a quick glance at the unfriendly crowd around Abby and her feet knew where to take her, even when her heart craved the other direction.

"Hey, Abby." Sydney touched her sister's shoulder and when Abby turned, her eyes lit up.

"Sydney!" Abby hugged her, stumbled, then leaned all her weight on Sydney. "What are you doing here? I missed you." That was the alcohol talking.

"Jake is closing up, so I popped by to give you a ride home."

Abby sent her a grateful, drunk-laced look. "You drove here? For me?"

I didn't have a choice.

Sydney nodded with a forced partial smile.

They would talk about this in the morning, or when Sydney got back from her trip. Sydney wouldn't be able to drag Abby from the sleep that would overtake her once they got back to her house at five in the morning, when they were leaving for Joan's house.

Five in the morning! That was only three hours away and Sydney was sure she hadn't even gotten a whole hour's worth of sleep yet.

"Awe, thanks Sis but I'm actually going home with...that guy over there." Abby pointed at a much older man. Flame and skull tattoos covered every piece of skin peeking out around his black tank top. His daunting eyes were watching them closely and he didn't appear to be nearly as drunk as Abby was. Sydney didn't like that one bit and was grateful Jake had been watching out for her sister.

Sydney made a mental note to call or text Kate in the morning in case Abby continued this streak throughout the long weekend while she was away. Peyton was forceful, able to relate and could handle Abby's drinking, but with her being pregnant, Sydney didn't want to put her in a situation like the one Sydney was currently partaking in. Kate was forceful in a motherly fashion and didn't fear chasing Abby down.

"Nah. How about you come home with me? I have cupboards full of candy." She was exaggerating, but Abby had a sweet tooth for candy.

"I'm just going to go with...with..." Abby laughed and Sydney didn't find the situation at all amusing. "I forget his name." That was the perfect reason not to go home with him, plus the strangely possessive looks he was sending their direction was creeping Sydney out. There was not a chance Abby was going home with creepy stare man.

"No, you're not."

Abby pouted at her like a child which was another good indication of her drunkenness. She wasn't likely going to remember any of this is in the morning. Jake's respectable words came to mind, *I'm not the guy who makes love to a woman who doesn't remember anything in the morning.*

Jake was an honorable man, unlike the creep heading in their direction.

Ugh. She didn't want a confrontation with him.

"Come on, Sydney," Abby whined.

"Let's go. Now."

Sydney thought Abby might pout again, but instead she wrapped her arms around Sydney and said all sweet and child-like, "I love you, Sydney." Then she gasped and Sydney felt her heart jump up her chest.

What? God what now?

Her eyes darted around the room.

"Did you see Jake? He was all ready to kill someone

today after you guys didn't have sex," she loudly whispered the last word right in Sydney's ear.

Sydney had seen him. How could she miss him? Why did Abby assume they were going to be having sex?

On their way to the door, she glanced over and saw he hadn't moved and neither had his eyes, locked on hers.

"He's totally into you." *I'm totally into him.* "Give him a chance." *I did.* "I bet he's a great bang."

"Abby!" Sydney didn't doubt it.

Just then Sydney felt a tug at Abby's weight and she stumbled backwards herself, knowing exactly who was pulling Abby.

Why couldn't they just exit without a scene? Why was Abby so drunk? Why hadn't Jake phoned her for her instead of this?

"Hey, hey now. This here lil' lady is coming home with me tonight." Even his voice was spine-chilling, in a disgusting, creepy old man kind of way.

Oh great.

What had ever possessed Abby to befriend these people or this person in particular? This was why Sydney didn't drink to get drunk, not to mention her dad was a recovering alcoholic and the night of the February dance was another good reason to stay on the game. At least she had ended up with Jake who protected her. Abby on the other hand had been heading down a dirty road.

Sydney turned to the creepy eyed man who had Abby's arm in his hand.

"She's coming home with me," Sydney told him, her skin crawling at the sight of his dirty nails digging into her sister's flesh.

He stepped closer to her. "I don't think you heard me correctly," he threatened, hovering over her but not nearly as threatening as the man by the bar that would protect her and Abby in a heartbeat, no matter what was going on between the two of them.

Sydney took a deep breath and tugged Abby back. "I don't think you heard me correctly." His grip remained solid on Abby's arm. "Let go of her."

"I didn't hear her complain." He smirked and flashed his yellow teeth, making Sydney's stomach turn.

Abby did a pitiful pull of her arm but his grip never faltered and she eventually gave up lying on Sydney's shoulder and yawning loudly. "I'm going home with my sister." Her week declaration was pathetic.

"Decision's been made." Sydney turned to leave when one of his hands grabbed her arm and dug his skinny fingers into her flesh.

"You're messing with the wrong guy."

Ouch, ouch, ouch! She flinched, there was no getting out of this as his fingers forced her to turn around.

Chapter Nine

THE SECOND THAT bastard put his hand on Abby, Jake was crossing the room. But when he touched Sydney, Jake saw red.

His thick hand gripped the shoulder of the man that thought he could lay a finger on Sydney and he had to do everything not to turn him around and drill him into the ground. He wanted too, oh, how he wanted to, and if the guy wasn't still gripping Sydney and Abby, he would have.

Jake's eyes caught those filthy fingers on Sydney's flawless smooth skin causing his grip to tighten and he was ready to rip the guys arm right off.

"I suggest you take your hands off them." There was no suggesting about it. This man was out of time and had better remove his hands before Jake removed them for him.

"I suggest you mind your own business."

Jake's blood boiled in an anger he hadn't felt in years. No one, absolutely damn well no one, touched his woman like that. *His woman. I wish, Not the time Jake. Focus.*

"These two gals are my business." He sent him a warning stare. "I'm not asking you twice." He was lucky Jake asked him once.

The douche-bag released Sydney but Jake didn't release him until Sydney pulled Abby behind him and out of harm's way.

This man was so damn lucky. Jake was already in a helluva bad mood.

"You okay?" Jake asked. Even if they weren't in the best of places, this woman meant the world to him and she always would.

Sydney nodded, biting on her bottom lip, pleading with her eyes that he let the man go.

Jake would rather throw a punch but he let go of the guy, for her. As he turned to him he said, "It's about time you and your friends leave." Jake nodded at the posse. "And you're not welcome back in my bar. Any of you."

The guy mustered up his pride and called his guys over with a nod of his head. When Jake let his eyes move to Sydney for a second glance, he had to make sure she really was okay, the guy took a cheap shot and threw a punch, hitting Jake right in the jaw.

"Jake!" Sydney cried.

Jake heard Chuck and Devon, who were not far behind, watching and waiting for such a move, rush over. He should have let them take over, that's what he paid them extra for, but this guy had gone way too far and it wasn't even about Jake's pulsing jaw, it was the way he thought he could treat women, Sydney to be more precise.

Jake turned and nailed the unexpected ass right in the same place he'd hit Jake. Only Jake was taller, stronger and had muscle where this guy was short and scrawny. His tattoo's, dirty clothes, and greasy hair didn't scare Jake, nor did they add up to much of a man. He'd seen worse. He'd dealt with worse. He had fought way worse...and won.

The guy went flying onto his backside and his posse rushed around to help him up and moved in toward Jake.

Jake stood his ground with Chuck and Devon on either side of him. This group of trouble-makers were his last customers. The bar was closed and Jake had been waiting for Sydney to arrive before asking these jerks to leave. The only crowds were the waitresses who knew to keep their distance.

The three of them, boasting muscle, against the six grease monkeys was no competition. They stood their ground. He didn't want to have to fight six of them...alright it wasn't the worst thing to happen tonight...but he wasn't about to back down either.

The prick on the ground stood up, obviously the leader of this group, and high tailed it for the door. His posse followed.

Chuck and Devon walked past Jake to watch them get in their vehicles and leave before locking up.

Jake took a deep breath before turning back to Sydney and really looked at her. There were no marks on her skin. *Good.* He could breathe soundly again. Then his eyes wanted to look at the rest of her. Her blonde hair was a tousled mess of untamed curls tumbling around the shoulders of a denim dress she wore. Her eyes looked tired, her body looked tired. She looked like she'd been spending her evening the same as him: thinking about them, wanting but not knowing how to fix this between them.

"Oh shit, Jake you're bleeding," Abby said.

***

SYDNEY SAW THE blood and was concerned about the cut under his lip, but when he turned and stared at her so intensely, she forgot about all of it and watched those blue eyes, waiting for him to make a move. The five words repeated in her head like a thundering stampede, *Sydney, I'm ready to talk.*

Jake touched the blood on his mouth and looked at his fingers like he didn't believe it.

Guilt chided Sydney. He had protected them, and ending up with a bleeding cut, and she was too busy waiting for him to say words she knew he wouldn't.

Sydney pushed aside her desire for Jake and decided to be his friend right now, which was what he needed more.

She sat her sister on a lounger and Abby lay back sprawling across it, her black dress hiking almost to her underwear. Devon and Chuck passed by trying their hardest not to look.

Taking a deep breath, Sydney yanked down the hem.

"You stay here," she told Abby.

Abby smiled dozily and Sydney was relieved when her eyes shut. Chuck and Devon would still be closing up, the waitresses counting their tips and cleaning up, so no one would let Abby leave without informing Sydney first.

Sydney took Jake's warm hand in her own, noting it swelled out under her touch. He was going to need to ice it. She needed his hands to run along her arm like they had at the beach, and slide around her waist pulling their bodies together. That wasn't happening any time soon and the thought made her sad.

She left Jake at the bar to sit on one of the stools.

"I'm fine," he grumbled, all manly and macho, wiping his lip with the back of his hand.

"Wait here." Sydney grabbed a frozen bag of vegetables from the walk in cooler for his *fine* hand and the first aid kit for his *fine* lip. He was the most stubborn man she'd ever encountered. No one questioned Jake, whether they were right or not and if so risked being thrown into Jake's big black book of *I don't like you*...Sydney was the exception. If you were on his payroll and questioned him, you might as well throw in the apron.

When she climbed onto a bar stool across from him, she couldn't help notice he'd changed out of his suit and was back in his jeans and black t-shirt which spanned across the width of his chest. His elbows were on the edge of the bar and he was rubbing his forehead.

Sydney glanced around the bar. Everyone was gone. The music was cut and Abby was still passed out, and snoring exactly where Sydney left her.

"I sent them home," he said as if reading her thoughts without even looking at her. That wasn't uncommon for the two of them. They had spent so much time together, a lot of instances they were completely in sync with each other.

Sydney opened the first aid kit and took out a cloth to wipe away the blood, but he was turned away from her; still being a stubborn ass.

"Let me see."

"I'm fine." She knew he was fine, that wasn't the point.

"Jake Stow, I swear, turn yourself around so I can look, or so help me I will turn you around myself." She wasn't sure exactly how she would manage that, but climbing on top of the bar or even better climbing on his lap would give her access to his face...for the simple act of cleaning the blood away. The throbbing ache between her legs was going a whole other direction with that image.

He turned in a huff with a straight lined mouth and a set of glaring eyes.

She ignored him and took a deep calming breath. She touched his chin, moving it sideways to look at the extent of the damage across his gorgeous smooth skin. Stubble or not this man had it going on.

Her eyes moved to his and in the dim light they looked almost navy. Time stood still between them. She wanted to kiss him so badly it hurt. She wanted him to promise her he would never leave her again without having to ask.

"You have a little cut," she said quickly and put all her attention into continuing to examine the little cut.

"Little." He rolled his eyes. "Why are you fussing about it if it's little?"

His hand caught her wrist and the touch instantly made her body aware of how close they were sitting. His legs were much longer than Sydney's and when he'd turned toward her his knee hid itself under her dress and against her bare center thigh. Even the slightest movement was rubbing desire straight up her thigh to her warmest woman area.

His face softened and he let go of her hand to gently touch her exposed bare knee. Her blood heated. Her breath caught in her throat and her womanhood drummed harder for his fingers to follow her legs right under her dress.

In all the years they'd been friends, never had they so intimately touched, gazed or wanted each other as much as the last twenty four-hours and his desire was written plainly across his face. Jake, who never let anyone see him, was exposing himself to her.

Sydney ignored his hand and wiped the fresh blood from his skin. She was fully aware he was still staring down at her and watching her every move. Moves that before today, before that family day disaster would have been much less strained.

As she touched his skin, she could feel his thumb pressing harder against her skin, not anything painful or remotely close to the jerk who'd gripped her with the intention of hurting her, but in a slow massaging motion that was leaving her skin tingling and wanting more. She thought about shifting so he would release her, or shifting to give him access to continue up her leg.

She sat still.

His jaw was swelled but the cut had stopped bleeding. She was about to put a small bandage over the open wound but his other hand caught her wrist again

"I don't need that."

She wasn't arguing. "Fine."

He let her go and she dropped it in the first aid kit. She had done all she could do. She didn't even bother pressing the cold bag against his face or hand but slid it across the counter toward him. He ignored it, his eyes focused on her, his fingers on her leg.

"I should go." She didn't want to and said it only because what else would they do.

Sydney didn't move.

Jake didn't move.

The intense air between them was increasing her breathing by the second.

His free hand, leaning against the counter's edge found her arm, slowly tracing more heat with his fingers. Her skin was melting at his touch, her insides were scorching.

"Sydney, that's not a part of my life anymore," he finally said, so strained it sounded like just the words hurt him. "Why do you feel the need to drag me back there?"

Sydney didn't even want to talk about any of that right now. Instead her thoughts were contemplating what it would feel like if he lifted her onto the counter and she wrapped her legs around his waist. Meanwhile he was trying to resolve their circumstances. Or was he?

So I understand why you left me. Why couldn't she just tell him the truth? Because I need to know what drove you away before I let you back into my heart. Because when you left the first time I hardly survived.

Too many people had left her. Her mom, Kyle, Henry and Gran had passed only last year. Sydney wasn't able to handle Jake leaving again and she needed to know what made him go in the first place.

His family—that's why.

Did she want him to say it? If he did, then what would she do? She couldn't stay. How could she when she feared him walking away again for them?

"I have to know what happened." Not want, if it was a want she would ignore it and kiss him now.

He shook his head. "I can't."

As much as it hurt she pushed his hand away from her leg.

"Then I can't." She slid off the stool and headed toward Abby, the reason she'd come in the first place. Any hope that the few short hours he'd realized he wanted to be with her enough to share a struggle in his life was extinguished.

His boots hit the floor louder than normal. "Sydney what do you want from me? I've waited over ten years for you to give me an inch and when you finally do, you cut it right off."

She spun. "I have waited over ten years for you to give me a reason to give you an inch."

"My past is not your damn business!"

***

THE MOMENT THE words came out of Jake's mouth, he regretted them. He especially regretted the hurt across Sydney's face before she turned, picking up her pace.

"Syd, wait," he called after her. "I didn't mean it."

She ignored him.

He kind of meant it. Sometimes knowledge was dangerous and that part of his life was extremely dangerous.

Jake wanted to grab her wrist and make her stop, but from the tense way she walked he knew that would be a mistake. Not the first one he'd made tonight.

"Syd, please."

She spun her cowboy boots, digging their heels in the plank floors. "What do you want from me!?" she yelled at him.

His eyes glanced at Abby. She was so heavy in sleep she didn't hear a word. Then he looked back to Sydney.

"I want you Syd. Isn't it obvious? I've always wanted you."

She laughed. "That's why you left me right? Why you didn't bother telling me and disappeared for over a year, right? Because you wanted me so badly?"

He wanted to step closer to Sydney and comfort the sadness his departure had left with her. Still, all these years later and she thought he'd wanted to leave her. He hadn't wanted to leave her. He hadn't had a choice. He didn't go about it right, not telling her had been his mistake. But if asked him not to, he would have stayed and his sister would have been in trouble. Adalyn had needed him, or so he thought.

"That had nothing to do with you."

"It had everything to do with me!"

"I was young and foolish."

"That's what I get? Blame your age for not picking up a phone and letting me know you were alive. For not telling me you were leaving in the first place. Not a word for over a year. That's not enough, Jake."

"It's the truth."

"It's the half truth."

He groaned. "Why are we doing this?"

The fight fell from her face. "If you have to ask then I don't know why we are doing this."

What the hell did that mean?

"Night Jake."

She shook Abby awake enough to walk her out of the bar.

Jake watched her load Abby in the car before climbing in, glancing at the door first. Every part of him wanted to chase her down and make this better, but the only way that would work is if he went back into his past with her and he wasn't sure if he could do that.

Chapter Ten

SYDNEY FOLLOWED BEHIND Haylee like a sad over-exhausted puppy, dragging luggage that felt like it held the weight of her sorrow. Inside, beyond the smiles and excitement she'd shared all morning with Haylee, she felt like a sad puppy.

Their sandals flipped and flopped across the marble floors through Joan's house...more like Joan's mansion. It was the home Sydney had raised Haylee in before they'd ventured out on their own into Sydney's small, but cozy house, where they weren't pampered with a maid and grounds keeper.

The glass French doors of the main living room, which were larger than Sydney's entire house, didn't make a sound as they pushed them open and found Joan waiting on the back porch for them.

Joan was an early riser and smiled widely at them, like she'd gulped down an entire pot of coffee already. *Mmm, coffee.* That sounded like the solution to kick-start Sydney's fatigued body, plus a couple hours of well-needed, solid sleep.

Joan stood straightening another one of her gorgeous white outfits detailed in blue nautical theme. Every trip they took on the boat Joan had a new nautical-themed outfit for the first day of take off.

"There are my two girls!" she said giving each of them a hug. "I'm so excited. It's going to be a beautiful weekend for us. I have fully stocked the refrigerator and alcohol cabinet." She winked at Sydney. "But not for you Haylee." She wrapped her arm around Haylee's shoulder and kissed the side of her head.

"I know Grandma."

"I also fully stocked that colored powder you put in your drinks, Haylee."

"Thanks. Did you get pineapple?"

"Of course. Plus, the big surprise..."

Sydney wasn't in the mood for any more surprises. Surprise, you didn't sleep with Jake. Surprise, Jake wants to kiss you. Surprise, not enough to have a simple conversation. *Surprise, surprise, surprise!*

But a surprise to take her sad mind off Jake sounded good. Then she could stop considering throwing in the towel and running back into his consoling arms. *No, stand by your beliefs or he will hurt you again.*

Joan's house wasn't located directly on the lake but rather on the river that split off from the lake called Crystal Cove where boaters could dock their boats for the summer conveniently in their backyard.

They walked to the dock, waiting for the big surprise Joan promised on deck.

Sydney needed to stop feeling sorry for herself. She decided listening to her daughter plan out the order of events since they only had four days to cram it all in was a better plan for today. This vacation, just the three of them was exactly what she needed to clear her mind of Jake and all the drama the two of them had created. He wasn't going to talk with her, that was clear, so she needed to let him go and stop wanting more from him than he was willing to give her. A sunny, hot gorgeous long Jake-less weekend was the perfect solution.

Sydney felt herself smiling for the first time since she'd dragged her objecting body out of bed for a shower.

They climbed aboard the sixty-six foot princess yacht, which was again bigger than Sydney's entire house. Below deck were three cabins with attached baths, one for each of them. Teak and white decked the cockpit which was divided into three sections. There were twin sun beds port and starboard, a dining area including a wet bar, storage, an electric barbeque and refrigeration under an electronically operated sunroom. It was extravagant.

The sun was just beginning to lighten the sky just as Joan planned so she wasn't steering the boat in the dark.

Joan headed to the cockpit. "Here's the surprise!"

Sydney was digging for her cell phone. She needed to send Kate a text about Abby so she could stop by her house before she opened the shop. That girl needed a good swift kick in the...

As Sydney causally glanced up at Joan's big surprise, she saw it wasn't just the three of them on board.

Jake? Jake! What was Jake doing on board? What kind of pleasant yet miserable surprise was this!

He wasn't looking as tired as she felt, nor was he looking even remotely close to miserable. His bright eyes matched the white knee-length casual shorts and polo shirt he was wearing. *White shorts? Polo shirt? What on earth was going on!*

Jake had never joined them on one of their annual

boating trips and he had certainly never worn white shorts.

"What's Jake doing here?" Sydney asked when Joan walked back, passing an excited Haylee who was heading up to greet her Uncle Jake.

"You always want me and Jake to communicate better and he showed some interest in coming, so I invited him." She shrugged and went below, like it was no big deal. It was a huge deal!

Showed some interest? What an hour ago? Why did he suddenly after all these years show an interest in joining them on a trip? What did he want? And why was he smiling at her like an excited child holding in a million things to say to her?

Now the monster of a boat didn't seem all that big.

***

"UNCLE JAKE!" HAYLEE shouted. She tossed her bag on the sun seat. "This is awesome. You've never been to Hastings Port with us before. This is going to be so much fun!"

He wrapped his arm around her shoulders and squeezed. At least someone was glad to see him.

She smelled like the suntan lotion from Sydney's store. He recognized the coconut smell after testing a sample Sydney had left for him at the Cliff House a few weeks ago.

"It sure is. Your stories every year intrigued me to come along." That was half the truth. Their stories were always full of excitement, but he'd never been invited along. He hadn't exactly been given an invitation this time either, but after a long few hours without a wink of sleep, and unable to get Sydney out of his head, he called Joan up and she was more than thrilled to have him along. Very

LAKESHORE LOVE

surprising.

"It takes six hours to get there, depending on what kind of mood Grandma is in. Sometimes she heads straight there and sometimes she stops and cooks, sits in the sun, then starts up again. So if we head straight there we will be just in time for their luau themed lunch that is extending into the evening with a luau themed supper followed by a dance." She took a breath. "They have themed days every long weekend and I looked up the themes so I could bring some stuff from home to dress up. Tomorrow is the casino theme and I brought decks of cards to staple together and make like these necklace collar things. Sunday night is a masked ball theme so I made me, Mom and Grandma feather masks already, but we can go into town and find you something. Then..." Haylee continued into fireworks and food and more. He tried to pay as much attention to her very specific details as he could, but his eyes kept wandering to Sydney.

She was back to wearing the flowing summer dresses that he appreciated so much. They were made from a teasing, torturous material that left his mind fascinated with what might be underneath. The white halter dress today was leaving little to the imagination, it was almost see-through, flashing a pink bikini that sparked heat straight through him.

Sydney sent him curious look. Of course she did. He had shown up on their vacation, last minute, after a terrible evening of arguing and she was probably wondering what the hell he was doing. If he'd gotten enough sleep, he might not have picked up the phone at the early hour and instead opted to wait until she got back to talk and by then he might have talked himself out of it. He didn't want to talk himself out of it. He *had* to talk to Sydney.

After she drove away that morning, which felt like a lifetime ago, he was left with this sinking feeling knowing all he had to do was open up to her, give her an inch and he could have all of her...if he wasn't too late...that's exactly what he'd always wanted.

Jake was prepared to tell her everything she needed to know and planned on walking off this boat in four days with her on his arm. Her as his. That was his plan and he could tell by the looks Sydney was casting him, she wasn't on board with the plan.

Sydney didn't shy away from him like he suspected that she would. She walked to the cockpit looking ticked as all hell. Haylee grabbed her bag and went under the deck with Joan, making a comment to Sydney as she passed about how great it was to have Jake aboard. By Sydney's stare he would guess she didn't agree with her daughter...but by the end of the weekend he would convince her otherwise.

"Hi," he said. Just her deep blue eyes were supporting his decision to board this boat. He needed to win those blue eyes back and to think if he had only agreed to talk to her hours ago, they might have been boarding this boat together, hand in hand.

He noticed the dark circles around her eyes from lack of sleep and it was at his hand.

"What are you doing here?" she snapped, very unlike Sydney. It would seem he had pushed her buttons to the max.

He didn't want to play games with her about why he was aboard this boat. He wanted her to know that he had come to talk, resolve and look into whatever was conspiring between them. "I don't like the way we left things between us, Syd."

LAKESHORE LOVE

She crossed her arms and he noticed the way the motion boosted up the top of her breasts in the pink bikini. Very distracting...pleasurable but distracting.

"So what? You thought coming on a boat with Joan and Haylee was a good place to...well...not talk about it. Obviously we all know how you feel about talking, so what are you doing here? And, besides what would we talk about...since your life is none of my damn business."

"I came here to, believe it or not, talk to you."

Her eyebrows rose and she snorted. *Snorted!* He didn't let the amusement show on his face. Maybe she needed to have a nap before they talked.

"Right. Talk. Jake Stow wants to talk." She said the words with a serious sarcastic manner. "See how all those words don't suit each other."

Yes, she was definitely lacking sleep.

"I didn't come here to fight with you." He almost offered to climb off the boat if that was what she wanted, but he couldn't bring himself to do it.

She cut him off before he could apologize. "I came to have fun and spend time with Joan and my daughter. Not sit around and talk...with *you*."

Ouch. She better have a full night's sleep before they even attempted to have a talk.

He decided that furthering this conversation would accomplish nothing. He said, "Alright. Let's get this boat started and get you girls to your destination for a fun weekend."

He turned to controls. Hopefully in the six hours before they docked at Hastings Port, Sydney either slept or relaxed because he hadn't come on board to ruin her vacation.

Chapter Eleven

TALK? TALK! DID Jake forget the definition of the word *talk* this morning when he crawled out of bed and made arrangements to crash *her* trip, with *her* family and throw around promises he wasn't going to keep? *Huh? Did he?*

Sydney jumped in the shower. After avoiding Jake for six hours, too piping angry to sit in the cockpit with him, and not wanting to lounge on the sun beds and let the comfort of his presence calm her down, she'd been forced into her cabin with a novel. After a few pages of not absorbing a single word, her eyes would no longer stay open and she'd fallen asleep until she felt the boat gear into reverse and knew they were at the slip.

Finally getting a good sleep, she felt refreshed as she helped tie the boat to the dock before returning back below to get ready for lunch.

Jake was in just as delightful of a mood now as he'd been at six that morning when she finally emerged from below, showered and changed into a summer dress with wooden beaded straps. Her stomach growled for lunch.

Haylee rose from one of the sun beds when she saw her mom and rushed over with a pink flower lei necklace she slipped over her head. "And, one for you." Haylee was wearing a purple lei necklace and at a glance around she saw

Joan and Jake also had color around their necks. They were a rainbow of lei necklaces.

"Who is hungry for lunch?" Joan asked, rising from the table. She'd changed into a white A-line dress and matching heels. She finished her glass of wine and, without waiting for an answer, headed to the back of the boat.

"It's kebabs!" Haylee called over her shoulder rushing to follow her grandma.

Jake was staring at Sydney. She could feel it without looking at him and her feet were frozen in place when she wanted to follow after the women and get out of his sight.

Why wasn't he moving? What was he doing?

Finally she looked at him and sure enough he was watching her. He hadn't changed like the rest of them, typical man, but he was handsome all the same. *Handsome? How are you going to last the weekend if your mind keeps going down this path...*

"What?" It came out in a snap of irritation from her inner thoughts.

"Do you mind if I join the three of you?"

Why was he asking her? Who was she to dictate where he could and couldn't go? He'd invited himself on this trip without asking her.

"Why are you asking me?"

"You were right about me bombarding your vacation. That was presumptuous of me and I definitely do not want to force you into anything you are not ready for. If you don't want me to join you for lunch, I will eat here. I won't mention anything to the girls, except some lame Jake excuse. Joan has packed so much food in this thing, you would think there were ten guys staying aboard."

LAKESHORE LOVE

Sydney couldn't help the smile that found her lips. Joan always over stocked them on food like they were going to get stranded on an island on the way to their destination. "Sometimes we eat like ten guys." Her joke relaxed the tense muscles in his face. "Of course you can come for lunch, Jake and you don't have to ask me. This is your family too."

"I'm not worried about them or me. It's you I'm thinking about. If you don't want me to come Syd, I won't."

His consideration for her was pulling chords in her chest. When had Jake Stow become such a fluent talker in thoughtful sweetness? *Why was he being so darn sweet when she was trying to stay mad at him? How would she stay mad at him when he was being so darn sweet?*

"It's kebabs. You can't very well miss kebabs," she said with a little nod.

He smiled. "After you."

Sydney led the way to the barbeque picnic that was gathering by the yacht club building. Like every other year, the club had gone all out with the luau decorations. Hibiscus flowers, straw bunting, and tiki men were everywhere.

Joan and Haylee already stood in the lineup for food, so they joined them and once they all sat down for lunch, Sydney's mood shifted. She didn't know if it was the appetizing smell of the barbeque kebabs, or the happy sounds of the tourists enjoying their lunch. It could have been the hot sun pounding down on them like a blanket of warmth. Whatever it was, the tension between her and Jake diminished and they both fell into their regular roles, laughing, joking, and smiling.

Lunch turned into a day of events set up around the yacht club building. They had traditional ancient Hawaiian games converted with current day props such as spear throwing using lawn darts and a watermelon as the target. None of them sliced open or even stuck a dart in the watermelon.

Rolling stones was a little easier and similar to horse shoes with sticks dug into the dirt. Only instead of horse shoes, you rolled rocks and the closest person to roll a rock to the stick, without touching it, won.

After supper the paper lanterns lit the marina and when it came time for the night scavenger hunt. Joan took a round out to catch up with some of the regulars who were also her yacht friends, while the other three grabbed a paper, their glow sticks and got to searching.

Jake and Sydney ended up with a group of girls, most of who knew Haylee and before they even got halfway through the list the two snuck away from the group, who were doing a fine job without them.

They walked back toward the low music coming from the dance at the yacht club and away from the bush where the girls were searching for a stick in the shape of an "S". In the dark, that seemed like a lost battle.

It had been a wonderful day, even better because Jake was there.

Jake.

What was she going to do about Jake? She could start by listening to what he had to say. He claimed he would talk about anything she wanted but she suspected there were "buts" involved in that statement. How could he change his mind so quickly from absolutely not discussing any of it to discussing anything she wanted? It didn't make sense, so she was leery about getting her hopes up and fighting the urge to

LAKESHORE LOVE

reach over and hold his hand.

"Where did you get white shorts with such little notice?" She smiled realizing where she let her question hang. "Let me guess, you're surprising closet."

He chuckled. "No comment."

"Who did you leave in charge at the Cliff House? You and Joan have never been away at the same time."

"Devon."

"Do you think he is ready to handle it for four days?"

Jake nodded.

That was good.

They stopped at the edge of the party.

"Do you want to go?" Jake asked.

She shook her head. Her body felt drained, after yesterday's fight with him, then picking Abby up and having another fight, then seeing him on the boat and having another battle inside her, she was beyond ready for bed. She also wanted to check her cell phone in case Kate had texted or called and, if not, she wanted to send a text to make sure Abby was alright. She was even considering calling Devon to keep an eye out for her, but felt that was asking a little much. If all else failed she would phone Riley.

Jake walked back to the boat with her.

"Where are you sleeping?" she asked, as they climbed aboard not even taking into consideration the three cabins were occupied until that very moment. Her mind had been on other things. Jake things.

He nodded at one of the sun beds. *Outside? He was sleeping outside?*

"No. You can have my cabin. I will crawl in with Haylee, she won't mind."

"No, I don't want to impose. Besides I like it out here at night." He stepped toward her. "Close your eyes."

She sent him a questioning look.

He grinned. "Just do it."

Taking a deep breath she closed her eyes.

"Do you hear that?" His whisper was low and so close she felt his breath touch her ear. All she could hear was her thundering heartbeat.

She shook her head.

"Listen," he whispered as his hands lightly moved her hair off her shoulders tucking strands behind her ears, giving them complete access to whatever he wanted her to hear. Her ears couldn't hear anything as she stood still and wondered what part of her he would touch next. When his hands did nothing she inhaled the night marina air and slowly released her breath, listening ro their surroundings. As she stopped thinking about how close they were standing alone under the stars she left room to listen to the soft hum from the dance, the insects singing a matching tune, the water hitting against the boat and she knew why he wanted to sleep outside with nature, it was beautiful.

"When Dad took us boating, I would always sleep out here. I acted like it was because I was so angry." He chuckled at his adolescent behavior and she smiled.

"I could see that. You were such a stubborn Stow." He had been as rebellious as Sydney had been obeying. "Still are."

She opened her eyes to find him closer than she'd expected. Without asking, he slid his hand around her back drawing their eager bodies together, while slowly slipping his hand in hers and moving them with nature's music. This was not how she'd imagined this evening's end when she dragged herself out of bed this morning. She liked it.

As her head pressed against the side of his, she closed her eyes and let the feelings she was burying deep down in her gut free and, for just this evening, she let herself feel what it would be like to be this man's woman: to be in his arms, to let him lead her, to trust him, and to love him fully. She felt the relaxing ambience she knew would consume and complete her. Why had it taken them so long to make a move for more than just friends?

"When I left you I thought I was coming back that night," he whispered into her ear resurfacing her fear and stomping the completeness back down. "That's why I left so early. I thought I could jump in my bike, drive the distance, get Adalyn and bring her back."

Why didn't you call the next day? Or the next? Ask him. I can't.

"When I got there a day turned into weeks then months and suddenly a year had passed," he said, as if reading her thoughts.

He was opening up to her which was exactly what she needed at the beach, but right now, after the arguments from the evening before still fresh in her mind, she wasn't as quick to just listen or want to understand.

Sydney pulled out of his grasp and stepped back, breaking the physical connection. "Suddenly a year passed?" She shook her head. That was unacceptable.

"I know you don't understand. Hell, I don't even understand what happened."

"No, I don't."

"I do understand that I never should have left you the

way I did. I picked you up that night planning to tell you that I was leaving and then one thing led to another and when I woke up I couldn't tell you."

"So you slept with me and bailed."

He looked hurt. "It wasn't like that for me."

"It was like that for me."

He stepped toward her. "I'm sorry. I can't take it back. I can't fix it. If I could do it over, Syd that would be the first thing I would change. I would never have left you like that."

"But you can't do it over."

"You're right, I can't."

She folded her arms across her chest. That was that. It was exactly what she wanted to hear, that he wouldn't leave her again. It didn't make her feel better. *Why not?* It saddened her that the peace she'd thought she would find with those words were missing. What more did she want?

"I can't do this right now." Because she didn't know what she wanted.

He nodded. "I can wait." He held the patience that was typical of her.

"I don't even know if I want to do this now." *Liar! Yes you do!*

Jake looked so sad. "That's your decision Syd. I support whatever you decide. If you want to be friends, I will always be your friend."

Ugh! Why was he being so nice? "Good night Jake."

"Good night Syd."

Sydney closed her cabin door and leaned against it. What was wrong with her?

Chapter Twelve

THE NEXT MORNING after a restless sleep Sydney cringed at the sunlight. Self control had never been hard for Sydney. She knew right from wrong, she knew when to speak and when not to.

During the night, envisioning a shirtless Jake sleeping just above her on one of the sunbeds, self-control seemed new to her. She'd had to dig into every deep part of her brain to keep herself from not to crawling out of her bed, climbing up the stairs and curling up beside him and asking him to promise to never leave her again.

Is that what you need? A promise from him? She had no idea, but after sleeping alone, craving Jake she wished she knew exactly what her mind needed so she could stop engaging in her self-control.

Holding her pick-me-up tea, she scanned the harbor. *Beautiful.* Sydney and Haylee were lucky to have the opportunity to vacation to such gorgeous spots via boat while Joan covered all the expenses for them, including their shopping. Sydney had long ago stopped trying to pay Joan for the outings and meals she bought for them. Joan never accepted reimbursed money.

Where was everyone?

Sydney heard Haylee laugh and found her on land playing horseshoes with Jake...shirtless Jake. *Really?* Was it that hot out already that he'd had to rip his shirt off? Thinking of ripped, it was amazing the body he'd acquired with his morning visits to the gym. That was his venting post. Jake wasn't a man who gave any consideration to how he looked, much less what other people thought of him, and the gym was no exception...no matter his teasing about glorious mountains as he called them...he went to pound out any frustration he was feeling.

Sydney straightened the grin that had crept across her face at the memory. *Glorious mountains.* The memory of the breathtaking comments he'd made about her body sent a wave of burning desire which jolted her awake more efficiently than the tea she was holding.

Joan came up behind her. "It's nice for Haylee to have someone her own age to play with," she said comically, passing by and settling on a lounger.

Sydney chuckled watching him run around acting like an adolescent cheering and flaunting his scores at Haylee.

Sydney settled beside Joan. "What are the plans for today?"

Joan flipped through a magazine and shrugged. "I don't know, your daughter has it all figured out. We are running late however, since you decided to sleep in." *Sleep in? What time was it?* "Jake had to practically drag her off this boat so she didn't wake you up."

A chuckle passed her lips before she sipped her tea.

"Does Jake's presence have anything to do with you?" Joan asked. "Haylee mentioned you've been acting weird around each other lately and after yesterday morning and then the two of you snuck off last night..."

Sydney wasn't sure how to answer Joan. If she told

her the truth and then it didn't work out between them she would be stuck in the middle.

"Mom!" Haylee yelled, boarding the boat and giving Sydney the break she needed to avoid Joan's question. She needed to figure out what was going on between her and Jake before she could talk about it with anyone else. "What are you doing still not ready?"

Waking up. Sydney cradled her tea and sent her daughter a *leave me alone* look. She'd just crawled out of bed and she needed a moment.

Jake was right behind her, shirt in hand and his tanned torso flexing another good morning to her.

Go away. As if I didn't see enough of that wonderful body all night wanting to reach out and touch and now first thing in the morning was the real thing. Ugh!

"Morning," he said.

Last night's conversation seemed so far away with the fresh morning and her groggy mind.

"Morning. This is a first, you up before me." There were days she'd arrived at the bar in the afternoon and he was still in his loft sleeping.

He hiked his finger at Haylee. "She's not a quiet morning person."

Haylee shook her head. "Suck it up," she said to Jake. She looked at Sydney. "And you, get up and go get ready." Haylee started listing their day and times.

Sydney stood up. "I'm going." It was way too early to cram an entire day into one minute without fully waking up, besides...Jake was distracting her.

Below deck in the kitchen, Sydney gulped the rest of her tea before jumping in the shower for a long warm, pelting, body relaxing private time to herself.

She wrapped the towel around her wet body, tucked the top to secure it, and then grabbed her makeup bag off the counter. Pulling it open she saw Haylee had been rummaging inside and her facial sunscreen was missing. She wasn't spending the day outside in the sun without protecting her face. Racoon eyes were not a good look and the body lotion was too oily for her face.

Groaning, she quickly slipped into Haylee's cabin looking for the sunscreen. The cabin looked like a tornado had gone through. Her suitcases of clothes now spread across the bed, her make-up across the trays on the counter, and...Sydney caught sight of one of her dresses. Then another one and another. Was she going to have any clothes left in her cabin?

Forgetting about the sunscreen, she grabbed the loose, above the knee rosette print dress letting her towel slip away. Before she slipped into it, she noticed the belt missing. Her eyes roamed the disaster of a room. *Haylee!*

Sydney tucked the dress under her arm and started looking for the belt with no luck.

The bathroom?

The sunscreen was likely in the bathroom. This bathroom was smaller than her own and she and Haylee hardly fit in together with a wood shutter closed around the bathing area. She wasn't complaining about the size and found it incredible they each had their own private baths no matter the size.

Her sunscreen was below the mirror. She took the three steps and reached for the small bottle when she heard the shutter sliding open behind her.

Her daughter was showering after the rush she gave her? Was she kidding?

Sydney opened her mouth to make Haylee aware of her presence as she turned and slapped straight into Jake's drenched water soaked and *naked* body.

Come on! It was like last night's dream come true.

She stilled, her eyes staring at the dripping tanned chest that had played wake-up in her dreams all night and now only inches away from her face.

She gulped.

The sudden urge to close in the distance and kiss...lick...away the water made her suck her bottom lip in and clamp down. Sydney never had thoughts like these and it was only Jake that brought them out in her.

Jake stilled and she was afraid to look up. She wasn't feeling embarrassed pressed against him, both of them naked...okay maybe a little bit...but it was the feelings their connection was pulsing through her body that she feared would be written across her face after she told him she wasn't ready. Ready to talk and ready to touch seemed like two entirely different things that second.

"What are you doing in here?" she snapped instead and could have sworn he chuckled at her flustered self.

"Having a shower." That was obvious, but why was he in Haylee's cabin? That was obvious too...he certainly wasn't going to shower in Joan's cabin. "Did you come looking for me?"

Her eyes fell closed. She couldn't tell if he was serious or joking. She couldn't tell if the answer, *yes* that flashed in her head should be taken serious or not.

"I needed sunscreen," she pushed out.

"You search for sunscreen naked? In your daughter's cabin?" Humor now threaded his words.

This was not funny. Nothing about his growing manhood against her body was funny. Did he not even notice? Of course he noticed...did he not care?

Back up. Walk out the door and put your dress on.

Her feet stayed suctioned to the floor.

"Did you find it?" he asked.

"Find what?"

"The sunscreen."

Sydney opened her eyes and braved a glance at him. Big mistake. His appetite for her met her straight on.

He pushed her damp hair away from her face and she couldn't wait to feel where is hand would land afterwards. "My body could use a rub down," he said

"Jake?" At the sound of Haylee's voice coming into the cabin and knowing the bathroom door behind them was wide open, Sydney shoved Jake back into the shower and pulled the shutter around them. The shower was smaller and there was no getting away from him now, but with her hands against his chest at least they were separated...a bit.

"Yeah?" Jake called.

Sydney felt the wet warmth of the arm he kept wrapped around her from the tumble backwards into the shower. She felt his lower body pressed against her and she almost forgot why they were in there.

"Have you seen my mom?" From the distant call Sydney was sure she was on the other side of the bedroom door, but she couldn't be positive so they didn't move.

Jake grinned down at her.

Sydney shook her head wildly.

"Uh, nope."

Sydney sighed in relief and caught Jake's eyes move to her chest with an approving gaze.

"Oh," Haylee said.

Sydney slapped his chest and glared at him. His blue eyes didn't hide the humor.

"Grandma and I went to go check out breakfast at the yacht club but when neither of you texted me back so I thought I better come tell you."

Thank God! That gave her an alibi to have already gotten off the boat.

"Your mom is probably already headed there."

"Alright. If not and you see her will you tell her?"

"Sure thing kid."

"Thanks."

The door didn't shut and that meant Haylee had stayed on the other side of the bedroom. Good because Sydney's towel was bunched up on the floor at the door.

How had they gotten into this predicament?

How were they going to get out of it? Sydney wasn't even sure she wanted to get out of it.

"I think the coast is clear," Jake said.

Sydney was standing in his path and until she moved, he was stuck, against the wall, naked.

"Sydney?"

Her eyes found his again. "Yes?"

His deep breath pushed their chests together. "I don't know what to do."

"What do you mean?"

He released the air and it danced across her face. "Are you going to walk away or do you want me to kiss you?"

I want you to kiss me. Kiss me now. Kiss me hard.

"Walk away Syd."

Why was he telling her to walk away after offering her a kiss? "What?"

He let go of her and pushed open the shutter. "We're not here yet. If we do this now it will only add one more thing that we have to figure out later."

Huh?

Jake lifted her, turned and wiggled his way out of the shower, wrapping a towel around his waist. He held one out to her.

She took it angrily and wrapped it around her body holding the corner, knowing her shaking fingers wouldn't be able to secure it in place. "Is that your solution to everything? Walking away?" She couldn't believe the words came out of her mouth when she knew he was doing the right thing. The right thing hurt. It felt like he was rejecting her, no matter what he was saying. He was good at walking away, she had a point!

"Damn it Syd, I'm trying not to make this any more of a mess."

"Why?" she snapped. "Is messy too hard for you to deal with? Don't want to talk about it?" *Why was she fighting with him?* "Oh forbid Jake Stow actually had to have to share a part of his life!" She threw her hands in the air dramatically.

His tone didn't raise in anger like her own which made her even angrier. "I don't want to hurt you."

"How is this going to hurt me?" She was yelling at him now.

"You're angry at me. Engaging in this isn't going to fix the problems we already have. You're all over the place, you want to talk, you don't want to talk..."

"Oh I'm all over? I wanted to talk Jake and you made it clear it was none of my damn business."

"I didn't mean it."

"When do you talk and not mean it? You watch and calculate every word that comes out of your mouth, that's why nobody can get close to you. You keep everyone at a short distance with warning stares and a clamped jaw."

He clamped his jaw. "It's a subject I don't like Sydney, but I'm offering to tell you anything you want to hear about it, but having sex before we've talked will end with you getting angrier with me or yourself..."

"Don't tell me how I feel!"

His patience was thinning. "Would you rather I kiss you, make love to you and afterwards when you're thinking straight, let you regret it?"

"Yes, Jake! It's my decision!"

***

JAKE KNEW HE shouldn't. Every single sensible part of his brain told him to walk out of the bathroom and let her settle down because she would regret it.

He didn't listen.

Letting all the restraint he'd been holding go he crossed the room and lifted her off her feet and against the back of the shower kissing her saucy lips. She'd never spoken to him so forcefully angry and damn it if her arguing to have sex didn't turn him on more.

Whether she'd been expecting or ready for him to claim her, she was quick to respond. Her hands gripped the sides of his face pulling his mouth deeper into hers. Her legs had worked their way around him and he felt her towel slip to her waist and she arched her chest against him. She wanted this.

He ploughed into her mouth and she matched his forcefulness, sucking, biting and moaning. In all the love making scenarios that had played out in his head, never had he taken Sydney for an angry lover.

His hands found her breasts and she arched back at the touch opening her throat for his mouth. He lifted her higher and his mouth found the mounds taking each one in. She moaned in delight her nails digging into his back. He wanted her. He needed her.

Lifting her away from the wall he carried her into the bedroom and laid her on the bed landing on top of her and finding her mouth again.

They could sort things out later. He'd given his word he would talk to her and whatever she needed he would give her. This would not ruin anything between them. It might even push her to talk to him sooner.

He reached his hand down and found the wetness between her legs. She was ready for him. She wanted him.

"Jake?" she breathed against his lips. He licked her word away and dipped in to search for her tongue while his hand played below, teasing her.

"Jake?" Her hand pushed his away and he stopped. He lifted his head and looked at her. Just as he'd suspected would happen, regret consumed her face.

He dropped his head against her rising and falling chest. Why hadn't he walked away?

Without a word, he didn't really think talking right now would be a good idea, he stood and walked away.

Chapter Thirteen

SYDNEY HAD NEVER dressed so quickly in her life. Carrying her sandals she high tailed it away from the boat before Jake and didn't slow until the clubhouse came into view.

What had she been thinking?

She dropped her sandals on the ground and slipped into them.

Was Jake going to come for breakfast? Her eyes darted the path behind her but no sign of him.

He would be furious. She wouldn't be surprised if he didn't talk to her again for the whole trip. She'd dangled herself in front of him then when she landed on Haylee's pile of clothes there was no way she could go through with it. Not when Haylee could be affected by their sloppiness. Not when she really didn't know what was going on between them, just like he told her before she got all wired.

She'd messed up now. *Great, just great.*

Lacking an appetite, but not wanting to explain why to Haylee and Joan when she found them, she went through the buffet then scanned the tables. They weren't in sight. Where were they? Had she taken that long on the boat that they'd already eaten and left?

Sydney sat alone and tried to eat, but her knotted stomach couldn't handle it so she quickly disposed of what was left on her plate...everything.

On the way back to the boat she saw Joan and Haylee sitting by the fire pit in the distance. No Jake.

Sydney didn't know how she felt about that as she walked toward them, noting they had their purses, so they were waiting to get the day started. Did she want to see Jake? Or was it better if she didn't?

"I don't regret it." Sydney jumped away from Jake at the sound of his voice and covered her chest with her hand. Why was he sneaking up on her? Where had he come from?

She glared at him. "Don't sneak up on me like that."

"I didn't really sneak. You were just lost in your own world." *Lost in our world.*

Sydney bit her lower lip. "Why is this so hard for us? I mean usually people meet, date, get to know each other and are looking for the same things to move forward. What are we doing?"

Jake didn't appear angry like she had thought he would be after her all over the place mind. "We've already known each other for years, better than most married couples. We've had breakfast, lunch and dinner together probably as many times as married couples. We know each other pretty good...except that time in my life I am waiting to talk to you about...so I guess we're already like an old married couple we've just been missing out on the intimate part..." He grinned. "...so it's making us a little randy."

Why did she even ask? "Randy?"

"Horny, lustful..."

"Yes I know what it means and that doesn't answer my question at all. Are we dating? Are we trying to date? What is happening between us?"

"What do you want?"

"I don't know. It feels like we haven't stopped fighting since that kiss." Sydney wasn't a fighter and the more she fought with him the more worn out she was becoming.

"I don't want to fight with you." He stepped toward her. "I hate fighting with you to be honest. We've never played the fighting game." It was true. Even in their youth, fighting hadn't been part of their interactions.

"It's exhausting," she admitted, never in her life feeling so emotionally drained.

"Well, I had a cold shower just so I could spend the afternoon with you."

She groaned and covered her face. Why did he have to bring this morning back up?

"Why don't we agree not to fight for the entire day?" he suggested. "And no naked body touching, kissing, or randy moves either until we have talked."

She slid her fingers down her face. "Alright. But, you know it's shopping day right?"

"I don't know what that even means."

It was her turn to chuckle, because by lunch he was going to be fighting to not run away.

***

WHEN JOAN AND Haylee walked through the Hastings Heritage Museum gate, arms looped together, Joan in her white and navy striped capris, another nautical outfit, and Haylee in short-shorts and a long, lose tank top that hung past the shorts on each edge, Sydney grinned knowing they would be lost in the town's history re-enactment for hours.

Sydney yelled to them that she would catch up in a bit

but they hardly registered her at all with little waves on their way to the souvenir shop. That was their first stop, had been every year to find the goofiest dress-up costumes before entering the village.

Sydney walked back to the beach and found Jake just where they'd left him, sitting under a weeping willow one leg stretched out on the grass while the other was bent upwards steadying a paper he was reading behind his sunglasses.

He had lasted longer than Sydney had given him credit for. All morning he shopped with them but clearly only enjoyed the first maybe half hour. He'd sent her warm smiles and they hadn't fought once. After lunch, he had abandoned them for the very spot he was sitting now.

Sydney stopped at a food concession and bought two bags of handmade roasted nuts before joining Jake. She wanted to take him back to the heritage museum to watch the actors walk around all dressed up like they were right out of the nineteenth century making butter, quilting, baking and so much more. There was no rush. The two girls would be staying for the supper they put on and into the evening when they closed.

The closer she got to Jake the faster her heart sped. He was wearing black shorts today, unusual for him being a denim man, but a nice change, revealing his toned-thick legs. He was wearing the white t-shirt with a Hastings Port logo on the front that Haylee had convinced him to buy.

Sydney watched as women passed checking him out and he didn't look up until her sandals stopped beside him.

"Is it over?" he asked, his eyes not moving to the paper across his legs and referring to the shopping.

She smiled. "Yes."

He over exaggerated a thankful sigh as she sat beside him and passed him the bags of nuts. He pulled his sunglasses off and his eyes lit up. "These are my favorite."

She smiled. "I know. I buy them for you every year and I promised you more than one."

"Where are they? I need a year's supply."

She laughed. "I'm never telling or else what would you need me for?" She teased but Jake's face went serious.

He covered her hand that was resting on the grass beside him with his own and squeezed. "I need you," he said. "That's why I'm here. You wanted to know what we are doing and it's hard to specify because we have already done so much of what couples do, but I guess if you need a title, I want to date you. Call you my girlfriend. Kiss you. Spend the night with you," he added with a wink.

Sydney laced her fingers between his. "I want all those things too," she said low then snuggled against his side and rested her head on his arm feeling him relax against her. "I'm ready to talk Jake."

The museum could wait, this was a perfect moment and she wasn't going to rush it.

***

"TOP HAT OR fedora?" Jake asked slipping each one on and posing for Sydney. She laughed sunshine around them.

"Do they have a cowboy hat?"

He frowned. "Listen here, I've narrowed it down and these are your options?"

She sucked in her naturally pink lips debating the

choices. "Fedora," she finally said with a confident nod. "You in a top hat." She shook her head. "It doesn't suit. However a fedora is like a gangster of that time, kind of a rebel."

He plopped the fedora on his head. "You like rebels?" he asked in a dangerous tone that got another laugh from her.

"I like you and you're known as the rebel of Willow Valley." She shrugged. "So I guess yes I do."

Rebel of Willow Valley. Boy, his reputation preceded him.

"Well then. What should my gal be wearing?" He glanced around the well stocked souvenir shop that had everything from hats right up to complete dresses and suits for every station from back in the day for tourists to buy.

Sydney had a large red brimmed hat in her hand which she was considering but his eyes landed on lace and ribbon.

He grabbed the corset off the rack and flashed it in front of her. "This," he said.

Sydney's face paled and she snatched the sexy bustier away, putting it back on the rack. He was already envisioning it around her tiny waist.

"I'm taking the hat." She pulled him toward the check out.

He laughed and paid for their hats.

Jake and Sydney took their time wearing their newly purchased hats, just like lots of other tourist bustling around.

Since Sydney was a regular visitor at the museum, she was excited to show Jake every little detail including a corner where Haylee and her name were written under a picture hanging on the wall. When no one was looking

Sydney quickly scribbled his and they rushed out of the house laughing and holding hands like two carefree teenagers.

Every time her excitement got the best of her, Sydney would wrap her hand in his to pull him a little quicker along or she would slow down and lean against his arm as they walked. Jake reveled in the feeling her touch gave him. The wholeness, the content and the more time they spent together the more he seemed ready to tell her as much as she needed to hear.

They rounded the corner and a small white church with a steeple came into view. The double doors were held open with purple cascading flowers coming out of urns.

This was the busiest area they had encountered and there was a closed off section with a tent and more purple flowers everywhere. Lilacs. Sydney's favorite. The smell had him curdling inside. They were too strong and too floral scented for his nosebuds.

"They're having a wedding," Sydney said.

They walked across the grass, stopping at the satin rope fencing off area.

She leaned against him and watched the commotion. "I've only ever seen one before," she said and he realized it wasn't the workers re-enacting a wedding from the eighteen hundreds, but an actual wedding. Guests dressed in their best modern attire flooded around the doors before the bride and groom exited for pictures, as a horse and carriage waited.

"Look how beautiful it is." Sydney touched the flowers on the post. "Lilacs." She told him. "Don't you smell them?"

Of course he had. They had overwhelmed every

sense.

He nodded.

She bent down and inhaled them deeply as though the smell wasn't strong enough already.

She stood back up and watched the wedding gathering for more photos. "How romantic. What a wonderful place to share vows where everything is so down to earth, you know." She looked up at him. "No cell phones, no Wi-Fi," she added.

"My kind of atmosphere."

"It's too bad I can't show you the church. It's so beautiful inside—antique pews and amazing paintings plus there are gowns you can try on." She smiled and started tugging him away.

What was with this family and playing dress up?

Eventually as Jake was starting to get hungry they found Joan and Haylee. They were not wearing fancy hats like the two of them. Instead, a plain peasants old-fashioned dress made Haylee look like she belonged in another time. She'd even rolled her hair into a bun and wore what almost looked like a bonnet. Joan on the other hand, not surprisingly, wore an incredible old-fashioned, sequined, beaded, ribbon-laced, velvet and satin ruby red with black detail dress that looked like it held the heat.

Sydney laughed, touching their outfits and pulling her cell phone out to take pictures.

"Uncle Jake I'm totally diggin' the hat. You look like a gangster."

"It suits him," Joan said and again it was missing the heat behind it that she was accustomed to dishing out.

"Give me your cell," Sydney said to Jake holding her

LAKESHORE LOVE

hand out.

When he dug it out of his pocket, she stood on her tiptoes, they're heads touched and she said smile and flashed a picture.

"Now when you see this you'll want to come every year." Jake wouldn't need a picture to remind him he wanted to spend every day with this woman.

Chapter Fourteen

JAKE GEARED THE boat down and looked at Haylee to make sure the position was right.

She gave him a thumbs up so he cut the engine.

"We don't want to get too close to the boat that is letting off the fireworks or our heads will be looking straight up in the sky," she explained, arching her neck to demonstrate. She peeked an eye at him from the awkward position. "See what I'm saying."

He laughed. "I got ya Haylee."

Haylee and her Hastings port friend, Kimberly, went to the front of the boat to wait for the sun to set and the show to begin while Joan stayed on shore visiting a couple at another dock.

That meant more alone time for him and Sydney. He found Sydney below deck preparing a tray of cheese and crackers. She'd changed into a longer dress and wore a beige cardigan.

He wrapped his arms around her waist pressing against her back and nuzzling into the side of her neck. "You smell delicious," he whispered.

She laughed, continuing to slice through the cheese. "You smell like exhaust."

He nibbled her ear. "Do you like it?"

She laughed. "Not at all."

His hand took the knife out of hers and set it on the counter.

"Not at all?" he asked as he spun her around. He wanted to kiss the laughter that escaped her but he didn't want to complicate things after the great day they'd had together. They needed to talk, but at the same time they wanted the same things...to date. Dating included kissing which wasn't sex like this morning's ordeal, but could lead to sex, but...he was confused as hell.

She tilted her head. "What are you thinking?" she asked her fingers playing with the front of his shirt but her eyes watching him.

"What are you thinking?"

"I asked you first."

He grinned. "I'm thinking about what you're thinking about."

She made a face. "What?"

He took a deep breath. "We haven't exactly talked yet and well I wanted to kiss you but I wasn't sure if I should because I didn't know what you were thinking and after this morning I didn't know if I should."

"You want to kiss me?"

"All the time."

She chuckled. "I have a confession," she whispered.

He leaned in close.

"I want to kiss you all the time."

That was all he needed. His mouth covered her soft lips in a gentle and slow kiss. She was as delicious as the night at the beach and as the evening at his place. Only this time there was no background noise in his head warning him because together they were going to figure all this out. Knowing he was going to get to kiss these lips for the rest of his life, he took his time savoring her. And not only her lips, he savored her touch too. First her hands pressing his chest, then as her hands clenched his shirt he relished her knuckles digging into his skin. He appreciated the way her body, her legs especially, naturally welcomed his to move between her. He also took delight in how she felt underneath his hands and his hands couldn't get enough. They wanted to touch her everywhere.

When she pulled her mouth away and ran her tongue across his, he almost pulled her back.

"I'm going to take the food to the girls."

How was she thinking about the girls?

"I'm going to have a quick shower." He smelled like exhaust from helping some of the other guys at the harbor with a boat. "Then I will be right up."

It was the quickest shower and he'd ever taken. He met the girls at the bow of the boat and watched an amazing fireworks show.

The two young girls took off for the nightly campfire at the yacht club building leaving Sydney and Jake alone. Again.

He wondered why he hadn't come on more of these trips with her since they were so easily getting in some quality alone time.

Sydney scooted close beside him, leaning into the nook of his body and touching his leg. Her touch sent desire straight under his zipper but he was trying to do the right thing here. Damn, nothing had ever been this difficult.

"As much as I would much rather pick you up, carry

you below, strip your clothes and step under the water with you..." She gasped and he felt her fingers tighten on his leg. "I think we should have that talk first."

Sydney looked up at him. "You're so bold," she said, surprise lighting her eyes.

"Only with you." He kissed her head. "Wanna try it?"

She looked mortified. "No."

"Come on." He gave her side a little squeeze.

She laughed. "No."

"I might like it."

She laughed harder. "Jake, Stop."

"Alright. Let's get down to business." As much as he didn't want to. But the faster they talked the faster they could get into that shower without causing suspicion. "I will tell you everything you want to know about those years in my life but I have one condition."

She arched an eyebrow. "Alright."

"I don't want to know anything about you, Kyle or Haylee."

Jake had been expecting her body to become rigid at the request because she wanted to tell him about her life after he left. He didn't want it to be said out loud. It was done and over and they were who they were. Life was good. He didn't want to mess with it.

"I know there is something about my departure that you need answered, something that scares you. I don't know it is but I want you to be at peace with it. But I don't want the Kyle/Haylee topic. Ever. This condition isn't for now this moment or this year...it's permanent. I don't ever want to discuss it."

He pulled away from her and turned on the seat so his

leg was between them. He needed to see her whole face and know she understood his condition.

"I would do anything for you, Sydney McAdams. Anything. But not the Haylee/Kyle topic. I can't do it. That's my condition and if you can't agree now take your time. I'm not going anywhere."

***

I WANT TO tell you. I want to tell you.

Sydney battled the words wanting to surface and a full-fledged conversation of rationalizations went through her head.

He doesn't want to know. That's his condition. He has a right to know. But he doesn't want to know and that is his right. Was it? He's offering you a life. Don't you want it? Yes. Then say alright. Say alright! But he doesn't know. But he doesn't want too.

Until his hand touched her face she hadn't realized how zoned out she had become. The warmth soothed her and she forever wanted his warmth to soothe her.

One condition. Take it.

"No rush Sydney," he said. He was so sweet. He was so good to her, good to Haylee. What more could she ever ask for in a man?

"I mean it." He bent over and kissed her forehead. She leaned into his touch taking deep breaths. "Tomorrow, the next day. A week from now...I can wait."

A week from now! She didn't want to wait a week from now. There was her answer plain as day.

She pulled away to look into his eyes. "This is hard because I want to tell you."

He nodded.

But she wanted him more. "But I will agree to your one condition if you agree that if the day comes and you want to know, you will ask me."

He kissed her. "Agreed," he said against her lips. "What do you want to talk about first?" He pulled away but held her hands between them on his leg.

Sydney took a deep breath. She didn't want to talk right now. Today had been a wonderful day with him and sitting alone listening to the distant music like they had the first night she wanted him to wrap his arms around her and hold her tight.

I'm afraid you will leave me again. It was that simple and yet so hard to say.

"Do you want to know about my mother?"

Not really. She knew his mother was a drunk and a drug addict.

Just say the words Sydney. Tell him flat out what scares you.

"Do you want to know about Adalyn?"

Why couldn't she just say it instead of keeping him guessing?

His confused and concerned smile tore at her heart. He finally wanted to talk and she didn't.

Still holding his hands, Sydney stood and walked in front of him. She settled his hands on her behind and he grinned up at her enjoying the position. He even gave her a little pinch that caused a giggle to escape. As she straddled him, his pleasurable surprise made her insides turn over with excitement. Was this what it felt like to be seductive? Because it felt so darn good.

"This is bold," he breathed, running his hands up and

down her back.

It was bold! And it was exciting! And it was nothing like Sydney!

Sydney kissed his reluctant lips. He wanted to talk. How out of the ordinary. But her persuading lips soon had his lips converted, kissing her back and once he had a taste he lifted Sydney and laid her on the bench settling between her legs.

Sydney moaned against him.

She felt his hands move from the back of her knee slowly under her skirt and up her thigh. She was jealous he got to touch her skin so she slipped her hands under his t-shirt. His stomach felt just as strong and solid as it looked and when she moved her fingers down to his pants he moaned against her. "Syd?"

Her hand moved down the front of his shorts and rubbed the hardness there. Her bold touch seemed to make him envious because his hands dipped under her dress and slipped under her underwear and...

"Take it into cabin Gees." Joan's heels tapped across the floor beside them.

Sydney froze.

Jake froze.

There was no way climbing off each other would be better than just staying put.

"Your daughter is just on shore children," she said as she past. "I'm calling it a night but there's not a ripple in this lake so if this thing is a rocking all night I will know it's not the weather."

The door to below deck slammed behind Joan.

Sydney's eyes found Jake's and she could not help

but laugh. The hard look on his face broke and he laughed with her. His hands were on both sides of her face and he rubbed her hair with his thumbs.

"That wasn't exactly the response I imagined with Joan," he said.

She smiled. "I don't think you ever really gave her a chance."

"I don't think I want to talk about that while I'm lying between your legs."

She bit her lower lip. "You should get off me before Haylee gets a glimpse of this show."

He kissed her. "I want to rock this boat with you."

She laughed. "With Joan's cabin next to mine it's not going to happen."

He frowned. "You started this."

She reached up and gave him a peck. "You started this with that kiss on the beach."

"I don't regret it."

Chapter Fifteen

JAKE WATCHED HAYLEE slurp another one of those raw oysters into her mouth and his stomach turned.

He pushed his plate of food away. He was done.

Haylee grinned at him. "It's delicious."

Joan and Sydney agreed with her, each happily eating their seafood plates while Jake had been enjoying his burger and fries. But he couldn't stomach watching them suck little slippery, raw fish out of shells.

After supper on their last night, Jake walked hand in hand with Sydney to the beach. The wind picked up and took her skirt with it a few times.

"It's going to be a rocky night on that boat," he teased.

Sydney playfully hit his arm that hers looped around.

"I was just saying. I had to have another freezing cold shower this morning."

He felt her giggle against him.

They walked to the beach and sat on the sand watching the sun set.

"Jake?"

"Yeah?"

"I don't need to know what happened when you left. Not the details you don't want to share. I will always be here to listen if you want to share. It's just..." She paused with a sigh and he waited. "It was so hard when you left. You didn't call, you didn't even tell me you were leaving. I just woke up and I was alone."

He wanted to tell her how sorry he was but he didn't want to interrupt her when she was finally talking, asking him for whatever she needed so they could move forward. He'd waited all weekend to have this talk and was excited she would be on his arm when they returned to Willow Valley just like he'd planned.

"If I ask you not to leave me like that again I know you won't."

He would never leave her like that again.

"You've already said that's the one thing you would change and that's the one thing I've been afraid of happening again. That's all I need." Why did he sense a "but" to follow? "I thought if you told me why you left, what you did and what was more important..." She paused and very slowly said, "than me."

He squeezed her hand but didn't say anything. His leaving had nothing to do with who more important.

"I thought if I understood why you left and could relate to you back then...I don't know...then maybe you wouldn't do it again or maybe I could prepare my heart for the next time you did." He was never doing it again. "It doesn't make sense I know. I just don't know how I would deal with you leaving again."

Jake wanted to tell her that he would never leave her again but he had listened to what she said and that wasn't what she needed to hear right now. She needed to understand why he left even if she was claiming she didn't. He was relieved that was all she wanted and not every single detail he couldn't share.

"You know my childhood story that Joan was our nanny and my Dad's mistress and my mom left us when she found out."

That was the underlying friction between the two of them all these years. It hadn't always been like that. When Jake and Adalyn were young and Joan was the live-in nanny there had been a time when the child in Jake would even say he loved Joan. She'd been around as long as Jake could remember, raising them when their mother would leave on her fancy trips. She was gone for weeks, sometimes months, at a time and his dad travelled for business. It was quite often just the three of them and Kyle until the shit hit the ceiling and his mother left.

"We moved to Willow Valley while my dad was having some midlife crisis and Adalyn found where our mom was. One day, months before I left, we got on my bike and rode out to see her. She wasn't the same woman that left us. She was a drunk, an addict...she didn't even recognize us. We came home confused and blaming Joan and Dad for what my mom had become. Adalyn thought her love could change my mom."

Sydney's head rested against his shoulder and her hand other hand stroked his arm, giving him the strength to continue.

"Adalyn left, but I wasn't going back." Only Adalyn knew that truth after she'd tried to convince him to help her save her mother. "That place was disgusting and I didn't see any good there. But Adalyn called me begging me to come help her." *She only had to ask once.* "She was in a panic, so I agreed. That was when I picked you up. I thought I would be back before you even noticed. I was young Sydney. I know you don't think that counts for anything but it counts for my carelessness. My thinking I knew everything while knowing nothing. I left. It was the hardest decision of his life. I was drawn into their world while trying to get them out and finally the day came that I realized neither of them were ever leaving. I walked away and I came home."

Jake stood up, unable to sit any longer. He held his hand out and helped her to her feet, pulling her close to him.

"I came home for you. I thought about you every single day more than once and every day I would have preferred to be home with you then there."

Softly she stroked his neck with her thumb. "I thought about you every single day you were away. I worried about you every single day."

He touched her cheek. "I'm sorry that I made you worry. I will never make you worry again. I will never leave you. I know it's only my word but I'm giving it to you. I am promising you."

***

SYDNEY HAD DECIDED she didn't need to know Jake's past as they walked hand-in-hand toward the beach on the beautiful warm evening, their last evening before they went back to Willow Valley and back to reality. She wished she'd taken Kate's offer to stay longer so they could spend more time together. Once Jake shared the past with her, she was happy he had. She felt closer to him after knowing what he'd gone through. Even though she hadn't thought she needed to hear the grounds for his departure after his first conviction to never leave her again, safeness settled around her now and a faith that he would never hurt her again. His every word loosened her heart. The love for his family was strong as was his love for her.

He was waiting for her to reply. She smiled at him and kissed him. The tension in his body dissipated in her embrace. Their kiss turned into a long hug accepting their future together.

"You're a wonderful man, Jake Stow," she told him. "You're kind, strong, and you give your heart like no one I've ever met."

"I give you my heart Syd. The whole thing."

"I give you mine," she replied. "The whole thing." She'd given him her heart a long time ago.

Jake kissed her again, then smirked down at her like he had a secret.

"What's that look for?" she asked.

"Since my presumptions this weekend have been a bull's-eye basically every time...Coming onto this boat to win you over, not having sex before we were ready, choosing a fedora instead of a cowboy hat..."

What was he going on about? "Is this going somewhere?"

"I hope so." He kissed her nose then walked her away from the beach and back along the path toward the boat. When the "y" in the path came along Sydney continued right toward the water where Joan's boat was docked while Jake pulled her left to a road of small rental cottages.

Excitement created a little more bounce into her step and she couldn't help wonder if he had rented one of these quaint little cottages, even though that would be ridiculous. Her stomach fluttered with anticipation, her grip around his hand tightened.

Stop being silly. Rented a cabin? Who does that?

Jake stopped in front of one of the cabins and pulled a key out of his pocket. Sydney stared at the key as more flutters occurred in her stomach. When she looked up at him, she didn't have to ask. He'd rented it.

"Was it too presumptuous?" he asked. "We don't have to do anything I just wanted to be alone with you without having to worry about Joan or Haylee."

He was so sweet. She answered by squeezing his hand then reaching up and grazing his cheek with her lips.

They went inside the small two bedroom cottage decorated plainly with a couch set, wooden kitchen table, chairs and boat scene paintings on the wall.

Sydney liked it.

"It's not the luxury of Joan's boat," he said, grabbing a bottle of wine that was chilling in the ice bucket and two wine glasses sitting on the table beside it.

"I don't need luxury." Besides she knew this man could afford luxury if he wanted and this was a last minute attempt to spend time alone with her. Which meant more than money ever could.

Her heartbeat pounded faster with each step to the couch. They settled down and snuggled together, leaving the wine on the coffee table.

"Like I said, we don't have to do anything. I could just hold you all night like this."

She snuggled closer. "Alright." She could let him hold her like this all night too, but her head knew they were alone. No Haylee in the next room or Joan walking past. No hiding. Most importantly, there was no fear between them. They had worked out everything that was holding them back and now everything was perfect. It was also the perfect opportunity to do more than just snuggle.

Sydney worked up the courage and touched his leg. She felt every muscle underneath her fingers tense and she wanted the same.

She remembered how he lifted her on the sun bed and landed on top of her so gently. How he'd picked her up in the shower a little rougher. Either way she liked. She remembered how she'd bravely climbed on top of him first. The memories delighted her insides. But she knew they didn't have to rush things because they had all night...alone. She also knew Jake was restraining himself, being the perfect gentleman.

Sydney stretched back on the couch, her head resting on the arm, and extended her legs across his lap wiggling her bare feet at him.

"My feet are aching from all that walking today," she said.

The look he leveled at her sent hotness through her body. He wanted her. She loved the idea of that.

She wiggled her feet, continuing the teasing torture. When Jake's hands found her feet and his thick fingers dug into her skin, she hadn't expected it to feel so good. Her eyes closed as he massaged his thumb into the arch of her foot, soothing it in a way she hadn't known she needed.

Wow.

He moved to her ankle causing jealousy from her feet. *Share,* she thought, smiling as her calf tingled beneath his touch. He took his time on each calf and Sydney felt herself sinking deeper into a trance with each rub. When his hands touched her knees, her breathing became more shallow still.

She felt him lift her legs and peeked to find him

turning toward her. Her chest was rising and falling faster. With him kneeling between her legs the urge to pull him against her was too much and she reached for him.

"Slow down," he said, keeping out of her grasp.

Slow down. Was he nuts!

His hand pressed against her chest, seemingly unfazed that his hands were against her breast. as he gently pushed her back down. All she wanted to do was pull him down with her. Slowly he slid his hand away down her stomach that dipped as he ran his fingers across the material and over the warm area longing for him. He stopped back at her knees, one hand on each gently rubbing.

"I have stared, watched and longed to touch these legs for years," he said as his the attention of both hands moved to one thigh.

She grinned. "My legs?"

He nodded, gently digging his fingertips into her skin. It felt wonderful. She wanted those fingers higher, under her dress.

"The summer is brutal with you wearing dresses and flaunting your legs."

"Flaunting?" She laughed.

"You think it's funny but..." He pushed her dress up over her right leg and touched her scar.

Ugh. Sydney grabbed his hand to move it away. Of all the places he could touch why did he touch there, a rippled piece of unattractive skin scarred from the accident.

"Hey," he said, taking her hand and kissing it. "Don't be like that. I like every part of you."

He let her hand go and went back to her scar.

She stiffened.

"Sydney."

"What?"

"It's beautiful."

She scoffed. "It's not beautiful."

"Do you want to tell me about it?"

The accident? Not at this current moment while you're rubbing me whole body down. "No."

"You've never told me about the accident."

Why was he talking about the accident now when his fingers were playing havoc with her body. Here she thought she was teasing him by making him massage her feet. The tables had turned on her, because she felt like his touch was driving her wild.

"You never asked."

"I'm asking now."

Now? Now! Why are you asking now?

"Why were you all in that vehicle?"

"I thought you didn't want to talk about Kyle and me." She didn't want to talk about it at all. She wanted him to move his hand from that area and continue right up her legs.

His face went serious. "That was the night my dad died." The sadness in his voice pulled at her heart and her legs could wait for his touch another time. Maybe later in the evening or maybe another day, they had their whole lives. Each puzzle piece of their lives was fitting perfectly together.

She sat up with her legs on either side of him and took his hands in hers. It wasn't like Jake to ask about the past. She hoped this would make him feel closer to her as she had with their time at the beach. She wanted to share this part of her life with him.

"We were going to get you," she told him. "Kyle

showed up at my house and he was determined he knew where to find you. A part of me lit up that night at the thought of bringing you home." *A part of Kyle had lit up too.* "Your dad was at the car waiting on the driver's side. We climbed in anyway. Kyle was determined to leave. I just wanted to find you. I don't remember everything they said but there was arguing and fighting. They knew something I didn't and weren't about to share it. They were talking in code. But your dad promised Kyle that you were safe and that someone was watching over you and would bring you home when they could. I don't know what he was talking about, but he was driving us in circles. That infuriated Kyle and then it all happened so quickly and I woke up in the hospital."

She'd watched his face while she spoke. He turned away from her, and he went rigid, his eyes drifting off into the distance. She knew what he was thinking as guilt played with his features. She liked this side of Jake—not hiding behind the mask he wore daily. For the first time since he left all those years ago, she also knew she could talk to him about it maybe even help him move past it.

She touched his cheek, noting he'd let his five o' clock shadow fill in again. Like her legs, she'd been tortured to touch the side of his face for the last few years.

"Jake, stop blaming yourself for their death." Sydney knew he carried that blame from the day he'd first met Haylee, and also learned of his father's death. The look on his face for both moments were one in the same.

He sent her a look that said not blaming himself wasn't possible.

"You wouldn't blame your mother or Adalyn for their deaths and they were the reason you left. So why do you blame yourself? Your father would never want you to blame yourself."

"If I had stayed home they would have lived. What did I accomplish when I left? Nothing. Mom and Adalyn stayed. If I had listened to my dad..."

"If I had listened to my mom I wouldn't have ended up pregnant at sixteen or broke my arm when I was five years old. We can't foresee what our actions will do. Maybe sometimes we should have listened better and other times not at all." She wouldn't trade the difficult upbringing of Haylee through her teenage years for anything. "But you didn't leave to hurt them. That wasn't your intention. You didn't know if you left they would chase after you and end up in a crash and die. You couldn't have known and you can't blame yourself."

Sydney hiked herself up on him and hugged him.

She knew he wasn't going to agree with her right away and she wouldn't press to make him see it her way. That wasn't how Jake worked. It was a guilt he'd carried for a lot of years, but at least now someone else's voice was in his head telling him differently.

"Do you want to know anything else?" she asked, hoping he would say yes and she could finally tell him.

He shook his head against her. "No." He kissed her shoulder and laid his head on it.

An uncomfortable pain went through Sydney's stomach that had nothing to do with the sadness she felt for Jake.

"I can finish that massage for you, if you want."

As she slid off of him she hoped that was code for something a little more intimate. He went right back to massaging her thighs taking his special time around her scar until she forgot it was even there. She was glad when his hands reached her panties and he didn't stop. As she was enjoying his touch, sliding beneath the lace, her body was growing hot and not in a good sensual way.

His lips kissed her throat, working their way down the front of her dress. His hands travelled under her dress and over her bare upset stomach.

She felt sick to her stomach.

He must have felt her stiffen or read her face because he stopped and leaned above her. "Is something wrong?" Concern stared down at her overriding the passion. *Bring the passion back, tear the mask of concern away!*

Wanting him to continue, it was their last night on vacation, she smiled at him. "A little upset stomach. Probably from the wine." *What the two sips?* Maybe it was too much sun during Haylee's cram a week into four days.

The answer pleased him and he kissed her lips.

Her stomach lurched.

Calm down. Do not ruin this over a little bit of sun.

But she was glad when his lips kissed the side of her face then her ear. A tightening started in her chest and hotness in her mouth.

I'm going to vomit.

His mouth was moving back to hers. She shoved his chest. "Get up. I need the bathroom."

***

JAKE LAID THE wet cold washcloth across Joan's sweating forehead and stood back as she groaned and rolled away.

He was damn glad he hadn't eaten those oysters now.

He had never seen her look so helpless and memories of when he was little and their positions were switched flashed into his head. One in particular. He had been around seven, fussing with a high temperature and the only person he wanted was his mother. But she wasn't there. Beth was always away. Joan had settled him down with a soothing song, rocking him in her arms. She'd been different back then. So had he and there were times in his life even now that he missed that bond they'd shared before she married his dad.

"There's a bucket on the floor beside you and water on the table. Do you need anything else?"

She groaned and he took that as a no and moved to the next cabin. It was empty. He knocked on the bathroom door. "Haylee?"

"I'm dying," her voice strained through the door miserably.

"You have food poisoning. I have a washcloth here to cool you down."

"I don't want it." Her snarky remark made him chuckle.

"Can I come in? Are you decent?"

"If you want to see what death looks like..." Her moans hadn't stopped since Jake and Sydney arrived back at the boat to find the two women as sick as Sydney.

"Is death dressed?"

"Yes, but I can't guarantee there's not puke on my clothes."

He was willing to take the chance.

He found Haylee curled up around the toilet with her head resting on her arm against the bowl. Her eyes only moved to him. "See." She pointed to the bottom of her dress with the wiggle of one little finger. "There's puke on my dress." There was in fact a stain on the bottom edge of her dress.

Jake laid the washcloth across her face and grabbed a new one wiping the material of her dress and trying to control his gagging reflexes. There were a lot of things Jake could handle: blood, punches...but not vomit. His stomach was worse than a rollercoaster after eating at just the sight of vomit and the smell. He shivered. Gross.

He tossed the washcloth on the floor in a pile of towels for Sydney to deal with later and sat down on the floor. It was small and he had to bend his knees against his body.

"Do you need anything?"

She shook her head and closed her eyes. "I'm going to sleep here."

"I put a bucket beside your bed."

"No," she snapped.

Jake had discovered something this evening (besides his decision to not eat the seafood). He learned Joan was a whiny sick person, Haylee was a cranky sick person and Sydney was a quiet sick person.

Jake wasn't going to leave Haylee on the floor, so he sat with her while she brought up more of that slimy seafood fest they'd enjoyed earlier, holding her hair, flushing it away, covering his nose, and cringing at the sound. When she finally decided to lie in bed, he carried her exhausted limp body and put her to bed, rewetting the washcloth and setting the bottle of water beside her.

"I will come back and check on you in a bit," he told

her while standing at the door.

"Jake?"

"Yeah?"

"Thanks."

He grinned. Cranky but grateful. "No problem Haylee."

He stopped in the kitchen and took a few sips of his beer before heading to cabin number three where the woman who had spoiled the private cottage he'd rented for them was sprawled on her back across the bed exposing her gorgeous bare legs as her dress, unnoticed to her, was up to her thighs. One arm was flared out beside her while the other lay over her eyes. She was sleeping. The three of them were starting to wind down, thank goodness. He wondered what time it was now.

Not wanting to interrupt Sydney when she was finally sleeping he tugged her skirt down gently and pulled the blanket over her. He set the water on the night table and turned to leave.

"Jake?" Her voice was exhausted.

"Yes."

"I ruined our night."

He chuckled at her whine. "We have plenty of nights ahead of us." He reached down and kissed her forehead. "I brought you a washcloth." He placed it on her forehead.

The three women looked like complete crap but they looked better then when the sickness started.

She pulled his arm. "Lie with me." She was wiggling her body toward him.

Jake glanced at the open door. "What about Haylee and Joan?" Not that he really envisioned them going too far

LAKESHORE LOVE

unless it was to their own bathroom.

"I don't mind."

Jake climbed into her bed and she cuddled her backside against his front, spooning. Her head of hair landed on his arm and she held his hand. With his free hand he repositioned the washcloth then ran his hand over the smoothness of her arm.

She groaned. "Stop it. You're reminding me of what we can't do." She took his hand and pulled it around her. "I'm never eating sea food again."

Another chuckle. He laid his head on the pillow, his lips against her hair. "Do you need anything else?"

"Just you." He liked the sound of that.

You're all I need too. Forever.

***

THE SCHEDULE HAD been to head back to Willow Valley following lunch. After a night of running back and forth, checking on the three women, then snuggling up beside Sydney for a few hours and then repeating the whole process, Jake was exhausted and fell into a deep sleep with the rest of them. They didn't pull back into Joan's dock until the sun was beginning to set that evening.

The girls rushed onto the dock so quickly, more than ready to get off the bobbing boat, that it added to the turn of their upset stomachs.

Jake was left carrying their luggage as they climbed into Sydney's car like little sleepless zombies. By the time he finished loading the bags he realized Sydney had fallen asleep on the passenger's side.

Jake left his bike in Joan's garage and drove the two women home. He carried the luggage in behind them.

"I'm skipping boat trips for the rest of the summer," Haylee said, slugging her way up the stairs. He was sure that notion would pass.

They looked better. Well their skin had color again and the sweating had passed. They all looked like they needed a shower and a good night's rest.

Jake found Sydney drinking a glass of water in the kitchen. She smiled at him but it didn't reach her eyes. "What a beginning and ending we had this weekend." She looked exhausted.

It was interesting.

"I want to check on the Cliff House. Did you need anything before I go?"

She shook her head. "No, I'm good. You go."

"Do you need me to bring you anything back?"

Sydney hugged him. "I stink," she said. She did smell a little bit. She pulled away. "It's late. I need a bath. You need to check on the Cliff House and I am sure Devon has a list of things for you. Don't worry about me. Go. I will see you tomorrow, or text."

He didn't text. "Or I can stop by."

"Okay."

Jake reached out, pulled her stinky body back into his, and kissed her forehead. She tried to object but her weakness lost the battle and she hugged him back. "Then maybe we can start off where we left off in the cottage."

"Mmm. I like that idea."

"It's a date."

"I like the sound of that, but can we just keep this between the two of us for right now?"

He wanted to tell everyone, but it wasn't only his

decision. They'd had a rough start getting to where they were so he definitely respected her wishes.

"Alright."

She smiled. "Thanks, I just want to get through Haylee's birthday first. You know, let her have her day before we drop the bomb and steal her thunder."

Sydney was always thinking of someone else, their feelings always came before her own.

"You don't mind, do you?"

He must have not answered right away. It wasn't because he minded, because he didn't, it was because he was noting what an amazing woman she was.

He shook his head. "You're the most thoughtful woman I know. I will wait until you are ready."

Chapter Sixteen

THE THUNDEROUS HARMONY of *happy birthday* filled Sydney's small back yard so loudly she was sure they were disrupting the neighbors evening. The rain was holding off and the cool breeze from the threatening weather felt wonderful, brushing the hot sun away from their skin whenever it peeked through the clouds.

Sydney's stomach was twisted in knots, but for a good reason and not because she'd had food poisoning. This was the first time she'd seen Jake since they got back. She'd been so busy at the shop all week during the day and he'd been busy at the Cliff House during the evenings. She'd thought about stopping by but time wouldn't allow it.

As the song came to an end her daughter smiled shyly from the opposite end of the picnic table. Completely surrounded by family, Haylee shook her head like an embarrassed teenager.

The song may have finished but the backyard exploded into light teasing directed at the birthday girl.

"Come on!" Abby shouted loudly, reaching over to squeeze the lace on her niece's shoulder. "Blow those candles out. We don't have all night," Abby continued to tease, while her hand stopped by the side of her cake to scoop a finger-full of icing that she stuck in her mouth. She grinned around the table.

"Abby!" everyone bellowed, not at all surprised and followed by laughter.

Abby mouthed, *"What"* innocently contradicting the wicked knowing-look her eyes sent them, laced in thick black eyeliner and glue-on eye lashes.

"Don't leave any burning," Peyton continued the teasing banter.

Sydney had a feeling this teasing was going to go right around the table.

"Each candle equals each boyfriend you have." Peyton's protruding stomach pressed against a white strapless dress and her chocolate locks fell around her bare shoulders like sprinkles on a cake.

Colt teasingly squeezed his wife's side. "I can't wait until your birthday and we will see how many candles you leave lit on your cake." He turned towards the family. "How many candles will that be this year?" He taunted about her age, causing a roar of laughter.

Peyton lightly hit his middle. "Stop it! And I can't wait to see how many candles are left on *your* cake." She poked a finger against his chest and Sydney knew she was referring to his false reputation as the ladies man rather than his age.

Colt wrapped his arms around Peyton's waist and pulled her tightly against him...as tight as one could with her middle. "Oh baby, there will only be one candle lit for you," he told her in a smouldering tone that caused an uproar of *take it to your room* comments.

A delighted feeling washed through Sydney knowing her sister was fortunate to find a man who loved her so genuinely.

She looked up at Jake who was standing beside her. She was fortunate to find a man who loved her so genuinely too. Once they told everyone that is. Then they could be open about their relationship and hold hands like hers itched to do. First they needed time to themselves and even though it was Haylee's birthday, she wanted this evening to rush by a little quicker so it was just Jake and her.

Colt simply kissed the tip of Peyton's nose before turning to the fussing table, disregarding all the remarks. "And for the record we are celebrating Peyton's birthday this year," he announced.

The fussing turned to cheering because everyone knew Peyton was taking a difficult first step celebrating the day she had not acknowledged since the death of their mother on the very day Peyton had turned sixteen.

Peyton flushed, not an ordinary occurrence for the outspoken brunette with a flare of the tongue. No blush for her husband's playful teasing right out in the open in front of all of them, but there was a flush for her past. Typical Peyton.

If it were Jake touching and talking to Sydney in such seductive tones in front of everyone, she would melt under the table from embarrassment. As it was she was finding it hard enough not to stand there and smirk like a child on Christmas Eve, anticipating what the late hour would bring them.

Peyton rubbed her middle. "Let's just hope these twins are not late and end up being born on the same day."

"Awe. That would be adorable," Kate said.

"Then you would have some explaining to do," Kent said, turning his attentions back to his granddaughter. He ruffled Haylee's hair.

LAKESHORE LOVE

"Grandpa!" Haylee swatted his hand away before smoothing down her locks. "I don't have a boyfriend."

"Kent leave her be." Elaine sent him a look.

"Don't believe her," Abby said. "I think his name is Damien."

Haylee shot her aunt a glare.

Hmm, Sydney had heard this name thrown around. The two had been walking to and from school together but it would seem she was sharing more details with Aunt Abby. It was probably easier to talk to Abby who sometimes acted her age than to get any into out of Haylee. Whether Haylee confided in Sydney about this little crush or not she trusted her daughter...but boys still scared the bejesus out of her. Sixteen and pregnant always flashed in the same thought as Haylee and boys.

Sydney felt a warm, rough hand engulf her own and didn't have to look over to know it was Jake, quietly telling her to wipe that look of fear away from her face. That wasn't the only thing she had to wipe away from her face as she enjoyed his tender touch.

Sydney sent him an exaggerated smile. No one was paying any attention to the two of them.

He arched an eyebrow as though to say *a little much* and her smile turned to a glare

Jake shrugged in comical defeat and winked at her sending a whole new set of feelings through her. *Was this party ever going to end?*

Sydney heard Haylee take an over-exaggerated inhale in preparation for distinguishing the thirteen candles wrapped around the cake.

"Ohh," Jake shouted in Sydney's ear and she found

herself staring at him...again.

"What is this?" Haylee asked staring around the still lit cake.

Everyone played innocent, poorly, with stifled grins and amused eyes, insisting she try again.

Haylee eyed them suspiciously. She wasn't an unobservant regular teenager but enlightened the older crowd by once again attempting to blow out the candles that burned even higher.

"Are you all kidding me?" She laughed. "Do you think I'm five?"

Five...Sydney recalled her fifth birthday. She'd been a super shy adorable sweetness and they'd celebrated at the beach. Jake had been there too. She remembered him also, setting up a game of ring toss with pop bottles and rings he made out of rope. All day she was able to drag Jake into her thoughts. She wanted to drag him into her bedroom.

"Does this mean we don't get cake?" Rosemary asked her parents.

Kate was laughing and snapping pictures but Marc assured the brunette darling snuggled on his hip that she would get a slice of cake.

Rosemary smiled, relieved and lay her head back on his shoulder to look at Haylee, but really she was eying up the cake.

"You have a lot of explaining to do," Kent roared and Sydney found herself smiling along with him.

Haylee elbowed his stomach playfully. "Grandpa!"

"Blow again!" Abby encouraged, reaching over for another dip in the icing. Elaine slapped her hand away before it made contact. Seriously she was worse than Rosemary...a five-year-old child.

Haylee shook her head. "I'm not trying it again."

"Do it," Abby said.

"You do it."

Sydney could indeed picture her sister leaning over to do just that but Joan scooped the cake away and carried it and the blow-less candles away.

Helping Joan, Sydney passed out the slices of cake.

As the night ended the sun dipped below the lake and filled the sky with a beautiful array of pinks and purples.

Sydney stood the front porch waving at the vehicles of her family members departing down the street thinking, *finally*. She loved her family but she was craving alone time with Jake. The cottage had just been a teaser that left her longing for so much more.

Haylee stood on one side of Sydney and Jake on the other. Jake always hung around a little later than everyone else, depending on the Joan/Jake mood. After the wonderful weekend they had, Sydney wasn't sure if she was ever going to have to worry about their troubled relationship again.

Today, however, she knew he had different intentions then their regular calming and friendly after hours chit-chat.

Sydney wrapped her arm around Haylee's shoulder as they went back into the house where Joan was pouring herself a mug of chamomile tea to help her sleep. Joan had decided to stay the night in the guest room and she took her tea to go, along with a goodnight hug and kiss from Haylee.

One down and one to go.

Sydney felt like a teenager sneaking her boyfriend into the house unnoticed to play tongue-tag all night. She had more intentions than tongue-tag. At that moment he sent her a look that said he had more intentions than a round of tongue-tag too.

Sydney turned to her daughter. "It didn't rain." *Go to bed Haylee, go to bed.* That was awful, it was her daughter's birthday. Then Sydney looked at Jake and found a smoldering look that was buckling her knees.

"Mom, it's never rained on my birthday. Not one day. I told you." With that comment the thunder roared. All their heads looked out the kitchen window and their laughter mimicked the thunder. It wasn't raining yet, but it was coming and there was a backyard that still needed to be cleaned.

Haylee gave Sydney a tight hug and kissed her cheek loudly. "Thanks for the party mom. Love you."

Sydney kissed the side of her face. *Finally!* "You're welcome. I love you too."

"Night Uncle Jake."

"Night Haylee."

When Haylee disappeared up the stairs, Sydney turned to Jake and they shared a *finally* look.

"Hey," he said, taking a step toward her.

She smiled wider, as if that was possible. "Hey," she said, taking a step toward him.

"Today has been the longest torture of my life." His hand caught her waist and pulled her against him and she laughed, gripping the front of his shirt.

"Kiss me already," she teased but barely got the words out and Jake's mouth plunged into hers.

A round of thunder tore a strip through the sky.

"First, let's get that tent taken down before it blows away," Jake said, already headed toward the back door. *Who cares about the tent? We were so close!*

The view of his rear caught her attention and she groaned, following behind...but not looking away.

Sydney rubbed the sides of her arms as the cool wind elevated and whipped her dress up. The rain began to fall. She pushed the material down and caught Jake watching out of the corner of his eye. She playfully hit his shoulder, enjoying his sneak-peeks before they both scrambled to grab everything.

The rain started as a light mist feeling good against her body, a cool-down after anticipating her evening with Jake. By the time the tent was folded down and the tables mostly emptied the sky had opened a downpour on them.

Sydney grabbed the last handful and dropped it on the patio table under the protection of the gazebo. Jake dropped the tent at their feet.

They were soaked.

Sydney moved the damp hair stuck across her face as she looked up at Jake. He looked like he'd just stepped out of a shower, unfortunately he was fully clothed. Water dripped down the hardness of his face and his shirt clung to every inch of his torso.

When their eyes found each other, both looking like wet rats, they busted into a loud laughter that had nothing on the deafening rain pounding above them.

Knock on wood, Haylee.

Sydney reached over and pulled his shirt away from his chest for two simple reasons: To touch him and to get the material away from cuddling every muscle across his middle that was making her want to touch him. She wanted to pull the t-shirt right off his body like he had earlier.

"You're soaked." She laughed.

"So are you." His fingers twisted around a piece of her hair and he tucked it behind her ear. His hand lingered at the side of her face.

The humor vanished...her awareness of him increased without warning...again.

Sydney stepped toward him.

Jake stepped toward her.

Sydney swallowed hard.

It was happening.

Sydney felt every one of his fingers digging through her hair and into the back of her scalp. She felt his thumb slowly rub the side of her face leaving Sydney standing...trembling. *Grip me more. Rub me harder.*

There, deep in his dark sizzling eyes, she saw his raw, hard desire for her and they were both on the exact same page...finally.

Chapter Seventeen

JAKE'S FREE ARM found Sydney's tiny waist through the dampness of her thin dress and heat scorched at the contact. He watched her blazing blue eyes begging him to make the first move.

Make the move, Stow! You waited all bloody week to get this close to this woman. Hell, you've waited over ten years...take her now!

He didn't care if the lightning took this whole deck down he was not letting this woman go.

Under the lace edge of her dress, that was now dipping lower then before the rainfall had soaked the material, her chest rose and fell with each deep breath she took.

His grip tightened and a tiny gasp escaped her wet lips. In that moment he lifted her and his mouth crashed against hers. She tasted warm like a summer day, soft like a rose petal and delicious like vanilla cake. It didn't take long to go from an unsure caress to passion, exploring the long lost island inside her mouth.

Sydney arched her supple body against him, digging her leg against the hardness between his legs. His mind was lost as her hands snaked up around his neck. He felt one hand stamp a print against his back while the other dug through his hair.

This is actually happening. They were both on the same page, it was perfect.

Jake pulled her body up higher, slipping his hands under her dress and grazing her lace panties as he found her hot, bare, wet back. The smoothness of her skin was amazing beneath his fingertips, the moisture slid his fingers across every area his arms would move him and he couldn't touch enough of her satin skin.

He hadn't noticed their contact had moved them across the deck until her back, or leg, or his arm...he wasn't sure...bumped a lawn chair and sent it falling backwards. The collision sent them off balance, out from under the shelter of the gazebo and back into the rain. Sydney let out a low surprised scream grasping the front of his shirt harder and their legs tangled together. They stumbled a dance, but he kept them in an upwards position. When they stopped, she was grinning at him through the rain pelting against her face. He carried her and partially dragged her back under the gazebo.

She smiled at him. "Let's take this to my bedroom." Her feminine voice was husky and he had a hard time concentrating on the meaning. Then his eyes, as if having a mind of their own, glanced through the glass door at the hall that led to her bedroom. Her most private room where she stripped her clothes away each night and every morning.

"Your bedroom?"

She kissed his bottom lip. "Where do you think this is going?" she teased, lightly biting his lip like she was trying to tug away his confusion. She slanted her head at him. "Do you want to give the neighbours a show?"

His eyes scanned their current surrounding. *Oh shit.*

LAKESHORE LOVE

The little white picket fence enclosing her backyard wasn't hiding anything. They clung to each other and his arm held one of her legs in the air while the other had her dress halfway up her back exposing her rear end to the neighbours.

No. No, he definitely didn't want to give anyone a show.

Jake scooped her into his arms. She laughed surprised, then trailed kisses down his throat all the way to the bedroom.

Like Sydney's gentle warm soul, her bedroom was softly decorated in warm creams and accented in light turquoise. The floral bedspread and lace curtains suited the antique white-painted metal bed. Her room was warm and welcoming just like the soft kisses she was generously pressing against every part of his skin like she on an exploration.

Jake shut the door, but before they reached the bed she said, "Just a sec."

He stopped.

Just a sec what?

Fear claimed him.

Was that it? Was it done? Had she come to her senses and realized what they were about to do?

Sydney reached behind him and pulled a towel off a hook on the door and wiped her face. "A little wet," she said. He liked the water dripping from her skin. He liked it even more when her seductive hands slowly wiped away any remaining water from his face. Each stroke and each caress was followed by a kiss. Her tongue even ran across his chin at one point, which aroused him to the point he couldn't wait for her lips to reach his and he took her mouth in his. Tossing the towel behind him she wrapped her arms back around his neck kissing him back. Her warmth, her softness, her sweetness was everything he had imagined plus more. The way her body moved against his and her lips with his own.

She pulled away again licking her lower lip. "Jake?"

"Yes?"

"Take me to my bed," she whispered.

It would be my pleasure.

Jake did as she asked and laid her down across the ruffled bedspread. Her hands pulled his collar down while settling his legs between hers, his arms on either side of her. If they were going to do this, he was going to take his time. She deserved to be loved.

His hands ran through her long blonde locks and grasped the back of her head. This woman deserved only the best.

***

SYDNEY'S BODY MELTED with Jake above her, running his fingers through her hair and lightly kissing her lips, her nose, her forehead... She wanted him to run his mouth across every inch of her naked body. *Naked, they needed to get naked.*

Her hands touched the sides of the face she cared so much about, the stubble tickling her fingers. He bent down and took her mouth again, plunging his tongue to taste hers. He tasted delicious, like beer and cake wafting with the smell of his cologne which was driving her body wild for him.

Her hands slipped under his wet black shirt and touched his hard sculpted torso. That touch alone was going to put her over the edge and they weren't even undressed yet.

Naked.

Sydney tugged on his shirt. He took her hint and, with a devilish smirk, ripped it away, pausing above her. He was gorgeous, but she already knew that from days they spent at the beach. Alone in her room the intensity of his body tremendously increased. When she was finished gawking, not satisfied but only beginning, she found his eyes staring at her like it had been her shirt ripped away.

She grinned.

"Hey," she said in a husky low tone.

A grin tugged those hard chiseled features. "Hey." He was so damn sexy.

"I'm still dressed." Even though she knew her dress was up around her waist, her legs craved to touch his bare skin under the denim he was wearing.

One of his sensual hands touched her leg as far down as he could reach slowly tracing a hot line to her outer thigh. It was breathtaking as his hand slid over her underwear, stopping to tug at them, but leaving them in place, outlining her stomach, and sliding her dress up.

"We can fix that." He leaned down and kissed her stomach. She sucked in a deep breath, pressing her head against the bed and arching her stomach at him for more. He pushed her dress over her breasts and his hands followed, rubbing and gripping. She could get used to his rubbing and gripping. His mouth wasn't far behind, kissing the lace of her bra covering her mounds. As he began to pull the dress over her shoulders so she would naked, exactly where she wanted to be, a loud thumping stopped him.

They stilled.

No, no, no. Whatever it is go the hell away!

They listened. It repeated wild hard thuds against her front door.

No, no, no.

Jake pulled her dress down.

No!

In a quick motion he stood up and left her alone on the bed.

No!

He held his hand out and she pouted as he pulled her onto her knees.

Who was at her door? Whoever it was she was going to skin them alive.

She was his height as she kneeled in the bed with him standing beside her. He was reaching for his shirt but Sydney wasn't ready to part from him so she pulled him to her and found his lips.

"Let them get it," she said against his mouth, referring to Haylee or Joan.

He chuckled against her. "What happens when they come looking for you?" He pulled away grasping her hands in his and holding them between their lips. "And, I'm here?" He kissed her knuckle. "In your bedroom?" He kissed the next. "Half naked?"

"I wish you were totally naked."

He chuckled again. "I wish you were totally naked." He kissed her nose. "Go get the door."

"I don't care what they think." She kissed him again. All she cared about was keeping his shirt off his body and...she unbuckled his belt and was unzipping his pants when his hand caught hers.

LAKESHORE LOVE

"Yes you do. And if you keep heading down my pants, I'm going to lose my restraint and..." He pulled away. "Go answer the door, Syd." He said it so softly, so genuine. But she was leaving him, leaving this cloud they'd finally created and fear she recognized that went hand-in-hand with this man was trickling into her stream of thoughts.

"Don't leave," she whispered, but it came out as a plea.

More wild pounding at the door. Really? What was so important? And where was everyone else who lived in this house?

He cupped her face with his warm hands, still shirtless, pants unbuckled and kissed her hard. "I'm not going anywhere," he told her. "I promise."

With his promise, she scrambled from her bed, cursing so very unlike her all the way to the front door.

Someone better be dead. She scolded herself because that was a terrible thought.

She should have changed her damp dress, but hopefully this was a quick open and shut, send them away and get back down to Jake, kind of visit.

As she unlocked the door, her eyes glared up the stairs with a huff of annoyance, again very unlike her to get agitated so easily. Neither Joan nor Haylee could answer the door?

A stick-thin woman had her back to Sydney staring into the driveway where a vehicle was idling. Even from this view the woman looked sickly thin wearing tattered, dirty clothes and when she finally turned, Sydney's mouth dropped.

No. Only the thought came out sad, long and

disappointed rather than annoyed. Her forgotten worries returned, slamming into her stomach with such a force it almost knocked her backwards. A woman she'd never met, but a woman who she knew all too well.

Why today? Why right this moment?

The same brown eyes that Sydney had just left in her bedroom stared at her, tear-stained, mascara running and spaced-out. A shaky hand raked through a long overgrown mess of black and grey hair, greasy and unwashed for what appeared to be days...maybe weeks, possible months. It was disgusting and the wind was blowing her unclean smell right into Sydney's nostrils, chasing away the manly scent of Jake.

Sydney didn't want to speak. She was tempted to shut the door and convince the man down the hall, whom she knew this woman was looking for, that it was a wrong house call. But it wasn't her place to intervene, even if her fear was accumulating by every twitch this lady made.

"Can I help you?" It was so forced Sydney hardly recognized her own voice.

"I'm looking for Jacob Stow." *Of course you are.* Her voice shook. She was strung-out on drugs and by the looks of the marks across her arms they were seriously bad drugs.

"Jacob?" the woman called past Sydney, as if Sydney was going to hide him from her. *The thought had crossed my mind lady...more than once.*

Jake's mom sent her a glare as if she read her mind and Sydney wondered if she should be more cautious of this lady instead of upset that she was standing on her door step. Sydney had never met Jake's mother, but she'd met Adalyn and, digging through the roughness of this lady, Sydney could see some of Adalyn in her.

LAKESHORE LOVE

What were the odds that after promising not to leave her, the very woman he left her for in the first place showed up on her front step just as they were about to engage in what would change the title of their relationship? *Seriously, what were the odds!*

Wary of inviting this scruffy looking lady in, Sydney did so anyways, but not without doing a quick scan of what was in hands reach, in case this lady decided to grab and hide. Beth was Jake's blood, his family. She was also a drunk, drug addict who no doubt would steal if Sydney turned her back, but what choice did she have?

When Sydney glanced toward her bedroom she saw Jake standing in the hallway. She also saw that all feelings, emotions and thoughts of Sydney were erased from his face. He stared solely at his mom, unmoving and uncertain. She just lost the game. *Oh, stop it...what would your reaction be to ten years of nothing then your mother shows up on your doorstep looking like this!*

When Beth saw Jake her face softened, as much as it could with drinking wrinkles and drug open boils. "Jacob," she called with a little wave.

Jake walked down the hallway carrying himself strong and solid, handsome and clean. He didn't look at Sydney, not once, and a defeated sadness weighed heavily in her chest. Sydney's fears stood in her hallway, in the form of Beth Stow.

Sydney climbed the stairs to go check on Haylee and give Jake and his mother privacy. She didn't...couldn't...go back to her bedroom where his smell combined with her wet sheets would be too much combined with the fears of whatever was about to unravel.

"What are you doing here?" Jake's hard voice followed Sydney as she turned at the top of the stairs. Hard, but underlying with concern and love. The big ruff, tuff guy had that soft spot in his heart for his mom, no matter how awful of a person she was. As much as that scared Sydney, it also warmed her heart because his love for the people in his life was unconditional.

"I stopped by the bar and you weren't there."

Sydney wanted to give the mother and son privacy to sort out their issues, but her feet simply planted them when she rounded the corner. *What had happened between them?* Her curiosity couldn't pull her away.

"What do you need? Money?" Yes, pay her, shut the door and come back to me. Please, let it be that simple.

"No." Her whiny voice crept up the stairs childlike and right under Sydney's nerves. It was hard to believe that his successful father was at one time involved with this sketchy woman. It was hard to believe she was Jake's mother.

"Is it Adalyn? Where is she?"

"I don't know." Irritation rose along with her tone. *Why was she irritated, they were logical questions.* Sydney was starting to see tiny bits of Jake in his mother. Tiny, tiny bits.

"What do you mean you don't know?" His tone matched her irritation for not answering the questions she didn't like.

"Enough with all the questions!"

"Are you high?" Isn't it obvious?

"Jacob!"

"So that's a yes." There was so much hurt in his caring voice that it pulled every string around Sydney's heart.

"I'm not giving you money for this." She could envision him waving his hand up and down at Beth's body, but she didn't dare look around the corner in fear of being seen.

"I don't need money."

No lady, you need rehab...and a shower. She scolded herself for the latter thought. Clearly, this lady needed serious help and hadn't the slightest clue she smelled like a garbage truck.

"Then what do you need? Why are you knocking on my friend's door?"

Friend? The term stung. At one time she would have enjoyed him calling her a friend, she would be proud to be his friend, but now she wanted him to use a different title. The chances of that seemed slimmer with every word. If he fell back into the man who had left ten years ago they would lose any chance of discovering what had been occurring between them. Oh, how she wanted to rewind and ignore the door.

"High? Drunk? Whatever you are."

Sydney felt a hand touch her shoulder and jumped. Busted.

"Who's that?" Haylee whispered.

Sydney's heart was beating wildly as she gripped the shoulder of the bright cartoon-printed pajama shirt Haylee had changed into, and sent her a glare for startling her. It went unseen as Haylee braved a peek around the top of the stairs.

"Jake's mom," Sydney whispered.

"Jake's mom?" Haylee caught a glance of Beth then came back to Sydney's side and sent her a, *whoa* look. Beth was probably accustomed to such looks, if she even noticed.

"Is everything ok?"

Sydney shrugged, not sure what was going on. Beth wasn't easily giving up details.

Haylee strained to listen, resting her head on her mother's shoulder.

"I had to drop something off for you," Beth said.

"I don't want it."

"Neither do I."

"Girls?" At Joan's voice they both jumped this time.

Sydney's elbow made contact with Haylee's chin and a little groan escaped as she covered her chin. "Mother!" she whispered in a painful snarl.

Sydney hugged her daughter. "I'm sorry."

Joan stared at them confused. "What are you two doing?"

Sydney shook her head and made motions to lower her voice.

"Jake's mom is down there," Haylee blurted out quickly without working the poor lady into it. Haylee didn't know any of the history between Joan and Beth that dated way back before they had moved to Willow Valley.

Through the dark hallway she could see Joan's body tense.

The three stood quietly as the voices travelled up the stairs.

Jake's mother was still going on about dropping something off for him because she couldn't find Adalyn and no longer wanted to deal with it.

"Mom, you're not making any sense."

"I have to go." That sounded familiar. Sydney brushed the trickles of awareness away. Jake wasn't the same young teenager he was ten years ago. He was a grown man and he had promised her he wouldn't leave. She would give him the benefit of the doubt, she believed him.

"Go where?"

"I don't know. Stop asking me all these questions. Damn it, you're worse than your father!" *Yikes.*

Jake didn't let her insult daunt him. "What about Adalyn?" His worry for his sister and the life she had chosen was a burden Sydney knew he carried every single day.

"She shouldn't have done it. I told her not to after all these years."

"Done what mother? Jesus can't you get out a simple answer?" Hmm, that also sounded familiar, Jake. Not so much fun on the other end of this conversation, was it?

"She's probably dead."

The three women at the top of the stairs gasped then looked around to quiet each other. *Dead?*

"Dead? Why would you say that? What are you talking about?" Jake was in a panic. "Answer me. Dammit, Mother."

"I have to get out of here."

"Where?"

"Get your hands off me!"

A loud crash came from below then the front door slammed shut and silence.

The three women stood unmoving until Haylee nudged her mom to go downstairs. Sydney glared at her daughter. There was no way she was going down there. Only Joan's eyes were telling her the same thing.

Sydney shook her head. Jake would need a moment to himself to process Beth and her apparent no reason visit and he certainly wouldn't want to talk about it.

Go, Joan mouthed, in a bossy mom way, shooing her with her hands.

Sydney reluctantly made her way down the stairs to an empty foyer.

Had he followed her?

That wouldn't be surprising. He'd left and now Sydney was standing alone, her dress smelling of Jake, the memory of his touch and the worry of where he went.

Jake walked out of the kitchen shrugging into his leather jacket just as her thoughts were going wild.

Relief invaded her thoughts until his perplexed face barely acknowledged her.

"Hey." She remembered the small word seductively coming out of both of their mouths only minutes earlier.

Sydney touched his arm and he walked past her conveying hurt from small action. He had the power to hurt her and it was all too familiar.

"Are you alright?" she asked even as she was breaking inside.

Jake stopped.

She felt his tense body through her fingers. He didn't want to stop. He was leaving. This was her fear and it was overtaking her body at an incredibly fast rate. *Get it together Sydney. He just had a huge falling out with his mother. Of course he wants to follow her. She claimed his sister might be dead.*

"I'm fine," he grumbled. A lie. He was anything but fine but he wasn't one to admit it.

"Are you going to find her?"

"Yes."

LAKESHORE LOVE

She understood, really deep down she did. "Jake, be careful. You don't know what's going on with her, or Adalyn." He would know she'd been listening but his safety was more important. "Please, watch yourself."

Jake pulled away like he always did and she let him go like she always did. She turned, watching him open the door and walk away as she folded her arms across her front and tried to repel the emotions from surfacing. Ehen Joan and Haylee tromped down the stairs, she didn't want them to know she was reliving her past.

Jake stopped abruptly.

Then Sydney heard a tiny little sniffle…that of a child. She quickly crossed the hallway forgetting her misery and grabbed the sleeve of Jake's jacket moving him aside for a better view of what was stalling him.

Standing in the cold rainy night were three sets of dark, tired eyes. Sydney's fingers gripped tighter to Jake's jacket. These children were so tiny, malnourished and dressed poorly. *This was what Beth had to drop off?* Sydney's eyes followed the direction of Jake's as he looked around for his mother. Nothing. Not a car in sight.

Jake stared at the kids like he was seeing things and without a clue what to do. Sydney bent down to their level. "Hello. My name is Sydney."

The two girls, no older than ten exchanged mistrustful glances while the younger boy, maybe three-years-old, hid behind them, whimpering. He looked exhausted behind the ruffled curly hair dropping over his eyes.

"This is Jake." Sydney pointed at Jake and the eldest's wary eyes looked up at him.

"Uncle Jake?" she asked.

Sydney followed her gaze to Jake's solid face as he took in the words. These were Adalyn's kids. *Jake, smile, these are Adalyn's kids!*

"What are your names?" Sydney asked.

Jake's lack of response received a glare from the oldest before she looked at Sydney with untrusting eyes. "Beth left us here for Uncle *Jake* to watch us. You don't look like our Uncle Jake, so what do you care what our names are?" There was the no-nonsense Stow in this young girl that so reminded Sydney of Jake.

Sydney's mouth shut and she slowly rose back to her feet beside Jake, who was dumbfounded and quiet. This was about to get very interesting and Sydney had a front row ticket.

"Where is Beth?" Jake asked, sounding harsher than she knew was his intention. He was still wound up from Beth and concerned about Adalyn's safety.

The oldest shrugged. "How are we supposed to know?"

Sydney sucked her lips, trying not to smile. This little one was full of attitude while the other two cowered behind her, scared and seeking protection from the unknown before them. Sydney suspected the oldest was scared too only she had learned how to hide it with an attitude facade.

"Your mother is Adalyn?" Jake asked, slowly eyeing each child up. Their resemblance was uncanny.

Big russet eyes rolled upwards and the oldest took a deep, annoyed breath. "Well aren't you a genius."

Haylee had never in her entire life spoke to an adult with such disrespect. Then again, Haylee had always been taken care of, and it appeared these kids were lacking adult guidance.

Jake ignored the saucy tongue. "Where's your mother?" His tongue sounded just as saucy.

She shrugged, all superior, but her eyes were sad and Sydney's challenge not to smile vanished. She suspected this little girl's tone was a direct result of her need to protect herself and her siblings rather than to give Jake...or herself...direct ignorance. "I don't know." It came out snappy.

When Jake still didn't invite them in out of the storm beating on the roof above, Sydney stepped in, bracing herself for a battle with the oldest.

"Why don't we all come inside," Sydney suggested, stepping back into the house and nudging Jake who wasn't moving.

Finally, acknowledging her existence, Jake looked up at her. His face masked of all his emotions in a hard stare. She wanted to reach out and touch him, but as he stepped aside and motioned for the children to enter, which they did, he left her no opportunity.

Sydney tried to send him a look of comfort for the whirlwind of drama Beth had whisked into his life. He didn't even acknowledge the look, or reach for her. Instead, Jake disappeared outside to look for Beth. At least, she hoped he was looking for Beth.

Joan and Haylee met them in the small hallway with open mouths. Sydney sent them a *quit it* look and they smiled, fake, forced and confused as the rest of them.

Since the children weren't keen on sharing Sydney introduced Haylee and Joan.

"Oh yeah we heard about you," the saucy one said to Joan. "You killed our grandpa."

Whoa! Sydney's eyes flew to Joan.

Joan didn't tolerate little mouthy children, the way she'd raised Jake and Adalyn made that obvious. Her silk, deep purple pajamas swished as she straightened even more while her eyes turned into heated little saucers. "Now listen here little missy, that's rude and inappropriate. It's also completely uncalled for and disrespectful of other people's feelings. You are in our house and I will not tolerate such ignorance." Joan voice held no tolerance.

The little unnamed girl didn't even waver. "So kick us out. It won't be the first time."

Where was Adalyn? Where was Beth? Where was Jake?

Joan and the young girl had a stare-off when Jake came back inside just after the firework show and Sydney sent him a questioning look, *did you find her?*

He shook his head.

The younger girl, whose short hair was cut blunt with an uneven edge just above her shoulders, looked at Jake. "Are you our Uncle Jake?" Her voice was softer, kinder, with a hint of sad curiosity.

The little boy peeked around the eldest at the mention of Jake's name and his eyes shyly found his uncle.

The older one shook the hands that connected her to the young sister. "Of course he is," she snapped as Jake said, "Um, yeah I think so."

The younger girl yanked her hand away from her sister and sent her a glare. She walked over to Jake lacing her tiny fingers in his big hand. Jake stared down at her like she was the plague, but she didn't notice, showing him a wide-eyed, trusting face. "Beth said you would keep us now." The

LAKESHORE LOVE

tired girl rested her head against Jake and yawned.

Sydney held her breath. How are you going to run away from this?

Chapter Eighteen

KEEP THEM? KEEP them! What did that even mean? Why had his mother dropped them off with him? Why did his mother have them? Where was Adalyn? What had she done? What was going on?!

The unanswered questions drove Jake's mind into a state of uproar. What was he supposed to do when he had no idea what was going on? He was thrown into a situation with Beth and Adalyn...once again...and blind-sighted without a clue.

Jake paced across the kitchen, back and forth, his boots scraping the wood with each step. He should remove his boots knowing the scuffs of dirt across the floor would drive Sydney mad. There was too much on his mind to think about *boots*, too much unknown.

Sydney. He stole a quick glance at her. Her eyes were locked on him. Her damp dress clung and outlined her body where his lips had dipped into the silky warmth of her flesh in what felt like a decade ago. He wanted to go back in time to her bedroom, agree to her suggestion and let Joan or Haylee answer the front door. Then he could take his time and wipe away all the worry laced across her face. Worry he and his family had put there...again. Truthfully, as much as he wanted to go back, sending young Haylee or Joan, the mistress, into Beth's path would have been by far worse...and this had been horrendous.

He turned away from Sydney's questioning gaze. She didn't care about his boots, she was waiting for him to explain.

How the hell was he going to explain anything when he didn't even know what was going on!

He'd heard the startled gasps of horror that crept down the stairs when Beth put Adalyn's name in the same sentence as death, so he knew Sydney had heard every word between him and his mother. That left nothing else, of the current situation, to discuss. There were things that had gone unsaid the night he talked to Sydney about his past, but he wasn't about to walk down that road either. He built a fence across that road to block enduring the pain it caused ever again.

Each time he passed the kitchen door, he glanced into the dimly lit living room across the hallway. The three kids, still nameless, were bundled up in blankets on the pull-out sofa. The youngest, a small, shy boy, a replica of himself at that age, was already sleeping away the evening's events. Jake wished it was that easy for him...this was just the beginning of his night. The middle-aged girl, who smiled at him with Adalyn's exact, trusting glimmer, was lying on her sister's lap engrossed in the television. The older one...the saucy one that rose her eyebrows in such a way there was no doubt she wasn't a Stow, petted the younger girl's hair while her other hand was wrapped around the brother's hand. She was the protector. He'd been in her shoes.

"I didn't even know I had nieces and a nephew," he said, ripping his stare away and starting back into the kitchen, out of their sight.

After the drug and weapon bust in the clubhouse Beth's boyfriend operated ten years ago Jake had left that life. He'd thought Adalyn would see there was no fixing their mother, a lesson he had to learn the hard way. He'd thought, he'd hoped Adalyn would give up the horrible life she'd been dragged into and come back home with him to start a life away from the damages of their mother's lifestyle. Jake had waited in the police station for the entire night and when everything had settled, he'd been told she didn't want to see him. After everything he had done...after putting his life in danger for her...she'd denied him the opportunity to even have a conversation. Now his mother left her three children saying Adalyn might be dead. *Was she? How would he ever know?*

"Jake, sit down."

His wired body would never be able to sit still in a chair. *I have to get the hell out of here.* He needed to jump on his bike and scope out the town in case Beth was still here. Rain or not. The local bars were a great first place to look.

"I have to go."

Sydney pushed herself away from the counter she'd been leaning against. "What? Jake, where?"

"To go look for my mom."

Sydney stepped in front of him with her arms folded across her chest. Worry claimed every inch of her eyes and he wished they would look at him with desire like they had in her bedroom just a few moments before. He wished they were still in her bedroom now.

"I will let you go..." Let me go? Who was she kidding if he wanted to go her little tiny self wasn't stopping him. "...but, you have to promise me you're coming back here tonight."

He stared at her. *Come back? Why would he come back?* What was he going to do here? He had to locate his mother and sister.

Sydney stared him down as if reading his mind. "Jake, their grandmother just dropped them off with strangers promising that you..." She poked his chest. He almost grinned at how the gesture that was meant to be bossy was in fact adorable. "...are going to be their keeper." That was a terrible promise. "If you don't come back you will break their little hearts."

Break their hearts? He didn't even know them. What in the hell was she talking about?

"What am I supposed to do with them? Take them home with me?"

She smirked. He was glad this was amusing to her, because he was ready to blow a gasket. "No Jake. You live above a bar. You can't take children to live above a bar." Did she just stifle a laugh?

See, that's how good at this I am going to be. I need to find my mother or my sister and give these children back. They don't have a chance with me.

Deep in the back of his brain he wondered what kind of chance they had with either of those women too. He pushed those thoughts away. He couldn't contemplate them at the present moment when time was an issue. He'd already wasted the first moments when Beth left, which would have been the easiest to locate her.

"You can go look for Beth. But, when you are finished you must come back. Don't leave these children here in a strange house to wake up with three stranger's."

"I'm a stranger."

"You are their family."

He glared at her.

She arched her eyebrows. "You can flash me any little angry look you want, but you are coming back tonight." He wanted to come back to her tonight, but that wasn't what she was offering. "Go look for your mom and when you are finished, check the bar, pack a change of clothes and come back here. For the night." *Was that an invitation?*

Sydney's hands wrapped around his, damp and cold from being caught in the rain earlier. How he could have warmed her if all this hadn't interrupted them.

"Jake you're not alone. I'm here, but if you leave tonight the children will be alone and scared." Her eyes fell into the living room, where all three sets of eyes had closed. "They need you," she whispered.

***

JAKE OBEYED SYDNEY'S orders. He drove around town checking other local bars, hotels and restaurants hoping to find his mother. Just his luck, Beth was nowhere to be found. He checked in at the Cliff House, relieved to find everything running smoothly. He was grateful to not be dragged every which direction for situations when he didn't have the energy to deal with any of them. It was mid-week and busy but it wasn't the weekend crowd so there were fewer problems.

Jake grabbed a change of clothes from his place and found himself parked out front of Sydney's house, thankful the storm had stopped and he was partially dry.

The only light from Sydney's house was streaking from a break in the living room curtains.

He thought if he sat there long enough Sydney would peek out the window. She never did. Disappointment gripped him. *What if being dragged into this part of his life changed her mind about him?* That thought terrified him and a shudder ran through his body.

He didn't know how long he sat there not wanting to go inside. That was a first. Sydney's house was always warm and welcoming, it was as close to a real home he'd felt since his dad died. He'd hardly been able to stay away all day, and had practically run through the doors that evening wanting to see, touch, and be with Sydney.

Now there were three kids expecting him to *keep them* and the fear that Sydney had given up on him already, like she had the first time he left, caused him to pause. *Don't go there.*

When Jake finally climbed from his bike he found the front door unlocked. He didn't like that when Beth was being so discreet about the situation. Who knew what kind of danger she'd gotten into now?

Sydney, Haylee and Joan's voice came from the kitchen. Jake would have preferred to walk in to only Sydney, so they could continue where they left off...if she still wanted that.

"This is exactly what Henry always feared would happen," Joan was saying. It irritated him that Joan was dipping her nose in something that had absolutely nothing to with her, but he wasn't surprised. She had always dipped her nose into everything, that was how she latched onto his father...by dipping her nose into his parent's personal affairs. "Jake or Adalyn falling into that awful woman's world of drugs. Now Adalyn has dragged her children into it. What is

Jake going to do with two girls and a boy?" That was a very good question.

"Joan." Sydney's voice was full of compassion that relaxed Jake's nerves...a bit. "Jake will take care of them." That wasn't the reassuring answer Jake was hoping for.

"How is he going to take care of them?" That was also a plausible question. "They are being forced on him." That was true. "He doesn't want them." That wasn't even up for discussion; he would do what he needed to do for these children it wasn't a matter of wanting them or not because they were Adalyn's children. "He's not father material." Whoa, whoa, whoa...that was jumping to conclusions. "And that older one. Hmm, no respect there." He couldn't defend the older child's saucy tongue, however he didn't like Joan's implications about her, about any of them.

"Maybe he will find their mom," Haylee suggested, giving a little hope. Unfortunately tonight that hadn't been the case. "Or their grandma."

"That wouldn't be much better," Joan snickered. "Did you see the children? They look starved and sick."

"Honestly." Sydney was sounding a bit exasperated and Jake was beginning to feel guilty for his eavesdropped, but he would call it square after the three of them eavesdropping on him earlier. He didn't blame them, just the sight of his mother would grab anyone's curiosity. She was in the worse shape he'd ever seen her. Finally all her addictions had caught up to her body. It was a sad sight that broke his heart after all the time he had spent to coax her away from that lifestyle.

"Stop all these assumptions and worries. Everything will be fine. We are Jake's family. The three of us and we will be there for him, so he will be fine. They can stay here..."

"What do you mean stay here?" Joan's shocked voice cried, causing a half smile across Jake's face.

"I mean Jake and the kids can stay here. He can't very well take them to stay above the bar."

"That's if he even comes back." Did everyone think he was a ticking time-bomb ready to explode at any given moment?

"He will come back." Why did Sydney's tone not match her words? He told her he wouldn't leave, he promised and he was standing by his promise. He would never make that mistake with Sydney again, the consequences of his departure thirteen years ago hadn't been acknowledged until it was too late.

Joan made a sound indicating that she didn't believe Sydney. Jake had the urge to turn around and walk right out the door. He didn't need this shit right now. Where was the step-mother he'd spent the weekend with? No doubt Beth's appearance was causing havoc in her too.

"It's temporary until he sorts this out," Sydney said. *Temporary? Temporary!* What had been transpiring in her room? Was that temporary to her? No, it wouldn't be. She wasn't the type of woman to allow a man into her bed temporarily. Why was she using that word?

"Hopefully he finds Beth and Adalyn. If not, maybe he will have to adopt the children and buy a new house." *Why couldn't they all live together here?* He was rushing. He was feeling frustrated listening to this whole damn conversation when all he wanted was to walk into Sydney's arms. "We don't know what's going to happen, so let's stop creating *what if's*."

"This is ridiculous!" Joan snapped, obviously not liking where this situation was headed.

"Haylee, can you give us a second?" Sydney said.

Jake was about to step back, but where would he go?

Haylee walked into the hallway, looked directly at him and smiled, understanding and supportive. Anyone could see this young woman was Sydney's daughter with her soft eyes and kind heart. Haylee climbed the stairs without giving him away and her bedroom door shut behind her.

"Joan, I love you." Sydney was saying. "But I expect you to be supportive of Jake. I would never turn my back on Jake. Ever." That was a relief. Maybe there was hope for them after all this.

Being busted anyway Jake slipped his boots off and dropped them with loud thump to warn the women he'd returned.

Sydney's warm smile popped out of the kitchen. "Hi," she said, filled with relief at his return. "Any luck?"

He shook his head.

Joan appeared shortly after. "I'm going to bed." She didn't even look at Jake and went straight up the path Haylee had just climbed.

Sydney looked down at the bag in his hand and more relief danced in those eyes.

"Did you think I wasn't coming back?"

She flushed, looking embarrassed. "You've been gone for hours. It's almost one." It hadn't felt like that long.

"Let me take that." She reached for his bag. Their hands brushed and she gasped. "Jake, you're freezing. Come into the kitchen and I will get you something warm to drink."

LAKESHORE LOVE

"It's late."

If she heard him she didn't let it show, dropping his bag at the bottom of the stairs then heading into the kitchen.

Jake turned the opposite direction. He stood hovering above the pull out sofa and stared. The girls looked just like his sister. They had her dirty blonde hair as a child, the color, not the greasy strands these kids had. They needed a good hose down. They needed a good mother...their mother. *Was their mother good?* Adalyn hadn't listened to him all those years ago, what made him think even if he did find her that she would listen now? It would seem she hadn't been taking care of these kids, and then giving them to the Queen of Destruction herself, his mother, was not the wisest choice for the children. But still, what was he going to do with them?

Jake felt Sydney's hands graze across his forearm and felt the blaze scorch through his body.

"It will be alright Jake."

He turned and the affection he saw guided his hands to the sides of her face and his lips came crashing down on hers. An expected gasp escaped her mouth and he swallowed it up hard and needy. He didn't take his time like he had been hours ago. It was hard and needy and he just needed to forget everything and this woman could make him do that.

Chapter Nineteen

SYDNEY HADN'T BEEN ready for his kiss. She hadn't expected it. When he crashed down on her lips so hard, in comparison to the soft sweet way he'd kissed her earlier, she knew he wasn't kissing her for her. He was venting.

He was strong and quick and before she knew it they were back in her bedroom and her back was being slammed against the closet door. He'd lifted her into his arms with a grace that she hadn't even noticed. Until her legs, having a mind of their own, wrapped around his middle like she never wanted to let go. She didn't ever want to let go.

Her lips were kissing him back, taking in his tongue and she was pulling him against her. She wanted him as much as he wanted her, but not like this. Not when he was using her as a distraction to avoid his current situation.

Sydney moved away from his mouth, panting heavily and sucking in deep breaths. If she wasn't convinced he was only venting, she would have thoroughly enjoyed this sexual, dark side of him. But her brain knew better. Her lips objected, her hands objected, the area pressed against his hardness was straight out yelling at her. "Jake," she breathed.

He was so busy kissing her neck...and it felt wonderful...that he didn't answer. But it wasn't because he wanted her, it was because he needed a distraction. He was using her as a distraction. Couldn't he see that?

"Jake." She grabbed the side of his face and pulled him to look her. She saw clouds of desire for her, confusion as to why they stopped, and, as she'd suspected, the real reasons he'd carried her into her room: avoidance.

"We can't do this." The words tasted awful in her mouth.

He stared at her as though he couldn't comprehend the words.

"I'm sorry. I can't do this." Not like this! Not when you have a plate full of your family drama and dragged me in here to vent. I will not be your venting tool! Your punching bag from the gym.

He let her go. Disappointment surged through her as his strong arms retracted and she slid to her feet, using the door to prop her into a standing position. She felt so small with him towering above her and casting confusing looks in her direction.

"You're blocking the door." A cold-stone tone sliced into her already aching body.

"Please, don't be mad." *Tell him to spend the night with you.* She couldn't bring the words up with him starting at her so angry.

"I'm not mad." He was furious, she could see it in his straightened posture and dark lowered eyes, the way his throat was pulsing.

"Jake..."

"Do you want me in here or not?"

Yes. No.

"I don't want you to leave angry."

"I don't want to leave at all." Those words were

beautiful to her ears. *Let him stay and simply hold him on your bed.*

Sydney stepped aside and he went storming out.

Sydney! Go get him back. Go talk to him. Go lie with him.

She held the door open, expecting to hear him slam the front door on his way out of her house.

He didn't.

She stood there for a long time, standing in the doorway, staring down the hall where he'd disappeared into the living room with his family. She had left blankets on the chair for him in case he wanted to watch over them for the night. Jake was protective and she'd figured that was where he would want to be.

Once they both got sleep, he would realize what he had been doing...wouldn't he? Or would he be too enthralled in his family to care.

When the lights shut off and the door still hadn't slammed shut, she walked to her bed and stared down at it thinking maybe she had made a mistake. No matter what he was feeling at the present time, it didn't take away from what he promised. A promise he made before his family showed up and she watched the old Jake surface. Was that what she was truly afraid of? That he was going to backtrack down a road where she would lose him?

Ugh! It was all too confusing to contemplate at this hour. She wanted to walk down the hall and bring him back, but instead she wrapped the blankets with his light scent on them around herself and went to sleep.

***

JAKE COLLAPSED IN the arm chair and pulled the

blanket he knew Sydney set out for him across his exhausted body. So he was never sleeping in her bedroom. He'd been right. His life's darkness was too much for her. No matter what her supporting words had been to Joan, they were only intended on a level of friendship, even possibly a level of family, but not the family way he wanted.

The long hours he had been scoping the town for his mother had given her time to speculate a life with him. His mother's arrival, no doubt, just reminded her of who exactly he was: a messed up nobody.

It will be alright, Sydney had whispered in his ear. With her by his side everything would always be right, but now he realized that was never going to happen. To make matters worse, he was stuck here, in her house, on her damn uncomfortable chair, because he lived above a bar.

Dammit. Why didn't he suggest he could take them to the cabin? *You know why.* Yeah, because he wanted to come back to her, back to Sydney.

He had to find Adalyn and Beth as quickly as possible to get these kids out of Sydney's house. First thing in the morning, he was leaving.

***

SYDNEY WAS RIPPED from her dreams in a panic and her feet took her down the hall, finding the corner chair in the living room empty, just as she'd worried.

Her stomach dropped.

She pushed the curtain hanging over the large bay window aside and found Jake's Harley gone. Before six in the morning? She hadn't even heard him go.

Sprawled out on her sofa were three little babes fast asleep and unaware they would be waking up without the uncle they were expecting and needing.

She needed Jake too. She needed him to reassure her and take away this feeling overtaking her body as she remembered all those years ago waking up just like this and finding him gone. It was her fault. She shouldn't have pushed him away last night. He had needed her, but her fear of this whole confusing situation scared her.

Sydney grabbed the stinky, dirty bag off the floor in the hallway. At least it was summer and the children weren't missing school...if they were even enrolled in school. Who knew what these poor helpless children had endured.

After brewing a pot of coffee, she was usually a tea morning drinker but she needed strong black coffee, she carried her mug in one hand and the bag with the fingertips of her other hand to the laundry room.

The bag consisted of hardly anything: a few dresses, a boys outfit and underwear. It was enough to get them changed when they awoke. She dropped everything in the washer and cleansed her hands before retrieving her coffee the only thing that was going to keep her going for the day.

All night she'd awakened wondering if Jake had snuck out. Embarrassed to admit, she had even crept down the hall a few times to check that the chair had still been occupied. Then, when her body couldn't handle the exhaustion, she'd fallen into such a deep sleep that she awoke in a panic, ripping her from her dreams. Her fears had come true: Jake was gone.

Hopefully he was out looking for his mother and sister. What time had he left? Where had he gone? Would he be safe?

Sydney was glad she wasn't opening the shop today. She'd arranged it that way, presuming Jake was spending the night...in her bed...with her. What another disappointment.

It was Saturday and Haylee would be going to the shop at lunch to work for a couple hours. If Jake wasn't back by then, Sydney was going to walk up with her daughter and take the kids to the beach for the day. They needed a distraction. She needed a distraction.

Sydney took her tea and leaned against the archway in the kitchen, staring down at the children Jake had pawned off on her to go find his family. She didn't mind, she hoped he found them and resolved this matter quickly and easily. Jake deserved happiness and peace. It seemed whenever Beth was involved he ended up with neither but a bag of guilt he carried around instead.

Adalyn was in trouble. Beth was running away and Jake was running right into the middle of everything, unprepared.

How did he know where to go? Had he been keeping in touch with them? Would he come home?

Please let him come home safely.

***

JAKE PARKED HIS Harley in Sydney's driveway. He took a deep breath and the cool morning briskness stung his lungs.

He wasn't sure what he was going to say to Sydney when he opened her front door. He grabbed the box of muffins he'd picked up at Mrs. Calvert's bakery. That hadn't been his intention when he'd awoken in a panic, left the house and driven out of town. A few miles out his brain kicked in and asked him, *Where the hell are you heading Jake?*

When he didn't have an answer with no leads to follow, he'd turned around.

It was still early. Sydney was an early riser but he hoped she wasn't up yet and he could sneak in like he had never left. Only he had a box of muffins. He felt like he wasn't going to win today no matter what he did.

He unlocked the door with his key. *His key.* He'd always had a key to her house, as a friend. *A friend. That's what she wanted. Wasn't it?*

He shook away the thoughts and pushed the door open.

The house was quiet.

Sydney's slim body leaned against the living room archway, sending his nieces and nephew a loving stare. The small hands that had pulled him away from her neck the night before, now cradled a mug. He wished he was that mug. He wanted to wake up beside her every morning and watch her slip into the silk robe that was now pulled around her body. He wanted to gaze into those sexy, sleepy eyes. They could cuddle. He wanted to cuddle with Sydney. They could have morning sex. Lord knew he wanted to have morning sex with her.

Jake shut the door with a little thud to snap away those thoughts.

Sydney looked surprised to find him standing in her doorway. She stepped away from the arch and stared at him as though she didn't believe he was really there.

He held out the box. "I stopped by Mrs. Calvert's and picked up some breakfast." That was half the truth.

Her grateful smile was beautiful. "Thank you." How could she smile at him and thank him after the way he'd treated her the night before. His tone, his words had all been harsh and mean.

She didn't move and neither did he. They were wrapped in the quietness of the early hour and he enjoyed every second of it, relaxing him, comforting him and he was felt like the day was getting better. Then she shook her head, as if waking her from the daze, and quickly took the box into the kitchen.

He followed and Sydney set a steaming mug of coffee on the table for him before sitting on the opposite side and pulling the muffin box open. She ripped pieces off and eating little bites, watching him closely.

"You're leaving today, aren't you?" she finally asked.

"Yes."

Her sad eyes fell to her hands ripping apart the muffin now with no intentions of eating it. "I will watch them while you are gone," she offered.

He knew she would, but as she said the words he felt a wave of relief a wave of love for this woman. He wanted to apologize for the way he'd treated her the night before but the topic of Adalyn just seemed easier.

"I have to find Adalyn, whether she is alive or..." He couldn't even say it. He couldn't envision his sister, like his mother, a drug attic and alcoholic, or worse yet dead. That wasn't the woman he'd left at the station.

Sydney's chair scraped across the floor as she pulled it beside him. Her hand touched his knee and heat scorched through the denim to his skin. "What can I do to help?"

Why was she so good to him? "I don't know where to

start looking. But I think Mia will."

"You will have to ask her." Sydney grinned. "She doesn't trust me."

He chuckled and nodded. Mia had made it clear Jake was the only one she wanted to talk to.

"I need someone to watch the Cliff House if I'm not home tonight."

"Joan will do it." Joan never watched the night crew, so he might have to call Devon to manage it while he was gone. Devon had done a great job while they were gone and he didn't know how long he would be gone this time. He didn't even know where he was going yet.

"She will be pissed."

"She will understand."

Would she understand as the lady on the boat the past weekend of as the step-mother he had growing up? "She never understood. Why would she now?"

"She always understood. Stop looking at her like an angry teenager and you would see she was just a mother protecting her family. Even you and Adalyn. In her own way."

Once he had seen her that way, but that was such a long time ago.

"I need to go home, shower and change."

"Didn't you bring clothes?"

He'd forgotten. He nodded.

She wrapped her hand around his and stood. "You can use my shower." *Her shower.* He liked the sound of that. He would like it even more if she stayed with him.

Jake didn't object to her guiding him out of the kitchen. He grabbed his bag from the hallway, not letting go of her hand, not wanting to. He knew where the downstairs bathroom was—through her bedroom.

The unmade bed taunted him as they passed where Sydney had slept the night away, unaware of the gruelling lack of sleep he had endured. His body longed to lie beside her. He was so exhausted, if she'd offered a rest with her at that very moment, he would have crashed against her unmade sheets and wrapped his arms around her.

Sydney let his hand go once they were inside the bathroom and started digging through the linen closet, pulling out towels which she neatly set on the counter.

He dropped the bag at his feet.

She turned and clasped her hands together sending him a shy glance. "So," she said slowly. "Oh there's shampoo and body wash." The words rushed out of her mouth and she pointed in the shower. "So I guess that's it." She dropped her hands sucking in a deep breath and started out of the room.

As she passed him, he slipped his hand around hers and she stopped instantly. Her side pressed against his, creating a heat wave between them.

Sydney's eyes closed and her lashes shadowed her skin. He watched her chest rise with a deep inhale.

He wanted to apologize for the night before, but the words would just not come out.

"She is my sister."

"I know that. I understand. I'm not the same young girl I was then and you wouldn't be the man you are today if you didn't go look for them."

He turned her to face him, leaving his hand wrapped around hers. His free hand ran up the silk sleeve, stopping on her warm throat. The front of the robe had opened revealing the light pink silk tank top and shorts.

She stared up at him with so many emotions it was hard to distinguish them. If only his face told her everything he felt, it would make life so much easier.

Then like someone else was taking over his body, more words he'd never spoken came out. "You're my family. I don't know if I've ever told you that." He knew he hadn't. "But you are my best friend. You've always understood me when no one else even came close. You've always stood by me. When I came back I was young and my dad had just died...I should have said sorry to you then. I should have done so much more than I did. Because you were my only friend. I'm sorry about last night." Finally he could say it. "The way I man-handled you. No one should ever touch you like that. My glares, my tones, everything, Syd. I'm sorry. I don't blame you for asking me to leave."

A smirk pulled up the sides of her lips. He did not know what part of his apology amused her. "I would hardly call it man-handled." She was giving him an excuse for his behavior and it was inexcusable.

He hadn't noticed she'd moved her free hand. It was now touching the side of his face.

"Stop punishing yourself. Your throat is pulsing like you're going to throttle someone...*yourself*. I didn't stop because you were man-handling me."

He was afraid to ask why. Was it because she didn't want him? He had to know.

"Why did you stop?"

Chapter Twenty

SYDNEY TOOK A deep breath of air and all that filled her nostrils was the smell of Jake.

"Because you were venting."

He looked hurt. "Is that your word for man-handling? Venting?"

"No. Oh, my gosh, Jake. No." He was always so hard on himself and the horror she watched flash in his eyes made her forget the deeper reason.

She hugged him.

He was reluctant, but her arms stayed around his neck until his found her waist and she felt the weight of him fall against her. His head rested on her shoulder. His squeeze tightened. He whispered another apology through her hair.

"Last night was a lot," she whispered back. "It was scary...it still is...and you were so upset. You were angry, scared and sad. I know it might sound silly to you but we waited all this time and then after the shower on the boat...it just felt familiar." She sucked in a lungful of strength. "I thought you needed to sleep it off is all. I didn't want you to leave, but I didn't know what else to say. I didn't want to be your venting post."

His body stiffened. He pulled away and she was afraid he was going to walk away. Instead his hands cupped her face. "You are not my venting post. You are my support. You are my courage. You are sunlight on the darkest of my days. And I would never take you to bed without the intention of more."

Where was all this coming from? The words were beautiful. Butterflies swirled in her stomach at his confession and she smiled.

"That was beautiful."

He grinned, lightening the mood around them. "Don't get too attached to it," he teased as his warm hands roamed down her neck and touched her shoulders.

"I wouldn't dare. Besides, it was a little sappy for me."

He chuckled at her insult. "This is why I don't talk."

Her eyes widened. "Oh, so you do know that you are not a talker?"

He shrugged. "I've been told a few times."

"You should do it more often. Look where it gets you." Sydney slowly moved her hands to her shoulder and slipped her robe away. It fell to the floor. His hands immediately grazed her bare shoulders.

"Hmm, this is nice."

She laughed and tugged at his shirt. He ripped it off letting her hands roam.

He kissed her then, softer, wanting and needing like the beginning of a brewing storm. No man-handling. His hands roamed under her shirt and against her bare skin.

No interruptions, she pleaded.

She knew he still needed a shower so she moved their melted bodies and reached in to start the warm water, but he stopped her.

He lifted her around her back and under her knees just as he'd done the night before they had been interrupted. He didn't need any instruction this round, and took her to her bed lying her down.

"I want to do this right with you."

She pulled him down to her lips. "It's about time," she teased.

***

SYDNEY TOWEL-DRIED her hair and slipped into a floor length summer dress before making her way down the hall.

They'd also ended up in the shower after lovemaking and she couldn't begin to explain how wonderful it was. Sydney could still feel his fingers touching, his lips caressing, and his eyes roaming her body. She turned around feeling like they were still gazing at her. But he wasn't behind her.

She shook her head, almost laughing at how silly she was being. Their lovemaking had been the most thorough body wash her skin had ever experienced.

She felt amazing. She felt alive. Jake was all in and the unity felt complete. She felt like dancing down the hall and spinning at the bottom of the stairs...

Joan's serious face halted her dance steps. Her arched eyebrows would have touched the ceiling if they weren't attached to her face. She eyed Sydney up and down suspiciously, taking in her wet hair and goofy smile.

Get it together. Sydney sobered. Too late.

"Where's Jake." The accusation was clear and very different then when she'd passed them on the boat. She'd expected this reaction in the first place from Joan. There was no point in trying to hide the truth from her when Jake would be walking out any minute with damp hair, answering her allegation.

"He's dressing," she said, quickly passing Joan to find something to occupy her hands with when really she wanted to scream and fall backwards into a pile of leaves like a child. It was July. There were no leaves. Maybe into a pool of water? Maybe just back into the shower with Jake...

"Where?" This woman always possessed a way of saying anything regardless of whether it was her business or not. Sydney loved her to the moon and back, but she could see why her and Jake butted heads. He was private: she was nosy.

"Down the hall."

"In your bedroom?" She made the sentence sound so dirty.

Sydney nodded.

"Was he in the shower too?"

"Joan," Sydney hissed, not mean but with a warning of surprise. She shouldn't be surprised.

"Well?"

"Well what?"

"You know what."

She couldn't deny it. She didn't want to deny it. She was ready to step up with Jake. "Yes."

Joan shook her head disapproving. "Sydney what are you doing?"

What I should have done a long time ago. She didn't answer.

"He will hurt you. That is what Jake Stow does. And do you want to drag Haylee into this? He's her uncle. Do you want to mess that relationship up? Do you want to mess up the relationship you have with Jake? A sexual relationship will unquestionably mess up everything that you have worked so hard to maintain. He will hurt you."

Sydney spun around. "Enough!" Her voice was so loud they both looked across at the sleeping children. They did not stir.

Where was all this coming from? It must be Beth's visit jumbling her thoughts. Beth's visit was jumbling everyone's thoughts!

"That's not who he is. He will *not* hurt me. He would never hurt Haylee and deep down you know that. You invited him to Hastings Port. You saw us about to..." She flung her hands in the air, not wanting to say the exact words. "...on the boat and you said nothing. Because you know Jake, you love Jake and he loves you. I can see it even if you two can't."

Joan's anger dropped and she looked sad. Sydney didn't know what to think. Was she comparing him to his father? What had Henry done to Joan to make her not mistrust Jake so much?

"He will leave you for them," she finally said. "I don't know what it is about those Stow men, Sydney."

Joan sighed and practically collapsed on a chair. It didn't look like she had slept well either. It was a houseful of exhausted and confused people with emotions and feelings flapping around like a flag on a windy day.

"He will always leave you for them." That's what Sydney feared! She hated hearing the words from someone else's lips. They made them so much more realistic and terrifying. Especially from Joan who looked like she was reliving a scary time in her life.

Sydney pulled a chair in front of Joan and took her

trembling hands in her own. Joan was shaking her head so slowly it was hardly moving.

"Jake is so much like Henry. He's strong, he's determined, he is cautious and he loves his family unconditionally."

That sounded just like Jake amazing.

"I know where you three were going that night." Joan's voice turned to ice and Sydney swallowed hard. "I know what Kyle got into his head, but you don't know why, do you?"

Sydney shook her head. Sydney remembered Kyle pounding on her dad's door, saying he was going to get Jake back. He gave her the option to come or stay home. She didn't think twice about climbing into that car.

"He found out the truth." *The truth? The truth about what?* Sydney didn't dare ask. "Me and Kyle had a huge falling out. He was furious and when he took off, I called Henry. I knew he was going to you. Jake loved you and you loved Jake. Kyle knew if Jake saw you he would come home." Sydney remembered by the time they got to the car Henry was in the driver's side and he wasn't happy, but he agreed to go. He agreed to drive. Then there were all the accusations and the yelling. They never clearly said anything and Sydney couldn't even remember what passed between them. She only remembered the crash.

"Why are you telling me all this now?"

"I love you Sydney. I love Haylee. I even love Jake." Joan snorted, but Sydney already knew she did. "I want you to be happy and I know Jake makes you happy. I have watched you two for ten years try to ignore your feelings and finally, I thought, 'This boy is good. This boy has grown up, he's left that part of his life.' I thought. 'He's good for Sydney. He is good for Haylee.'"

Sydney squeezed her hands. "He is good for me Joan. He is good for all of us."

Joan ignored her. "Then Beth showed up and it was like I was looking at Henry. I've been where you are and I know he makes you feel safe...special, but in the end, they win. In the end he will fight for them until his death." Joan looked up at her. "Like Henry."

"Wasn't it worth it? To love Henry and have him love you as long as he could?"

"Yes."

Sydney breathed in relief.

"But you're still young, Sydney. You could have a guy that won't chase after demons in his past."

Sydney didn't want that guy. Sydney wanted Jake.

"Thank you Joan for sharing with me. I respect your opinion, but I don't want another guy."

For the first time in ten years, Sydney knew with all her heart that Jake was the man she couldn't live without.

"I know."

"It doesn't have to be me or them," she said.

"I'm scared for you."

"I'm scared for Jake. You should be too. You know what he's getting into, don't you? You know what this is about and you're afraid he's going to get hurt."

Joan nodded.

"Let's support him, together. He needs you too. I am not leaving Jake's side ever again and I won't let him leave me. I will fight for him."

Joan gave her a proud smile. "You're a strong woman

Sydney McAdams."

Sydney smiled. "I learned from the strongest woman I know. *You.*"

"Now you're just buttering me up so I will smile and play nice.'

"I would love it if you would play nice."

LAKESHORE LOVE

Chapter Twenty-One

SYDNEY, HAYLEE AND Jake sat around the kitchen table with their three small guests, who enjoyed the muffins Jake had picked up. They'd finally revealed their names, as though it was a secret they weren't allowed to share, along with small tidbits about themselves from the mouth of Lucy. After she'd had a good night's sleep and nibbles on a chocolate chip muffin she had become a little chatterbox.

Lucy was the middle child. She was six years old, her birthday was the first of June, but she didn't get anything this year because her mommy wasn't with her. She liked movies and playing in the sand.

Eleven-year-old Mia was quiet and observant, and she had laid a continual stream of *hush up* looks in her sister's direction all morning.

Benjamin, who answered to Benji, was a shy three-year-old attached to his oldest sister, the sole caretaker of this group.

Jake had a muffin in front of him but he wasn't eating, instead he had a strange look on his face. He seemed lost since he'd emerged from her bedroom, like all the worries had slammed into him the moment the water stopped.

Sydney shot him pleading looks to get the ball rolling. The faster he got some answers and left, which she was having an especially hard time dealing with, the faster he would be back. If it was as dangerous as Joan feared, Sydney wasn't sure why they hadn't phoned the police. However, neither she nor Jake was open to that discussion. Hopefully one of these children gave them something to go on.

Jake looked the children over.

"So..." he began, slowly going from one to the next. "...How did you end up here?"

"In a car," Mia answered.

His eyes widened and shot back to Sydney. She could tell her didn't know what to do that elusive answer. He had to keep going.

"Whose car?" Sydney asked, trying to sound casual rather than the prying they were pressing.

Mia ignored her and continued eating her muffin.

Jake, please don't leave them with me.

She felt like jumping on his motorcycle and finding the two MIA women would be easier than watching Mia. The motorcycle was her downfall but it was looking like a better option than this crowd.

"Beth's friend," Lucy supplied.

"Lucy," Mia scolded.

"What?"

Mia rolled her eyes.

"What was Beth's friend's name?" Jake asked.

A shrug.

"What does he look like?"

"A man," said Mia.

"Brown hair," said Lucy, followed by another glare from Mia.

Jake ran his hand through his hair looking fed up and

frustrated. Sydney stood to offer more juice, sensing where this was going, but Jake dove in deeper.

"Alright, listen here. I understand that Beth told you that I'm keeping you and dropped you off and you have it in your little heads that I'm your new watcher or whatever. Now, let's clear something up. I'm not."

Sydney slunk back down in the chair. She was tempted to throw her muffin at his face.

Haylee sent her a surprised look but what was Sydney supposed to do? It wasn't her family, so she shrugged back at her. Haylee looked like she wanted to hide behind a muffin.

"I'm going to find your mother and grandmother and figure out exactly what is going on with the two of them. And I'll drag them back so they can keep you."

It sounded so much more awful then he could possibly understand.

"Good," Mia said. "Cuz we don't want to be stuck here with *you* forever. We didn't ask to be here."

"Good. Then help me find them."

Lucy reached across the table, unfazed by Jake's aggression or her sister's attitude and grabbed a slice of apple. "I don't mind staying here. I like it here." She sent Sydney a shy smile, which she returned. *Well one of these kids kind of liked her.* That would make Jake's departure a little easier.

"Where are they?" Jake demanded.

Mia shrugged.

"Where did your grandmother say she was going?"

"We don't call her that."

He sucked in a deep breath before rephrasing his sentence. "Where did Beth say she was going?"

"Away."

"Away where?"

"I don't know. I'm ten."

Sydney saw another war building up in Jake so she quickly stood up. "Will you excuse us?" She rounded the table and grabbed his arm, surprising him.

***

SYDNEY'S WARM FINGERS let Jake's arm go once she had dragged them onto the porch. He didn't like the stare she was giving him since he'd had plenty of attitude from Mia. He was tired of fighting. He was tired of defending himself. He was tired of trying to figure out how to fix this. He was just plain tired.

His hand reached for her crossed-attitude arms and pulled her against him.

She giggled. He liked her giggle, her smile, the way just her presence comforted him.

He grinned down at her and asked, "You trying to sneak a private moment with me?"

Pink colored her face, and then she sent him a seductive smile. *Seductive!* It wasn't the first one she flashed at him in the last day, but it still surprised him that she had such a smile. Her seductive smile triggered a desire in him to sweep her off her feet and back into her bedroom.

"No, but I'm not objecting to the idea." The sexiness of her tone doubled his reaction.

He chuckled. He knew she had dragged him out here to give him a speech about how to talk to the kids, but he would rather just hold her in his arms and feel the stress of his day diminish.

He tenderly bent his head and kissed her warm lips.

LAKESHORE LOVE

Instantly he felt the all-natural high that wasn't a result of the wonderful flavor of green ginseng tea, a morning staple for Sydney, but rather her intoxicating lips.

If only Joan's words weren't burrowing a hole of irritation into the blissful embrace with Sydney.

After catching another conversation that he had no right eavesdropping on in less than twelve hours he was beginning to feel like a busybody listening in on everyone else's business. Normally he would have made himself known before letting all the details reach his ears, but when he realized it was him they were talking about, his legs simply stopped moving and his ears were locked on every word.

Jake pulled his head away and her eyes gazed up at him with the same bliss he felt. Her tongue ran across her lips and he wanted to take them into his mouth again.

He will hurt you...That's what Jake Stow does...The words were scalding hot in his brain. I will never let him leave me...I will fight for him.

"What are you thinking?" she asked.

What if Joan is right? What if I hurt you? What if I will always hurt you...?

"I'm not getting any answers in there."

"With that snappy tone of yours the only things you are going to get are snappy answers."

"I don't feel like taking all day." He would rather search out Adalyn and Beth, reunite with the three kids, maybe even help them figure out what to do next. More than that, he wanted to be with the woman in his arms and never let go.

In the end, I will fight for them until my death.

"Replace your frustrated tone, you know the one that furrows your brows and makes the veins in your neck pop out..." He was sure she was exaggerating. "...with an understanding tone and listen to their answers to find the right questions to ask." That was no more helpful than the rationalizing battle taking place in his head.

He stared at her dumbfounded.

She shook her head with a little giggle at his unawareness. "Give me your phone." Her little hand popped up between them waiting.

He reached into his back pocket and handed it over breaking the warm contact.

Sydney quickly jotted some questions down and he looked them over.

"Ask them these questions."

She sent him an encouraging smile and he pulled her into a simple hug. He needed her right now more than anything. He would never be able to do this alone, he wouldn't want ,to. He wanted her for the rest of their lives. He wanted all of her more than their friendship, more than the last ten years and he never in his life wanted anything more than a complete and fulfilled life with this woman.

As they walked back into the kitchen, he skimmed the questions once more and used the advice she'd given him about his furrowing brows, which he noted were already furrowing and his neck pulsing.

He will always hurt you...

Jake would never intentionally hurt Sydney, or anyone else for that matter. He wanted to protect Sydney —even from the pain and hurt he had inflicted on her. So, in the end, would she end up hurt at his hand? In the end, would it be a continual path of pain for Sydney if they were together? He didn't want that. He wished his dad were here. Moments like this he missed the advice his dad would dish out...and his dad was always keen on dishing out advice...if only Jake had listened better.

Jake sat on the chair and all eyes were on him. All he could think about was if he would hurt the only blue eyes, encouraging him with all her caring heart.

***

STANDING IN THE driveway, Sydney watched as Jake straddled his bike, wishing it was her instead. She felt a deep worry about him leaving. Mia had answered his questions...sort of...and he was leaving to an address she had finally spilled that they had lived at before Adalyn left them with Beth.

She leaned against his leg with her arms folded in front of her. "Be careful."

"I will."

"And you use your phone. Call or text me when you get there, when you leave. Just so I know you're okay."

He made a face at her like she was overreacting. Maybe she was, but she didn't know what he was walking into, not like he knew, not like Joan knew.

He grabbed for his helmet and she grabbed him for a kiss.

He'd been acting a little strange since the shower, a little distant, but it was probably his departure and having to talk to the kids and all the worry he was carrying, so she let it slide.

When he pulled away he grinned. "Out in the open. How very brave."

She smiled. "Let me know when you get there."

He nodded.

"Promise."

"I promise."

"And when you leave."

"I promise."

She breathed a bit easier as she watched him drive away on his Harley. A bit...she was still scared of what he was walking into. She watched until his bike turned at the end of the road before heading back toward the house. This was going to be an interesting day.

Chapter Twenty-Two

THE ADDRESS MIA had given him turned out to be an apartment building. Not just any apartment building, a deluxe high-rise condo in a high-end of the city. Jake hadn't been prepared for that. Where did Adalyn get the money to afford a place like this? Jake had Adalyn's money from their dad put away in an account but she didn't have access to it.

Drake? The thought infuriated him.

This could definitely work to my advantage, he thought, setting his helmet on the handle and raking his hand over his head.

He found the manager button and listened to it ring as he thought about everything Joan had said to Sydney. He hadn't stopped the steaming sentence repeating through his head since he climbed on his bike and left Willow Valley.

"Hello?" A young voice crackled over the system and he shook his head. *Deal with this first and think about that later.* Who was he trying to kid? He'd been thinking about it the whole drive up here.

"Hi, my name is Jake. I was wondering if I could have a moment of your time to ask some questions about my sister. She used to live here."

There was silence. Maybe he'd given too much information and should have waited for him to come out.

"Be out in a second."

On second hand, maybe not. The term *on second hand* had been drilling his mind the long drive up here. He'd even needed to pull over a couple times to shake away the emotions building up inside him. He couldn't help think that Joan was right about him. He wasn't good enough for Sydney. His life brought pain, his past was dreadful and there were secrets about him that Sydney still didn't know.

Sydney was smart, sweet and so full of life that if she spent the rest of hers with him, he feared he would drag her down.

Curious eyes stared out behind black-rimmed glasses. A tall, skinny man wearing black dress pants and a button-up shirt came out to meet Jake. He pushed open the glass door and offered his hand. "Hello, I'm Robbie Dalton, Manager," he said.

Jake met Robbie' weak handshake with his own —forceful and solid. "Jake."

"What can I do for you?"

"A year ago my sister lived here with three children. Mia, Lucy and Benjamin."

Robbie nodded and a light broke his suspicious eyes as he recalled Adalyn's family. That was good right? That light lit up his eyes?

"Yes, Maria. I never had a problem with Maria and her family. They lived here for almost eight years and were one of my better tenants."

Jake shook his head. "Adalyn," he corrected.

The man shook his wavy hair. "No, her name was Maria."

That was strange. Why was Adalyn using the name Maria? Why hadn't the kids said anything to him? Why did they still refer to her as Adalyn?

"I have never rented to an Adalyn...is that what you said her name was?"

Jake nodded. *Adalyn, what is going on?* "Do you know where Maria may have gone?"

He shook his head. "No, she left in the middle of the night while her boyfriend was in the hospital after he was involved a car crash." More information that the kids could have shared with him. "When he was released two weeks later, Maria and the kids were gone. I noticed them gone, but it wasn't until he came pounding on my door that I knew something was wrong."

"Maria didn't say anything to you?"

"No."

"Was she acting differently before she left?"

"She was upset about the accident, but that's normal and I thought they were at the hospital while he was recovering. Again, I didn't know anything was wrong until he came pounding on my door."

"Did he call the cops? Report them missing?"

He shrugged. "I'm not sure. He left shortly after, so I assumed he'd located them. He packed everything up, paid the rent and left. He didn't say anything and I didn't want to pry."

"Do you know where he went?"

"He left a forwarding address for his mail."

That was perfect. "Could I have it?"

The man eyed him up suddenly as though maybe he had said too much and was now starting to regret it.

"What did you say your name was?"

"Jake. Jake Stow."

"But you're looking for an Adalyn?"

Yes, that was right. "Maria is her middle name."

It wasn't and this guy wasn't buying it.

"Listen, I'm not looking for any trouble. I am worried about my sister's well-being and if this guy knows where she could be I would be grateful to be able to reach him. What did you say his name was?" He hadn't and he wasn't about to now.

"I will see what I can do. What's your cell number? If I find anything I will let you know."

Jake was feeling defeated but there wasn't much more he could do. He jotted his number down for the guy then offered his hand. "Thanks."

The scrawny man shook his hand and simply nodded.

On Jake's way out he turned back. "Hey, how were they?" he asked. "How were the kids? Maria? Did they seem alright?" *The guy whose name you won't tell me.*

He smiled again and nodded. "Like I said, I never had any problems with them. The kids seemed happy and friendly and didn't cause me any trouble. They paid their rent and weren't loud. They seemed like a happy family." His face was solemn. "Is there a reason you would think they are in trouble?"

Jake didn't want to involve anyone but in the same thought he wanted that address. He nodded. "There is and I am very worried about my sister."

With that, he left and climbed back onto his bike, shot Sydney a quick, *I'm leaving* text and hit the road.

He hoped his phone vibrated with the address to Adalyn's boyfriend so he would have another lead. If he didn't get the call, he would be asking Mia and this time he wanted all the answers.

But you're still young, Sydney. You could have the guy that won't chase after demons in his past.

That was exactly what Jake was doing, chasing after demons from his past.

If Adalyn's boyfriend didn't give him a good lead then he would be left with no other alternative then to return to the darkest place he'd ever experienced. Possibly he would find his mother there, possibly he would find Adalyn. Either way, if he ended up back there they would know Jake was the snitch that landed them all in the slammer. He wondered who was in charge there now. Who he would have to face. He didn't want to face any of them and if he did...Joan's words haunted him...Sydney deserved better than this.

The life he had thought he was done with was now thrown back at him. The bottom line was: that was his life. He would always be the son of the drug addict. He would be the snitch to save his family.

Sydney deserved better. Sydney didn't deserve the life he could offer.

Dammit. The thought made him so furious he pulled his bike over on the side of the gravel road...again...and tore off into a panicked pace...again.

He should have never initiated a relationship with Sydney on that beach or chased her down on the boat after she reminded him of his past.

What had he been thinking? He'd been thinking he didn't want to live the rest of his life without her, but now he was dragging her into the darkness of his life.

Who knew what was going to happen now that he had thrown Sydney and Haylee into the middle of his disaster of a life. What if Beth returned when he was away? What if Adalyn dropped in? What were all the horrors these two women would bring with them?

Jake screwed up and big this time. He needed to fix it.

Hopefully, Robbie would send the address and he could get a location on this guy and drill him for some answers.

First, he had to talk to Sydney.

I am not leaving Jake's side ever again and I won't let him leave me. I will fight for him.

Sydney was going to put up a fight and he needed to be prepared with a plan that no circumstances would put an end to her fight. He needed to give her closure to move on with her life and find a man that could take care of her and not put her into danger.

Since Sydney was no longer employed at the Cliff House, it made day-to-day run-ins not an issue and as soon as he sorted out the Adalyn situation, they could part peacefully. He hoped.

Jake climbed back on his bike for the long drive home. But as he passed the Willow Valley signs in the black night, he didn't go straight to Sydney's house. It was past midnight and the bar was open until two Saturday nights, so he stopped in.

Devon was managing the place and filled him in on Joan's departure later than usual but not into the evening crowd. Devon walked with him toward his office, informing him quickly of the day's numbers. The numbers were the last thing from Jake's mind and they went out just as quickly as they came from Devon's mouth. Normally he would compare to last year to make sure they were maintaining the same numbers or picking up, but today sadness pushed all other thoughts away. And as much as the horribleness that he was aware with Adalyn and her kids, it was Sydney that stole all his attention.

"Keep up the good work." Jake shut his office door. He ran his hands across his face. He was exhausted, which wasn't like him for the hour. It was his early rise before six and driving all day long that had done him in. He collapsed onto the loveseat in his office and threw his feet up on the arm-rest.

He just needed a minute to himself before going to face Sydney.

He felt like shit as he planned to put a stop to the life they were beginning together. His guilt was immeasurable but it was his heart that was bothering him the most. A part of that organ, that he'd never known existed, was tearing up inside him and he was having a hard time working up the strength to face her. She would be waiting, and she would be expecting answers but she would be expecting him in a way that he couldn't give her in fear of the pain it would bring.

He just needed a minute, and then he would go to her house and face her. *I just need one minute,* was his last thought before his eyes drifted shut.

***

JAKE WASN'T ANSWERING his phone. Sydney had called him and texted him but she hadn't heard anything since he had texted that he was on his way back. That was almost eight hours ago.

Sydney was in a panic. What if he crashed? What if

he was in the hospital? What if he was lying somewhere in the road dying?

Oh stop!

She grabbed the phone and dialed the bar. It was one-thirty so they would still be open. She got the evening staff and asked if Jake was there.

"Um, just a sec Sydney."

Just a sec Sydney? Just a sec Sydney? She didn't know if her nerves had a second to spare before they exploded in sheer panic.

"Yes, he's in office did you want me to get him?"

He was in his office? He was in his office! Her fear lifted and a cloud of anger pulsed through her.

"No, thanks."

She hung up the phone, fuming. He was in his office back in Willow Valley and the stupid jerk hadn't let her know.

Sydney knocked lightly on Haylee's door and entered to a sleeping murmur. "What? What is it? What happened...what time is it?" she said, rolling over.

"Nothing." Sydney touched her arm to keep her from standing. "It's late and I'm stepping out. Can you listen for the kids please?"

Haylee sleepily agreed and rolled over, falling right back into her sleep.

Sydney stepped out into the cool night, tucking her hands in the pockets of her denim jacket and started for the Cliff House.

She was angry he hadn't called her, but worried at the same time. Why hadn't he called? Did he learn something that he was having a hard time facing?

They were just flipping the sign as Sydney pulled the

door open. The music had been turned off, but the staff was in their regular, loud bustling closing as she headed toward his office.

She knocked lightly on Jake's office scared of what she might find. Had he found the truth out about Adalyn and he was having a hard time dealing with it? She would stand behind him every step of the way, whatever he needed.

When Jake didn't answer, she pushed the door open and found him sleeping on the sofa.

Devon walked past as she stood in the doorway. "He got in around midnight and hasn't been out since." He snuck a peek and frowned. "Is he alright? He looked stressed when he came in. I was giving him the numbers but his attention was somewhere else."

Sydney had no idea and shrugged, sending Devon an unsure smile.

He understood, another year-round employee who got what Jake was all about. "I will lock up behind us." He said, giving her shoulder a squeeze. "You take care of him."

She smiled at him. "Thanks Devon. I will."

Sydney closed the door behind her and left her anger in the bar. She wanted to know what happened but she didn't want to wake him up when he was in such a deep sleep. Obviously, something had happened that he was having a hard time dealing with and she didn't want to interrupt the solitude he was finding.

She stared at him for a long time, but as she felt the night stealing her energy. Finally, she pulled his jacket from the coat hook and lay down beside him using it as a blanket for their arms.

This was the man she wanted to spend the rest of her

life with. She fit against his side, her head nuzzled perfect against his arm. They were meant to be together.

Jake stirred a bit but didn't wake. Sydney closed her eyes and let the night steal both their dreams.

***

THE LOW BREATHING hum and heat penetrating against Jake's side pulled him from his sleep. The familiar vanilla bean cream Sydney wore drifted from her soft skin and filled his early senses with a verification of the person lying next to him. His eyes remained closed as his breathing was slowly drifting back into the relaxing sleep blanketed in the warm peace Sydney conveyed.

Sydney?

His breathing stopped.

Why was Sydney sleeping beside him?

His eyes snapped open and darted around the room determining their whereabouts: his office. *Why were they asleep in his office?* His eyes rushed for the clock on the wall. It was early morning again just after six. *When had Sydney snuck into his office...and how had he not noticed?*

He let out the breath. Just lying on the couch, bodies pressed against each other, even fully clothed, he could feel his decision to end things with her slipping away. It wasn't only the loss of her physically that he would long to have, it was Sydney, his friend, that he feared losing when the words he didn't want to say passed his mouth.

Unsuccessfully unable to move even a centimeter from her, he lay back down and stared at her.

She was latched onto his entire side, her cheek resting against his chest and her neck curled into the nook of her arm while her free hand burned each fingerprint through his shirt.

LAKESHORE LOVE

Her legs were so entwined with his own that he couldn't tell where hers began and his ended. Sydney's heap of wavy blonde hair spilled everywhere like waves in the lake, over his arm, across his chest, around her head. He would rather sweep away the stray pieces falling across her face and kiss her good morning, but with his decision he no longer had that right and he wasn't going to kiss her just to leave her.

Where were the kids? Joan? Haylee?

There were so many reasons why they needed to get up and yet none of them convinced him to shake her awake.

What time had Sydney arrived at the Cliff House? Did she brave the late hour and walk up when no woman should be on the street? He didn't have to ask because he knew deep down that was exactly what she had done.

He should have called her or at the very least sent a text when he got into town. He'd been selfish not wanting to face her and wanting to hold onto her for only a little while longer. As a result, she had ended up walking to the Cliff House at the crazy late hour. Something could have happened to her. This was another prime reason why he wasn't good for her. He was selfish.

Sydney stirred and her fingers tightened around his shirt as her body stretched across him sending heat to every place. She pressed harder with a long, sexy, low moan that caused one to commence beginning deep down in his groin.

Her sleepy eyes found his and she smiled, a sexy, soft, drowsy smile that pulled the sides of his mouth into a pleased grin. "Morning." Her voice came out just as soft and sexy and his instinct was to wrap his hands around her tighter, pulling her up to his lips. He didn't move.

"Did you sleep well?" she asked with a half yawn that

ended with a little squeal.

He had never slept so well in his life. "Yes."

"Me too." Sydney snuggled up closer against him, if that was even possible, and her free hand found his chin where she stroked the roughness with the smoothness of her long fingers.

"Did you walk here?" It came out a little gruff, but why wouldn't it when he was well aware of what her answer was going to be and how it would displease him.

"Mm-hmm." Her eyes drifted back shut her lashes sweeping her soft skin.

The answer infuriated him and he didn't want to ask the following, but he did so anyway. "Alone?"

"Mm-hmm."

He was about to tell her exactly what he thought of that when her finger touched his lip. The touch sent excitement down his body and he had the urge to suck that finger into his mouth.

"I have to get home," she said.

Suddenly after trying to escape her grip, he didn't want her to leave.

With the hand hiding under her body, he moved the fallen hair across her face. "Syd, you have to get up, I can't move," he whispered quietly to her.

Her hand travelled down the front of his shirt. A casual touch, but intimate in every place it touched.

She looked back up at him. "Are you alright? You didn't call me last night."

"I'm fine."

"Did something bad happen?" She worried about him like no other person on the earth, which made what they needed to discuss even more difficult.

He shook his head and then smiled. "In fact I learned some good things about Adalyn."

She smiled back at him. "Like what?"

"How about I tell you all about it on the walk back to your house?" He needed her off him and fast before he dipped into her morning mouth and ended with both of them naked.

She pouted at him. "I guess you're right. I left Haylee in charge." She didn't move.

"It would be quicker if you got off me."

She didn't move.

"Jake I thought something bad happened to you. I was terrified." The morning hour was allowing the desire to creep into her eyes again and he felt like he might let his restraint go.

He sat up, forcing her legs away from his and she slowly sat up beside him, curling them under her.

He threw his legs over the edge of the couch and ran his hands across his face. "I'm sorry. I should have called you."

"Yes, you should have." He must have had her worried to snip at him like that. "I'm just glad you're alright." Sydney climbed to her knees and walked over to his side. In one quick motion, she sat on his lap and wrapped her arms around his neck, tucking her head in his shoulder. "You should have come to my house last night, then instead of rushing off we could have snuggled and played together all morning in my bed." Her abruptness heated his body. She nibbled on his throat before standing up, slipping into her jacket and waiting at his office door. "Are you coming?"

How was he going to tell this loving, caring, teasing, and gorgeous woman whom he'd loved his whole life that there was no future for them? He felt the day's events come to weighing heavily on him as they walked back to her house, hands laced together.

He needed a strong black mug...maybe pot...of coffee before he even attempted to explain his view on their relationship. Besides, he was enjoying telling her everything Robbie had told him, and the lead he might get to Lucy and Benji's dad. If he didn't get a phone call from Robbie he was sitting Mia down again for a nice long chat. That chat seemed a thousand times easier than the one he needed to have with Sydney.

For someone who avoided long, or small, chats he was getting himself into a hill of them and none were pleasant.

LAKESHORE LOVE

Chapter Twenty-Three

JAKE SAT ACROSS the picnic table staring into the very intimidating bright blue eyes of his niece. If eyes could tear someone down into shreds, hers would surely do so right that moment. She didn't like his request for a private conversation any more than he did. But it had to be done. Living in limbo for all of them would be far worse.

Lucy and Benji were content playing in the sandbox where Jake could see them behind Mia.

He was totally shocked that Sydney had actually left him alone with all three kids for almost the whole day to take her shift at the shop until five. There hadn't been a right moment to talk to her about the relationship and it was lurking in his head, distracting him, confusing him, but he knew what needed to be done. For now, his time would be better spent getting the answers they needed because Robbie hadn't called him back and he had nothing.

Sitting in Sydney's backyard after a barbeque lunch...he made a nasty barbeque if he did say do himself...it was time to get some answers.

Mia was prepared to deflect him. She was prepared to protect herself and her siblings, just as she had been doing for the last year since they were dropped into the laps of Beth. He knew this child all too well from his life with his mother. But Mia would answer him. He needed answers to find her mother.

"Straight forward and honest," Sydney had told him, "Firm but loving. Nice not mean."

Alright. I can do this. I would rather be shot in the foot, but here it goes.

"I drove to the address you gave me yesterday." No movement in her face. *Did you really think it was that easy?* "I talked to Robbie." There was a shimmer of knowledge shadowed in those eyes. *A start in the right direction...looking good.*

Jake was more nervous than this girl.

"He told me that you, Lucy and Benji, left the condo six months ago."

She stared at him.

"He also told me that you three kids were wonderful and your mom and your dad were good, nice people."

That didn't seem to faze her.

"He said you left in the middle of the night without telling your dad and he didn't know where you went or why." He wished he had asked Adalyn's boyfriend's first name. Hopefully, by the end of the conversation, he would know.

Silence.

"Where did you go?"

She folded her arms across her chest telling him *not a chance in hell* was she answering his question. *Be nice. Be nice.*

"Your sister likes me," he observed out loud, glancing over her shoulder at Lucy who was a ball of sunshine compared to this girl.

"Lucy likes cockroaches," Mia said flatly.

Hmm. Was she calling him a cockroach?

"Your brother likes me."

"He's three. He eats sand."

Jakes head snapped back over at the two in the sandbox. Benji was digging a hole, no sand in the mouth. *Phew!* He wasn't good at this taking care of children thing. It had been a long time since Haylee was young and he'd always been there for her but Joan or Sydney had never been far away.

It felt like Sydney was in a whole other country right now.

He leveled a look at Mia. "I want to find your mother."

"She will find us when she's ready."

"So you do know where she is?"

"No."

"Did she tell you she would find you?"

"Does she know where you live?"

Of course she knew where he lived. So, yes she'd told her that.

They were getting nowhere and he didn't like the games.

"Alright Mia...can I be honest with you?" he asked in a serious tone, slowly folding his hands in front of him on the table. Nothing else was working and he really didn't want to be mean. These kids were his family. They were scared and alone and Adalyn loved them. For whatever reason she thought they would be safer with him.

Nothing.

"Your mom is my baby sister. I love her. And I am worried about her. More than likely she's in some kind of trouble."

That sent a little terror to her face and Jake felt guilty for putting it there. *I'm sorry Mia, but I need some answers.*

"I can help her if I can find her. Please Mia, tell me what has happened since you left six months ago. Tell me everything because it might help. Or anything before you left that was a little strange.

For a long time she stared at him silent and thin-lipped, but he could see he had gotten through to her. In her eyes she was struggling to keep a secret...or perhaps fear of talking. He hoped she would find it in herself to trust him.

"My mom said you're not the bad guy." Relief filled Jake. Maybe he wouldn't have to fight so much.

"She said we could trust you and you would take care of us."

"I will." His voice almost caught in his throat. For two years he'd tried to convince Adalyn of those very words.

Mia looked up at him shyly as if scared to say the next words. "We don't want to go back with Beth."

"You will never have to go back to Beth. I promise."

"My mom dropped us off with Beth the night we left our house. She promised Beth would take us straight to you." Mia looked hurt. Jake guessed that hadn't happened and Jake felt a ping of anger at his mother for keeping these three healthy children and dragging them into her warped world instead of delivering them directly to him. He also felt angry and confused to why Adalyn didn't drop them off personally or call him so he could have helped with whatever mess she was in.

"Mom said she was protecting me, Lucy, Benji and Dad."

LAKESHORE LOVE

"What's your dad's name?"

Her mouth tightened then relaxed. "Julian." *Julian, the dad.* "I don't know why she needed to protect us or what she was protecting us from. We were happy until we went to Beth." Mia made a face. "Beth was taking us to you but then she didn't and she kept calling some guy and having arguments. Every time there would be yelling and she would get mad and leave us for days."

Damn his mother.

"Do you remember anything about the guy she was talking to? Did it have to do with you three or Adalyn?"

"Both I think. Beth would make us leave the room but we could hear her through the walls. He had a weird name."

Jake stilled. This was the road he didn't want to go down.

"Can you recall the name at all?"

Mia's little face squished up. "I forget. I heard it once, and it rhymed with snake and every time she was yelling we would say she's talking to snake again."

Cold slivers of danger and fear sliced through his preparation for the name. If he was involved nothing was going to turn out good. *Was he out of prison? How was he out already?*

"But then Beth said it would never come. I think she meant money and she left us with you."

This doesn't mean Adalyn's with him. This doesn't mean Adalyn's in danger. But what else did it mean?

"Anything else?"

She shrugged. "I don't think so."

"Where did you go to school?"

"We were home schooled." *Home schooled?*

"Can you tell me anything about your dad? Do you know where to find him? Does he have family? Where is he from? Anything?"

Mia thought for a moment. "They met through work and he doesn't have family. Our last name is Kasper if that helps." She frowned.

"Where does he work?"

"At the office." She frowned. "I really miss them both, Mom and Dad. I'm not sure what happened. We were happy living in the condo and then Dad got in the accident and was in the hospital. My mom was very upset after that happened and she said we needed to go to you and that Dad was going to be okay once we were all with you. I'm sorry...that's all I know."

"That's alright. You've been very helpful."

That was enough for now. Jake knew who was involved. He would give Robbie until tomorrow for a phone call then he was going to have to phone Jason. There was no way he was walking into that clubhouse again without consulting Jason first. Jason had saved his life and he would forever be grateful to the man. Jake trusted him and he would know what to do.

"Can I ask you one more question Mia?"

She nodded.

"Did Beth or whoever she was with hurt any of you?" He didn't want to ask but he didn't have a choice.

"No." The answer came quick.

"Ever?"

She shook her head and he believed her. His mom was a lot of things, but violent had never been one of them. "Sometimes she didn't feed us and we were always in the house and not allowed to go outside, but she never hurt us. She talked about you and my mom sometimes. She would say this was her fault and she didn't know how to fix it. She would say she..." Mia looked bashful and it was a nice change from the scared anger she usually wore. "...loved you two."

Jake loved his mother too, no matter what. Beth was his mother.

"One more thing," he said.

Mia arched her eyebrows.

"Sydney, Haylee and Joan..." Sometimes Joan. "...are my friends and they are very nice women. So, could you maybe give them a chance?"

The "my friends" term next to Sydney's name stung his chest. *My girlfriend, my fiancé, my wife sounded better.* That was an impossibility that made his chest tighten, making it hard to think about anything except Sydney.

Mia agreed a little too quickly, so he hoped she would follow through on her promise. She ran away from the table with less worry to play like a young child should play.

He compared the fear, worry, sadness in Mia because of what his family had done and noted that was exactly what he didn't want to do with Sydney. He never wanted Sydney to experience the worry, fear and everything else negative that came with his past. He was saving her in the end. He was letting her go to find another man who could protect her...the thought pissed him off...to love Sydney...no one would ever love Sydney with the depth he did and to stay by her side.

Anyone who hurt her during her road to happiness Jake would destroy. However, when she got home from work and the sun dipped behind the lake, he was forced, for her own good to hurt her, and because of that he wanted to pound the shit out of himself.

LAKESHORE LOVE

Chapter Twenty-Four

"THESE ARE CALLED spider dogs," Haylee explained sliding a hotdog onto the end of Mia's campfire stick. She'd already cut each end twice before sliding it on but it didn't look like anything special. Mia gave her an, *are you sure* look that made Sydney smirk.

"Roast it," Haylee insisted, then turned to Lucy and started hers. "Here's yours." She passed Lucy the stick and Jake helped her roast her hotdog.

This was their alternative to the barbeque Jake had planned. He had given a little child-like pout when he couldn't grill his steak. It made Sydney smile. He was a big child when it came to his barbequing and he liked to show off the talent.

The hour was touching seven and the sun was just beginning to hang low over the lake on its way to sleep for the night.

Joan opened the screen door and stepped onto the deck wearing a lovely, freshly-pressed peach pant and blazer outfit over a black silk blouse. Her hair was fluffed at the top with a claw clip twisted around the back. She looked beautiful and her face had some color of happiness that Sydney hadn't seen for a long while.

"I'm going out for supper," Joan called from the back

deck. *Supper?* This was the first Sydney had heard of her having plans, but then again she'd been distracted with all of Jake and his plans lately.

"Oh Grandma you look gorgeous!" Haylee called, but her attention turned back to the girls as the eight legs she'd cut into the hotdogs began to curl forming the spider she promised.

"With who?" Sydney called.

"A friend." Joan did not get all fancied up for a *friend*.

"What friend?"

Joan wiped the front of her outfit off as though it had gotten wrinkled from her walk down the stairs. Her eyes darted at Jake who was lost with the girls. "His name is Chester."

His? His! Oh she was going on a date.

"Chester?" Sydney ran the name through her mind, contemplated the familiarity and then the night of the March crash came back to mind, She remembered Joan had gone to the hospital that night to visit a friend that had been committed after having a stroke. And the name was Chester! *Oh, this was Chester.*

Normally Sydney would have pried more conversation about the only man that Joan had talked of since Jake's dad, but when Jake's head jerked up, Sydney was sure what was behind his eyes. Was he angry? What right did he have to be angry? The woman had waited fourteen years since her husband passed to even talk about a man, let alone go on a date. Joan deserved to go out on dates, meet a man that would make her happy and that she could grow old with. Sydney wanted that life for Joan.

Sydney abandoned the wooden lawn chair to meet

Joan eye to eye on the back deck where it was more private.

"Is it a date?"

"Chester and I have been friends for quite some time now, so we thought we would have a more formal dinner."

"Like a date..."

She shooed her away, irritated by her persistence. "Why do you have to label it?" *Because it was absolutely wonderful.*

Joan's face was getting flustered and she even looked like she was about to forget her untitled date altogether.

Sydney touched her arms gently. "Have a good time," she said, before kissing her cheek and sending her on her way.

Sydney was going to have to meet this Chester, depending on how serious they were about each other. Joan was spending the night again, so maybe Sydney could get a glance of this Chester when they got back home.

Sydney caught Jake watching and smiled at him, trying to ease whatever bad thoughts he was thinking. Once these kids were in bed she was going to take advantage of their alone time and she would ease him entirely, all night long.

***

JAKE CARRIED A sleeping Benji up Sydney's stairs to the small guest bedroom with a sleepy Mia and Lucy in tow already dressed in their pajamas, as promised which permitted more time around the campfire so they could see Haylee stir in three packets of Rainbow Fire, coloring the flames beautiful blues, greens and white. They all sat tranquilized by the amazing colors and quiet singing of crickets in the distance until finally, Jake called it—bedtime.

Now, they climbed into the bed, overly exhausted, in a zombie-like state.

Mia and Lucy climbed on each side and Jake laid Benji in the middle. As he was about to pull the covers over, them Lucy stood up on her knees and reached around him for a hug. "I love you Uncle Jake," she whispered drowsily then curled up beside Benji.

Jake was frozen for a second, taking in the affection and remembered the story Mia had told the two younger ones about how he would rescue them. He felt guilty for staying here with them all day instead of searching out Adalyn but he hadn't had much of a choice.

He caught Mia watching him through skeptical eyes. Unfortunately, it was going to be quite some time before this young girl truly trusted again.

Jake tucked them in and slid a wayward hair away from Lucy's already closed eyes.

"Goodnight," he said, then looked up at Mia again. "I love you three too."

A smiled tugged at her lips but she didn't give it any more distance. Her eyes drifted shut, content.

Sydney stretched out under the star-filled night by the fire pit. The fire flickered across her beautiful body, face and he felt himself wanting to stretch out beside her on the lounger and simply hold her. His body urged him to let the last few day's events slip away with the feel of her beside him. But that would be selfish and in the end when he said what needed to be said, it would hurt her even more.

Her sandals sat on the ground at her feet and her toes wiggled when she saw him.

"Did they go to sleep alright?"

LAKESHORE LOVE

He nodded. *Tell her now, this is the perfect opportunity.* There would never be a perfect opportunity to hurt her...to take back everything he had promised her.

He sat beside her tiny feet at the edge of the lounger, prepared to tell her.

"You definitely broke through to them today," she said. "It was nice to see them behave as children instead of terrified little adults."

It was nice to see them smile laugh and not fear their surroundings.

"What did you say to Mia to break that shell?"

Jake sighed. He supposed her curiosity had been itching to ask all night, with not opportunity to do so. And it was the reason he still hadn't told her his decision. So he could answer what she wanted to know before starting the conversation that would define their relationship permanently.

"Exactly what you suggested: the truth."

Sydney sat straighter and her hand touched his sending both comfort and desire through him. How had he lived this many years and ignored these feelings that were escalating now beyond his control.

"It was just as hard for her to hear it as it was for you to say it. Both of you needed to get it out because you four need to unite."

He wanted to turn his hand over and let her fingers lace through his but he didn't dare.

"When Adalyn left six months ago she took them to Beth and Beth promised to bring them to me." He didn't tell her about Drake because the name wouldn't register to her.

"For the past few months, Mia told Lucy and Benji

that I would rescue them. That I was their hero."

Sydney smiled softly at him. "You are their hero. They are the luckiest three kids to have your eagle eyes protecting them. Now and always."

He hated that she saw him as a hero when he was about to divide them.

"I want to go look for their dad. The manager at the apartment might call with a follow up address and if not Mia gave me his name so I was going to make a call and see if I can locate him." He wanted her to watch the kids. He could take them but he didn't even know this guy.

A car door slamming caught Sydney's attention, dragging it from him. "Joan's back." She scrambled to the edge of the chair, pressing the sides of their bodies together. She stopped. "Oh yeah. I wanted to talk to you about her friend Chester." She sent him an arched eyebrow. "Quit making angry looks when she talks about him. What did you expect—for her to stay single forever?"

He hadn't expected her to go find some guy named *Chester*. What kind of name was *Chester*? Who was this man? And was he after the money his dad left her? These were important questions not to be taken lightly.

"Is that what you think I should do after Kyle? Never date again?"

Well of course not. He didn't have to say the words and she smiled at him, victoriously making her point. "Exactly."

Sydney abandoned him and her shoes to sneak around the side of the house. He followed her bouncy shadow creep up the side and peek around the front porch towards the driveway. By the time he caught up to her, she was squatting beside a bush and peering around like a nosy child.

This was ridiculous.

He walked over and her hand pulled him to his knees.

"Shhh," she said, pressing her hands against his lips. *His lips!* Not over her own where he wouldn't have the desire to kiss every inch of her warm knuckles.

She snuck around the bush on her hands and knees, which was completely unnecessary, trying to sneak a peek at the couple. They were hidden in darkness but Jake could see Joan being escorted to the deck by a well-dressed, handsome older man. Jake thought dating at his age was hard, he couldn't even imagine how people in their sixties did it.

They were exchanging quips about having a good night, but Jake's eyes drifted to the hike in Sydney's dress that showed her long slim legs all the way up to the back of her thighs.

"They're so cute."

His head snapped up and she looked at him, smiling. "Really?" she asked catching him staring. Her tone was shocked but her expression was amused. This was not a good way to end their relationship.

Ticked off at himself, he wasn't sure what to say. Even in the dark, he could see Sydney's smile turn seductive. She slowly rose to her knees and moved against his body. That's when he should have spoken up. But her hands grabbed his and then her fingertips trailed up his arms to the collar of his shirt. She was unbuttoning his shirt.

"Joan's right there," he whispered, a good argument but not the one he should be using.

Her lips kissed his ear and she whispered. "I will be super quiet." Then she bit his earlobe and pulled away before a giggle escaped.

How the hell was he supposed to stop that? Not only was he crazy about this woman but he'd never seen this spontaneously...naughty side of her. Damn, it was hot.

Her mouth pressed against the side of his throat, hot and wet. She designed patterns along his throat with her tongue. The outline of her hand pressed against the back of his neck, forcefully keeping him in place, while her other hand massaged his exposed chest.

In the distance...a very far distance with the envelope of desire clouding his ears, he heard the front door shut and the cheater's vehicle drive away.

Sydney had taken complete control over his body as her mouth moved down his chest with slow, seductive kissing, nibbling and licking.

Then he felt her hand caress where his jeans had tightened and his mind snapped back. He couldn't do this. Not to her.

His hand caught her wrist. "Syd, wait." Barely a whisper, but filled with pleading.

He heard her giggle and her hands moved up his body and snaked around his neck. She kissed his lips. "Take me to my room then."

Yes. No.

He didn't move. His body stiffened and she must have sensed it because she pulled her head away to look at him, keeping her silky dress pressed against his bare skin and her body heating every place she touched.

"That was an invitation," she clarified.

He took a deep breath.

"Jake, what's wrong?" Her worry masked her lust.

"We can't do this."

A smile crossed her lips. "That's why I said take me to my room. Seriously, I would have pegged you more adventurous, but if you're not comfortable..."

He wanted to. Oh, his whole damn body wanted to. But she deserved better than a life of ups and downs.

He raked his hand across his face, purposely not touching her with his hands. "I'm not taking you to your room." He didn't mean for it to come out so rough.

His word brewed hurt and confusion across her face. "What?"

"You and me Sydney, it isn't going to work."

"What are you talking about?"

"Us. In a relationship...a couple. It's not going to work."

"O-kay." Her eyes were searching him for a sign but he was working his hardest to hide everything from her. "Why not?"

Because you deserve better. "Because I said so that's why." Why did it have to come out sounding so horrible. Probably because he felt horrible.

She was shaking her head. "I don't understand. What happened?"

"Nothing happened." His entire horrid past happened.

"Well, something happened or else you wouldn't be changing your mind about us?"

"What us? There was never an *us*."

She didn't like that way he said that and sent him a glare. "There was an *us* in my bedroom."

"Your bedroom was a mistake."

"It wasn't a mistake. Jake, stop it. Where is this

coming from? You followed me onto a boat for crying out loud to win me over and bared your soul before taking care of me and now you're calling it all a mistake? Talk to me now. Don't shut me out."

This was her fighting for him just like she said she would. He'd come prepared with the big guns to ward her off.

Sydney continued her fight for him and he knew he was going to push her away, but he savored her strong feelings that she felt were worth fighting...for him. "I don't believe you. Not after everything that we have gone through to get here. Tell me what's going on. Tell me what happened while you were gone that has scared you."

Your safety. Your future. I'm not scared...I'm terrified!

"I'm tired of always having to explain myself to you," he practically yelled at her and she jumped startled, but not afraid of him like others would be if he raised his voice in that tone.

"I thought I felt something for you all these years and finally this morning we were connected," he paused because the words were so harsh but needed, so he pulled out the courage. "There was nothing there. I didn't feel it like I thought I would. I mean the sex was good, but I didn't feel that connection between us that I was convinced I would." *I felt it, I'm so sorry, Syd. I didn't need to make love to you to feel that connection.* "I think maybe ten years of waiting for the real thing just didn't live up to the expectations. We are better as friends, you and me. You know what I'm saying?"

He watched every word cut the confusion away from her face and dig deep hurt throughout.

LAKESHORE LOVE

This is better for you baby I promise. I'm sorry it has to be like this."

"Loud and clear." She pushed her hands against his chest away from him. Thank goodness. He didn't know how long he could hold up this gig.

Before she stood, her hand sliced through the air and made contact with his cheek and surprisingly, for the tiny little thing she was, his face stung like a son of a bitch.

"Screw you Jake."

He deserved it, but he had hoped they wouldn't fight like this. She was usually rational and sweet. He really made her angry as she stomped with her bare feet away from him.

He caught up to her in front of the house where the dim porch light cast a glow across them. He touched her arm. He didn't know why or what he would say, he was just having a hard time seeing her so mad.

She yanked out of his grasp and spun. "No!"

She turned and stormed up the wooden stairs. They creaked below each foot. At the top, she turned to face his frozen body. He wasn't exactly sure what to do.

"The kids will be fine with me for the night and tomorrow, but you're not welcome to stay the night Jake."

He could see her better with the porch light casting a glow across her face. She was ready to cry. He'd made her cry.

"You know Jake, I know what you're doing. You think you're outsmarting me, trying to convince me all that garbage you said yesterday is true when the truth is you're hiding from something." So close Sydney. "And I want to fight for you, but I don't think I can win this one. I love you Jake. I want the future together that I know would be great, but if you need me to let you go, I will."

As she said the words, he had to build a shield around his heart to deflect them or he would march up those stairs and kiss her. She was right on, but it still didn't change the fact that a life with him wouldn't be easy and could be even dangerous.

"Let me go."

"Just walk away," she said sounding hopeless. "It's what you do best."

LAKESHORE LOVE

Chapter Twenty-Five

SYDNEY TEXTED HER sisters and arranged a girl's night out. It was last minute but she needed it after all the ups and downs Jake had been playing. Unfortunately, only Abby could make it.

Peyton complained about being too fat to go to a bar and Kate used the Rosemary card...Sydney definitely didn't hold that against her since Rosemary had just come back into her life this year.

Let him go. Let him go! Fine, she would let him go, but first she was going to shove exactly what he was walking away from in his face. Walking away, that should be Jake Stow's middle name: Jake Walk Away Stow. *Idiot.*

Abby was thrilled to join her and she showed up at the front doors of the Cliff House with Isabelle Caliendo on her arm.

"Sydney!" she called waving and picking up her pace in the black stilettos she was wearing. In her skin-tight black mini dress with a hollow collar, Abby looked sexy. Super-hot sexy, making the dress Sydney chose to wear look Plain Jane. Sydney had tried so hard too, picking out the shortest dress with a plunging neckline.

Then her eyes fell to Isabelle who was also sporting a super sexy black dress and Sydney just felt old.

Abby greeted her with a hug and looked her over.

"You look...cute."

That was not what she was going for.

"Hey Izzy we will meet you in there," she called. Isabelle nodded and was already having a conversation with some random guy on her way in the door.

"Are we here to give a Jake a little show?"

Sydney blushed. Was it that obvious? Abby didn't have details and Sydney did not fill her in.

Abby grinned. "That's what I thought. Did something happen?" Everything happened. "Do you want to talk about it?"

Sydney shook her head.

"Alright well this isn't gonna work." She waved a hand over Sydney's outfit. "Come on, I have some spare clothes in my car." *Spare clothes in the car? Who did that?*

Sydney didn't argue and followed her sister. Abby popped the trunk and pulled out a pair of skinny black pants, which she pulled on under her dress.

"Abby!"

"What?" She shrugged and looked around. "I'm not naked."

Abby grabbed a large black knitted off the shoulder studded top and put it over the dress and with amazing talent she slipped the dress off from under the top and handed it to Sydney with a smile. "Put this on."

"Where?"

"Right here. In the back seat. I don't care."

Sydney wasn't about to strip in the parking lot so she climbed into the back seat of the car and, feeling even more like a foolish teenager, she awkwardly changed into the skin tight dress that pulled and tugged her every curve.

She climbed out and Abby dangled an extra pair of black stilettos in front of her.

"Who has an extra wardrobe in their vehicle?" Sydney asked, leaving her cowboy boots in the back seat and slipping into the three inch heels that boosted her high into the air.

"You never know when you might need extras." Abby stepped back and examined Sydney with a nod of approval. "Now you're hot."

"I feel underdressed."

"You look amazing. Jake will be regretting every dumbass word he said."

Sydney was beginning to wonder if this was a good idea.

"Just wait." Abby pulled Sydney's side low ponytail out and ran her fingers through her hair, tousling it all over. She whistled. "Damn sister, you're looking better than me."

Sydney swatted her sister playfully. "Yeah right."

"You do."

Sydney didn't believe her. "Well we better get a drink in me before I change my mind."

"Let's get two." Abby grabbed her hand.

***

"SYDNEY IS IN the house," Chuck called, nudging his head toward the door.

Jake didn't see Sydney at first. He saw her sister Abby and two blonde friends but it wasn't until the one blonde turned that his jaw hit the floor.

Sydney? Sydney! He even had to do a double take because he'd never seen her wear anything so...provocatively sexy hot. Then he noticed he wasn't the only guy in the house ogling the blonde beauty. Her longer than long legs carried her through his bar in such a skin tight dress it was almost as if she wasn't wearing anything at all.

Her drinking buddies were Isabelle and Abby. That was a bad combination, but at least they were in his bar.

Two hours later, he regretted that thought. He didn't want to watch Sydney dance, laugh and touch other guys. He certainly didn't want to watch other guys touch her. Even if he'd sent her away for that sole purpose to go find a guy. He hadn't meant for it to be one of these drunken fools and he hadn't meant for her to go out and get drunk!

Did she not remember what happened the last time she had too much to drink? She'd ended up naked in his bed. This time maybe she wouldn't get so lucky. This time? There was not going to be a this time.

"No more for Sydney," he barked at the staff behind the counter.

"Jake she's only had one cooler and a shot," Devon challenged.

Jake shot him a look. It wasn't up for debate and Devon took a step back nodding his understanding.

Jake tossed the towel on the counter and pressed his hands against the surface. He felt frustrated. Was he doing the right thing? Of course he was. *Then why did if feel so damn wrong?*

"That one's got eyes for you buddy," Devon said and for a second Jake looked up hoping to find Sydney staring at him, but she was laughing and having a blast without him. Instead, a set of green eyes and a head of long red hair was sending him a look.

He wasn't interested. In fact, he didn't need this shit

right now at all. All he wanted was Sydney. If it wasn't Sydney it wasn't going to be any other woman. Ever.

Jake pushed his way from behind the bar.

"I need a break," he growled at Devon.

"Sure man I got this covered."

He glanced at Sydney. "Keep your eye on Sydney and Abby, would ya? Call me if anything is off."

"Sure thing boss."

Jake didn't care what Sydney drank, but he wasn't letting her get out of control. If she didn't like it then she could leave. He didn't want her getting into trouble on his watch.

***

"DEVON, ANOTHER ROUND for me and my sister." Sydney ordered, sliding onto the stool and tapping her hands on the counter in beat with the music.

The music was good, the company was good...it would be better if Jake were there. Sydney shook her head. *No more Jake.*

"Sorry, Sydney you've been cut off," Devon told her.

She laughed.

Devon didn't.

"What do you mean cut off? Who cut me off?"

He looked reluctant and before he even said the name, she knew. "Jake."

Jake? Jake! Why that controlling ass.

"Where is he?"

Devon shrugged as she was sliding off the stool. "Maybe in his office," he called after her as she stomped her way in that direction.

Cut off! Was he kidding?

If she wanted to drink and get sloshed then she would very well do so and he couldn't stop her! Even though that was not her plan after what happened last time. However, the comfortable buzz she had was helping to keep her from searching Jake out, which was exactly what she was doing. How confusing.

Sydney didn't bother knocking and shoved his office door open, ready to put up a fight. He wasn't in there.

She almost laughed at how foolish she felt except she was still so damn angry.

Sydney heard Jake's low murmur down the hall and her body moved to the end that led to his apartment. How dare he just decide they weren't going to be together and then think he could cut her off alcohol. He was sure fooling himself!

Sydney rounded the corner, ready to tell him exactly where to shove it but, at the sight of a red heads lips all over his neck, she lost her voice.

She lost everything. Her broken heart shattered into a hundred pieces and she wondered what this woman had that she didn't besides heels that were six inches too long.

Was this why he didn't want her? Was this what he'd be doing into the late hours at the bar? Bedding other women? He wasn't lying. She was wrong about him. So terribly wrong.

Sydney couldn't think. One day after he announced he wasn't physically attracted to her he was with someone else? One day!

She felt sick. Her stomach lurched and the tears

sprang. Coming to the Cliff House had been the worst idea of her life!

***

JAKE GRABBED THE red head's wrists to stop her from touching him. Just the thought of her fingers where he wanted Sydney's made his skin crawl. The red head was forceful, drunk and way more aggressive then he'd expected.

Couldn't he catch a break? All he'd wanted to do was go have a cold shower. Alone. He certainly didn't want to deal with a drunken tourist looking to get laid when his mind couldn't move past Sydney. That's how she ended up all over him so quickly because his thoughts had been on Sydney.

That's when he heard a gasp. And not just any gasp, the tiny inhale of Sydney.

He yanked around the mane of hair, and sure as shit, found Sydney witnessing what he knew by the look of horror on her face was taking it all the wrong way.

When their eyes met even more pain then he'd caused her earlier stared at him as her eyes filled up with water.

Oh, shit.

She turned and took off.

"Sydney wait!" he yelled, which startled the red head away from his neck and he pushed her off, chasing Sydney through the bar.

Her tiny little legs moved so quickly, he didn't catch up to her until she was outside.

***

THE BURST OF fresh air was not freshening and the little alcohol she'd consumed burned up her throat. She leaned over the bush, bringing up all her evening's food.

Why did I have to come here tonight?

Why was she punishing herself because Jake didn't want her? And now it was worse. Now she was the fool who was watching his family, helping him while he was banging some red-head.

He doesn't want you. He's not yours. And now she knew why.

She needed to get out of here.

"Syd?" She felt Jake's hands pull her hair up.

She retracted out of his grasp immediately. "Do not touch me!" she yelled, turning and losing her footing on the heels Abby had insisted she wear. She stumbled backwards and landed her rear on the gravel.

He stepped toward her to help and she could see red lipstick across his neck that made her stomach sick.

She held her hand up. "No!" she yelled.

"Syd, you know that's not me. I wouldn't do that."

"I don't know you at all."

"She followed me. I was not taking her to my apartment."

"Clearly you were taking her right there."

Sydney heard a car rumble into the lot and she scrambled to her feet.

What difference did it make if he was planning on sleeping with her or not? The fact was he didn't want her.

Why was he chasing her into the parking lot? Why was he sending her all these mixed signals? Why had she had any drinks at all tonight!

Tears streamed down her face.

"Sydney I promise I was not going to have sex with that lady there or anywhere. I promise."

"What does it matter?"

"It matters to me."

"Are you never going to sleep with another woman?"

"Not tonight."

She took a deep breath. This was pointless. This whole night had turned out to be a disaster. So much for making him jealous. She had gone and made herself jealous instead. Not only jealous, but completely and utterly heartbroken. She'd thought he was protecting her Jake-style, but now discovering the truth was like a kick in the stomach, a slap across the face, a hard reality that was crushing her heart the longer she stood and stared at him.

In a hopeless tone she said, "And not with me." The reality stung like a wasp sting and she wondered if the pain would ever go away. "Night Jake."

She turned and started toward the beach to go home...alone...and to forget about Jake Stow.

Chapter Twenty-Six

JAKE STORMED INTO the club-house left with no other options. Robbie hadn't called him with Julian's phone number and his sister was still missing. He considered calling Jason again, but that would lead to days...months of paperwork and doing everything right. Jake didn't have that kind of time. He needed to find Adalyn even if this route was likely going to get him killed. His sister wasn't the only one he was thinking about either.

After last night, and the torture he was putting Sydney through, he knew he had to get all this over with and let her move on without him. The faster, the better.

Nothing had really changed inside the clubhouse, just like nothing had changed outside. It was still dark and grungy with naked women's posters on the wall. There was a bar along the far wall and tables, couches and a pool table filled the room.

Jake knew exactly who he was looking for and exactly where to find him. If his mother had in fact been talking to a man that rhymed with snake, then that was Drake. What was he doing out? What did he want? Who did he want? Jake needed answers.

A couple of guys tried to get in his way as he approached the door, but he was hardly in the mood and drilled each one down with an unexpected punch, then threw

LAKESHORE LOVE

the door open.

Jake found the head man of the club-house at the end of the table just as he'd thought. Although he hadn't expected to find a woman sprawled backwards over the table as well, he wasn't surprised.

Drake looked up, unalarmed, at being barged in on and interrupted in the middle of banging some black-haired tramp. His stare told Jake he was surprised to find Jake Stow interrupting.

Not in any hurry to get rid of the woman in front of him, he casually said. "Well, well, well. Haven't seen this face around in over a decade."

Just because Drake was in the middle of satisfying his manly needs didn't cause Jake to falter or shy away. He'd come for answers and he was damn well going to get them.

"Where are they?"

Drake slapped the naked behind and sent her on her way while he sat down on the chair and lit a smoke.

"Always right to the point with you. Never any introductions."

Several heads bobbed in behind him, making sure everything was alright.

Drake waved them off. "We're fine."

The door shut, leaving them alone.

"What were you asking?"

As if he didn't remember. Jake wouldn't show up in this hole for any other reason. It had been the same reason over ten years ago.

Jake had to contain himself from crossing the room, grabbing the man by his throat and slamming him against the wall for answers. He knew better. This man could have his hide. This man was dangerous.

"My mother and Adalyn. Where are they?"

Drake slowly enjoyed inhaling and exhaling his cigarette. "Why the sudden interest?"

He didn't want to play games.

"Is Beth here?"

He never answered a question right away. Drake always had to ponder as he spun the round cylinder in his fingertips. "No."

"Adalyn?"

"Adalyn?" He said her name like he was picturing her in a way that made Jake's skin crawl. "Funny thing about Adalyn. She disappeared at the same time you did. At the same time I was put in the slammer." He sent Jake a threatening look. "I assumed she went back to her big protective brother."

Bullshit. He wouldn't let her leave just like that.

"Don't lie to me."

He held his hands up. "Hey, I wouldn't."

That was a lie from Drake the Snake himself.

"Beth on the other hand comes and goes whenever she runs out. Like an obedient puppy."

Jake cringed at the way he talked about his mother. A protectiveness...a guilt for being unable to protect her from this man washed through him as it did every time his mother came into his thoughts. But he couldn't save her. He'd tried. He'd tried for years but he couldn't save someone who didn't want to be saved.

"Your dad was a fool thinking he could save that woman. All she cares about is her high."

Jake cringed even more at the nerve of this man

talking about his father. He had no right. He didn't know him, and Drake had helped play his part in destroying his mother. His mother's way had been what Henry had been trying to tell Jake all those years, but he didn't listen. When he'd finally come to terms with the reality he'd returned home to his dead dad. To the only person in his life that loved him. Except Sydney. But he couldn't go there right now. He had to stay sharp in here or he would end up leaving in a body bag.

"You see, I thought it was Adalyn that gave the detectives what they needed to send me away. She didn't like me and she made it clear." He tilted his head as if going back in time, without ever letting his eyes leave Jake. He trusted Jake about as much as Jake trusted him. "I sat in jail, thinking it had to be her. When I got out..." He sent him a smirk. "...you only need one good lawyer to reduce a life sentence...I planned on finding Adalyn. She had to pay for what she did."

She didn't do a damn thing. It had been Jake. Panic shot through him. *Please be all right Adalyn. It was me, not her.* Jake didn't dare say anything until he knew what Drake had done or was planning to do.

"But it turns out she wasn't the snitch after all. She was just hiding her own secret."

Secret? What secret was Adalyn hiding that she didn't tell Jake? The pressing question was how did Drake find out about Adalyn's secret? He had been talking to her. *Where are you Adalyn? Please be all right? Why didn't you come to me first instead of sending your kids to me?*

Again, Jake wasn't about to start talking, he wanted to hear what this man had to offer first.

"Which in turn leaves only one other person I can

think of that would cross me like that." Drake knew.

A sick feeling washed over Jake. "What did you do to Adalyn?"

Drake waved his hand. "Nothing. Calm down Princess. Life is full of surprises. I wasn't about to hurt Adalyn after her secret came out."

What was he talking about?

"I just wanted a chance to meet her."

Meet who?

"But Adalyn hid her from me and surprisingly I didn't think of her being with you."

Her? Like the kids? More specifically eleven-year-old Mia.

"There you got it figured out, Jake. Mia is my daughter." The end of his sentence went low and cold.

Every drop of blood in Jake's body boiled.

Adalyn had gone into hiding to protect Mia from Drake. Did Jason have anything to do with his sister's protection?

Jake turned and crossed the room in a flash, but Drake was expected it. Drake didn't fight it and Jake was disgusted as he grabbed this sick bastard by the throat and slammed him against the wall like he wanted to the first time he'd touched his sister.

"Where is Adalyn?"

"I can't keep track of that lass."

"You stay away from Mia."

"She is my daughter."

"I don't give a shit. She is my niece."

Shit. Jake had to get the hell out of here. He had to phone Jason because he had just put every last family

LAKESHORE LOVE

member in Willow Valley into danger. *Sydney.*

"Last I heard Adalyn was tired of shooting it up here and landed herself back in rehab. See, Beth thought she could come back here and lie to me and try to hide Adalyn but once an addict always an addict."

Rehab. Back in rehab.

"I bet you had something to do with the relapse."

He shrugged a guilty look. "I can't deny it. I can be very persuasive."

That was the problem.

Jake's fist met Drake's face and sent him to the floor, Jake was out the back door and on his bike before anyone even noticed.

Once he got far enough away, he called Jason and was put straight through this time. Jake took his instructions and sped all the way back to Willow Valley.

***

SYDNEY LAUGHED SO hard at Lucy's impression of a dolphin out of the water...she still wasn't sure how that question ended up in their paper pile for charades...that she didn't even hear the front door open until it slammed shut.

Her stomach hurt, her sides hurt and it wasn't about Jake so it felt wonderful. Sydney hadn't cried so hard over something so adorable in a long time and after crying all night over Jake it was refreshing.

Lucy even had Joan laughing—full out laughing. This game had been a fantastic idea, Haylee's of course.

"That doesn't even make sense!" Mia cried, standing up and snatching the paper out of Lucy's hand. She read it to herself then flashed it in front of everyone. Obviously the writing was too small to make out, but she stated what it said. "It says dolphin," she clarified, turning to Lucy. "It doesn't say dolphin *out of water*. You made that up."

Lucy shrugged. "It was more fun and you couldn't guess it."

"Because it didn't make sense. Sit down. You don't get another turn."

Lucy stuck her tongue out but plopped on the couch beside Benji, giving his side a tickle. He squealed in delight.

Sydney barely caught her breath when Jake appeared, staring down at her with such a look that it stole the rest of her breath away and not in a good way.

What was wrong?

Sydney stood up immediately and followed him quietly toward the kitchen, or so she thought.

"We will be right back," she said, watching Joan and Haylee both acknowledge the look. Mia was watching as well.

"What happened?" she asked, as she turned back to Jake.

Oh no. Were Adalyn and Beth all right? Hurt? Dead? The thought was terrifying, but she didn't sense that kind of feeling from him. He almost seemed in a panic.

Jake didn't answer her or stop in the kitchen. Instead, she watched him go down the hall and into her bedroom, quickly, like he was on a mission.

She followed, even though her legs didn't want to and the red-head flashed in her head ruining whatever happiness she may have savored in her bedroom.

When she got to the doorway, she fully guarded her

LAKESHORE LOVE

heart and saw him pulling her closet open.

Did he not get the same vibes she did in this room now? It was like torture sleeping in here, having a shower after what she'd thought she would get to feel for the rest of her life.

Stop it. He's not in here to sweep you off your feet. Focus on the present, not on the past.

"What are you doing?"

"Pack some outfits and your overnight wear," he said.

"Why?"

He grabbed a handful of her dresses and pulled them out of the closet throwing them on her bed.

What was going on?

Sydney crossed the room and caught his hand before he pulled another handful out. "What are you doing?"

He turned and his eyes burned worry into her soul. "We have to go."

"Where? Why?"

"You, Haylee, the kids and Joan. Now."

That didn't answer her question.

"Right now."

"Jake, slow down. I don't understand what's going on. Where are we going?"

"I own a cabin in the woods." He owned a cabin in the woods? Since when? And why?

Whisking her away to a romantic secluded cabin would have sounded sweet, but his lack of explanation was terrifying her.

She was putting her foot down. She planted her hands on her hips and sent him an, *explain it before I pack it* look. "Why?"

Jake ignored the look. "We don't have time for me to explain. I will tell you when we get there." *Yeah right, and dolphins could actually live out of water.*

"You better try because I'm not going anywhere until you do."

He groaned, frustrated. "I don't want to upset you and if I half-ass explain this you will just keep pumping out questions and like I said we don't have time."

"I'm very upset."

Jake stopped then and turned to her. "I love you Sydney." Like an emotional roller coaster Sydney could have cried right there. *He loved her? He loved her!* He sure had a strange way of showing it. Then her heart sank. He loved her like a friend, like family.

"When we made love the expectation was nothing in comparison to the real thing. It was amazing. You were amazing. You are amazing."

He loves me!

"You were right. I only told you that load of crap trying to protect you from what I have dragged you into." What had he dragged them into? Why did she have the feeling it wasn't his fault and he was taking the blame?

The tears slipped down her cheek.

He wiped them away with his fingers, and then kissed her softly. "I'm so sorry, Sydney. I want to continue this conversation, but you need to trust me. We have to go. Do you trust me?"

Sydney would always trust this man and the protection he had for her.

She nodded.

"Alright, pack a bag."

Her bedroom door burst open and Joan came in with a worried look across her face. "What's going on?" she demanded, her attention solely on Jake.

Didn't she find it a little odd that she just burst into Sydney's bedroom when Jake was with her? They could have been...Sydney wiped away her tears.

"Where were you?"

Jakes face was solemn and he leveled a look at Joan. The two seemed to share a moment that was lost to Sydney.

"Oh Jake you didn't." A deep fear played along Joan's smooth features, sending a deep fear into the pit of Sydney's stomach.

"He was just released."

"How is that even possible?"

He shrugged. "I don't know, but he's out."

"Why would you go there?" Joan sounded horrified and her beautiful face warped into a mass of fear that aged her drastically.

"You know why."

"You should have given Beth a few more days."

"And Adalyn? What about Adalyn? Obviously she's in trouble."

Joan's eyes found the suitcase and her frown deepened with worry. "Are we in trouble?

"We need to go. Now."

"Did you call Jason?"

Jason? Who was Jason?

Jake nodded. "I have a cabin he wants us to go to," Jake said, then eyed Joan warily. "How do you know about Jason?"

Joan sighed. "Now's not the time, Jake. But if that's

what he said, let's go. I will tell Haylee to pack and you finish up here." She sent Sydney a look. "Meet you at the front door." She turned to leave and paused at the doorway. "Did they follow you?"

"No. But they know what town we are in so it won't be hard to locate us."

"What about the Cliff House?"

"I had Devon close it up and send everyone home until we get this sorted."

"Alright. Quickly then." Joan disappeared leaving Sydney with Jake.

"I have to call my sisters."

"You can do it once we are at the cabin. The quicker the better."

Sydney nodded and tore a couple dresses off the hangers before finishing packing her bag. Jake stood at the door waiting, looking at the clock, tapping his fingers on his arm, making Sydney feel like she was moving as slow as a turtle.

When she was finished and zipped the bag up, Jake was at her side lifting it off the bed.

He grabbed her arm on the way out. "I know now is not the time, but nothing happened between me and that woman at the bar. Nothing was going to happen. I was mending my broken heart," he said. "Now I know the only way to mend it is if I am with you. I want you."

He was right, now was not the time. More tears fell down her cheeks and he kissed them away. She couldn't speak and he must have known because he took her hand and led her out of the house.

Joan already had the kids loaded in her car and

LAKESHORE LOVE

Haylee stood by Jake's motorcycle waiting for them.

Sydney gave her worried daughter a hug. "Jake will explain when we get to the cabin."

"I can ride with Jake if you want Mom," Haylee said understanding Sydney's fear. The offer made Sydney's insides smile. Haylee would use any opportunity climb on the back of Jake's bike, but the answer had always been a forceful no.

Haylee was reaching for the helmet in Jake's hand when Sydney snatched it first.

"Get in the car," she told Haylee in her no nonsense tone.

Haylee pouted away.

Sydney stared at the bike as Jake climbed on. *Get on the bike Sydney.*

She didn't move.

"Syd, we have to go."

She stared at the bike like it was the ride to her death. In some ways that was exactly what she felt.

"Sydney." He held his hand out to her. "I'm right here. Trust me."

Always.

Chapter Twenty-Seven

JAKE LED THE way down the familiar dirt road only a fifteen-minute drive out of town, watching behind them to make sure they weren't being followed. When he was certain they weren't, he slowed before the gravel laneway that looked like just another path in the bush. He drove under a leafy tree archway that opened up into a picturesque cabin in the woods with a wide gap beyond where the crystal clear sparkling lake glistened.

It was incredible. Jake often came up to this piece of land to check on the log cabin with a wraparound deck. It was his investment. His only investment and he was eventually planning on moving up here, when the time was right...whenever that was. He didn't know what his future held currently but he hoped he hadn't lost the one woman he wanted to spend it with.

He parked the bike and felt Sydney's embrace relax. The strength of her arms was revealed with her deadly grip from the moment he pulled out of her driveway.

Jake had so much he wanted to tell her and apologize for. Mostly about the mistakes he had made with her in the last twenty-four hours, but now wasn't the time.

He handed Sydney the keys to the cabin to settle the kids in, promising to talk after he did a perimeter check.

Drake claimed to only think of Jake when he walked

LAKESHORE LOVE

through the door, but Jake wouldn't put it past him that he already had his men watching Mia. Mia, that poor young soul. He wouldn't let a damn thing happen to that girl. Drake would have to personally go through Jake before he laid one of his filthy fingers on her and Jake was not about to let that happen.

When everything came up clean, Jake found Sydney and Joan waiting for him on the porch. They stood when he emerged from the brush and met him in the driveway, waiting for an explanation.

"Mia is Drake's daughter," he said straightforward. No more games and no more secrets between any of them. Jake was tired of hiding half-truths and tired of having half-truths hidden from him. From now on he was going to give and expect a life of honesty from these two women.

Joan let out an exasperated cry which, under the circumstances, he had expected. Joan knew Drake was his mother's dealer and a dangerous man. She closed her eyes. "Did he tell you that?"

Jake nodded. "Yes."

"Who's Drake?" Sydney asked, completely in the dark about this whole situation. Exactly where he had wanted her and why he'd never wanted to have this conversation, but now wishing she knew everything.

"What were you thinking?" Joan asked, as though she didn't hear Sydney's question. She very well may not have, running the startling news through her head.

"I needed to find Adalyn."

"And was she there?"

"No."

She scoffed. "Where is she? Did he say? Has she been

there?" There was worry in her voice and distress in her eyes for his sister's well-being.

Jake shrugged. "I assume she was there because Drake thought Adalyn was the snitch." Jake said it that way on purpose, including the snitch part after her comment about Jason as he was curious exactly how much Joan knew.

Joan's response answered Jake's suspicion as a warranted horrified look crossed her face and her fingers pressed against her lips in worry. "Oh no Jake, she could be..." *Dead*...yeah he was well aware of that.

Joan definitely knew more than she had ever let on. She knew Jason and she knew about the snitch. Before Jake continued, he needed to know how. "How do you know Jason?"

"Through Henry."

"How did Dad know Jason?"

"Excuse me," Sydney said stepping between the two for their attention, her eyes finding each of them and pulling them to her. "Sorry to interrupt, but I want to know who Drake and Jason are before this goes any further. I want to know if we are safe. Then you two can continue clearing up the crap load of secrets you've been keeping from each other and from me." Sydney took her time to send each of them a glare. "However, I am more currently concerned about our well-being."

Where did he even begin?

"Drake is my mom's drug dealer who is the owner of the club-house where I went those years ago to find her and Adalyn. He is dangerous and he went to jail for manslaughter." Jake shot Joan a look before continuing. "Jason is the undercover detective that I helped to put Drake away. Drake is out of prison and looking for me because I was the snitch that helped put him there." He hated how bad that sounded. Jake didn't look like a snitch and he wouldn't have been if Adalyn hadn't been guaranteed a ticket out of that life if he helped Jason. "And he's looking for Mia because she is Drake's daughter. I called Jason the second I had put good distance between me and Drake. He instructed me to gather my family and stay here where we will be safe until he contacts us."

"So we are safe?"

"Yes." Jake turned back to Joan. "I want to know how Dad knew Jason."

Joan's face softened. "Your dad was the snitch, Jake. Not you."

What was she talking about? His father didn't know these people besides being his ex-wife's drug dealer. "That doesn't make any sense."

"That's because you don't know the history."

More skeletons hanging in her closet. "How about you enlighten me."

"I didn't ever want to taint your image of your father, Jake. It's not fair that I tell you what I am about to and you judge a man that is not here to defend himself."

Why did his dad need defending?

"He loved you and Adalyn more than you will ever know. Everything your father did, he did it for the two of you. Everything in his life that he changed was for the two of you. To protect you and give you a good life."

When she paused to give Jake the opportunity to comment, he remained quiet. His dad loved him, he got it...the question bothering him was what had be done that would make Jake think otherwise? And how on earth was he the snitch?

"Henry was a very smart man. He started life with nothing, but learned quickly how to flip money fast. Before you were born, he was hungry for money in a bad way. He had a clean business front buying, selling, renting properties for a good profit, but there was another side to him." She took a deep breath and Jake knew this had to do with Drake. "Henry illegally invested in gun smuggling, through Drake. He never got his hands dirty and he knew how to take out the right money and put it back without causing suspicion. Or so he thought."

At first, Jake didn't believe her. He needed a moment to register everything. How could this even be possible? Not once had Henry, Drake or his mother mentioned his involvement in the clubhouse. Jason hadn't mentioned his involvement when he pulled Jake aside and listed him his options: jail or snitch.

How had his dad, the man he looked up to, the man he trusted, the man who raised him, managed to keep such a part of his life hidden? At the very thought, Jake's eyes found Sydney's in a wide, confused stare. Jake was closer to Sydney than any other person in the world and he had managed to keep all of this from her. What would she think of him when all this was done and there were so many things he hadn't told her at Hastings Port when they were sharing their past? Jake was right ticked at his dad for all the deceit...is that how Sydney would feel?

"Through his connection with Drake was how Henry met Beth and most likely how the cops connected the two together. I don't know the details, I never asked because I didn't want to know, but Henry thought he and Beth were in love." Joan was pouring the details of the past out like she couldn't say it fast enough, like it had been weighing on her all these years and as every word past her lips, it looked like a piece of guilt was lifted from her soul. Jake felt like every word she spoke was doing the opposite to him and dragging him down into a puddle of mud he was having a hard time trudging his way through.

"How or why a business man like your father ended up with Beth is beyond me. She was an addict when he met her. She was addict when he married her..." Joan was shaking her head. "...I never understood it. Henry thought a life for them away from Drake was possible and that they would be happy. But every time she took a trip for a week or a month or longer, she wasn't on vacation like we told you. She was either back with Drake or back in re-hab." That meant Henry pulled his mother out of a life of drugs and she hadn't run to him because of Henry and Joan, she'd already been running to him.

"At first I suppose they were happy and it was enough. Not long after they had Adalyn, Beth went back to Drake. Henry knew me through my family...my rich family... and when he asked me to watch Adalyn between your mother's disappearances, I agreed. Mainly to spite my father who later disowned me. His daughter could never be a nanny, but I was young and rather smitten with your father...I always had been. Then you were born, and some months were good, some years were good, while others weren't. That was when your dad and I began to really get close. He didn't have anyone else. No family and no friends and I was living in the guest house, so we bonded."

Jake shook his head. "I don't want to hear about your relationship with Dad." The last thing he needed on top of the fact he just learned his dad was a criminal was about his romance with his mistress.

"Alright," Joan took a deep breath sounding frustrated at the interrupted. "Henry was gathering evidence for Jason and making himself a deal in exchange for putting Drake away. Your father invested money illegally but he wasn't a murderer like Drake. Henry had enough proof to put him away for a long time. He was working out the details and then you left. Your dad died and Jason had nothing."

Jake held his hand up. "Jason knew Dad died and didn't tell me?" This was getting more ridiculous by the moment.

Joan frowned. "How could he tell you? You were in over your head and as a favor to your dad, Jason involved you to keep you safe." Jake was fuming, they should have told him. Damn it, they should have told him.

"Is that what Kyle found out?" Sydney asked. "Is that what they were fighting about the night we were going to get Jake back? That Kyle learned about Henry's involvement?"

Joan shook her head.

"What were they fighting about?" Jake asked.

Joan pressed her perfect pink lips together, this time not wanting to spill the truth. Another secret.

Jake folded his arms across his chest. "What were they fighting about, Joan?" He mustered up his very best firm tone, but for a woman who had changed his diapers, it didn't faze her.

"Your father and my affair."

That didn't make any sense. They all knew about the

affair, it wasn't a secret.

"After Adalyn was born." *Had he heard her right?* "Nine months before Kyle was born."

Jake's anger paused, taking in her confession. *What the hell was she saying?*

"Kyle was your half-brother. That was why he went to get you."

Kyle was his half-brother? Kyle was his half brother! Kyle was a year younger than Jake. That meant his dad had been cheating on his mother the whole time they were married! No wonder she went back to Drake. Did Beth see Henry in Kyle when she looked at him? Did she know about the affair? What kind of life was that for his mother to live?

"Your dad was mortified after we were together. You have to understand Henry and I were friends for a long time before Beth came around and that night it just happened. We were never together again until after your mom left for good."

"Does that justify it? Does that make it right? What about my mother? Did she know? Did she know Kyle was Dad's?"

Joan looked hurt. "Beth didn't know about us and Kyle. Thankfully, he didn't take on your blue eyes and thick features. Beth left of her own free will and neither your father nor I had anything to do with it. Jake, your father would have stayed with her forever if she'd stayed with him. He was committed to her."

"What else did you two put her through that I didn't know about?"

"Beth left when you were Mia's age, so I don't think you remember a lot."

"I remember plenty."

"You remember from a child's perspective."

"Don't try to butter it up."

Joan laughed a strained gloomy laugh. "Butter it up? Let me see if I can refresh your memory. Do you remember the night your mother left you in a bath during one of her highs and Adalyn had to call 911 when she found you underneath the water Jake, unconscious?"

Jake didn't remember that.

"How about the time your dad came home to a houseful of high strangers and you and Adalyn were locked in the garage?"

He sort of remembered something about being in a garage.

"I was also the one that raced over to help you and Adalyn out of the situations she left you in. I was the one who took you to the hospital and sat in the waiting room for hours hoping you were okay. Jake. You only see what you want to see. You've always been like that. I know Beth's your mom, but I didn't push her away and your dad didn't push her away. She did it to herself."

This was too much.

"Jake, as hard as this is to believe, I loved you and Adalyn. I wanted the best for you two, just like your father. But you two were always so angry with me and there was no way of changing your minds, so I hoped you would grow out of it. I never expected you or Adalyn to go look for your mother. That part of our life was coming to an end and we were starting over in Willow Valley. We wanted to be a family."

Jake turned, unable to take anymore, and headed

toward his bike.

Sydney was at his heels. She touched his arm and he turned, knowing she was going to try and talk him out of leaving when right now all he wanted to do was ride.

Her supportive smile took away some of his anger. "Take me with you," her low voice said, surprising him.

Take her with me? He'd been astonished Sydney made it to the cabin on his bike the first time and now she wanted to climb back on with him? For him. She was amazing.

"Are you sure?"

She nodded. "The kids are with Joan and Haylee. They're alright."

Jake handed her a helmet. He was never letting this woman go again.

SHANNYN LEAH

Chapter Twenty-Eight

AS THE WIND continued to whip around Sydney, she wouldn't say by any means that there wasn't fear rumbling through her body, but she felt safe with the man controlling the machine. She also felt heartbroken for him.

There had been far too many secrets between Joan and Jake and so many they'd kept from her that she was going to need an instruction manual just to figure out what was going on and to keep up.

But her own sadness didn't compare to what she knew Jake was going through. If riding his bike down side roads was going to help him deal with the newest secrets in his life, then she wanted to be strapped to the back with him. Literally, she would prefer to be strapped to the back of this monster machine then knowing her arms were the only security she had.

Jake dealt with too much on his own. It was time they let the love between them build a team and deal with all the ups and downs of life together...and if that meant climbing on his motorcycle every single time life was too overwhelming for him, then she was willing to take that step. No matter how much quivering was going on inside her and right now every organ in her body was jiggling around.

Darkness had fallen around them quite a while ago, which meant it was well past ten and into the night. That also meant they had been driving for hours on his bike and yet it didn't feel like hours. That was how he always ended up out so late like a night owl.

When the bike pulled into the bush at the cabin, and the engine cut, Sydney would admit she was relieved. That was certainly enough driving for one day...one year...but if he needed her again she would clamber on and force her anxiety down.

The cabin was black besides the outside light.

Jake had pulled the bike over as the sun was starting to set and she phoned Haylee with a quick, less terrifying brief of events and confirmed everything was okay. Haylee had paused from the board game they were playing and Sydney relaxed when she heard laughter and teasing in the background.

Jake climbed off the bike, hanging his helmet from the handle bar before taking hers and doing the same. "Are you okay?" he asked putting her first when he was the one hurting.

She touched his worried face. "Are you okay?"

Without another word, Jake wrapped his arms around her waist resting his head against her breasts. His sadness tugged her heart and she stroked his hair with her fingers, cherishing in the way he was letting her comfort him through one of the hardest times in his life like he never had before. If only they had been this close when he returned, maybe things would have been different between them.

He kissed the bare flesh above her breasts and she almost went weak in his arms. She couldn't help think he was sad again. She knew she shouldn't go there. She knew now without a doubt in her mind that he loved her, but there was so much going on in his life maybe they should just...

He kissed her again, a little higher at the bottom of her throat and she swallowed hard.

The distant thought in her mind that they should stop and talk stumbled around and she almost laughed, even as Jake trailed more slow kisses up her neck and her body was reacting to every spot his lips touched. Jake wouldn't be able to handle anymore talking tonight.

His mouth reached her chin and she managed to pull her face away. It wasn't that she was afraid he was venting or using her, she just wanted to make sure he was okay.

His strong hands caught her face and pulled it back so their noses were touching. His shadowed eyes were so serious. "This is not because I'm scared or sad or dealing with my family shit. This is because when I was at the clubhouse today and realized I'd put my family in danger you were the top of my list Sydney. You were the flash in my head, the panic in my chest and the fears of losing you took me to a whole new level." There he was being charming again, sort of, in a serious, stone-cold kind of way. "I never want to lose you. I never want to be away from you again. I never want to *walk away* from you again. I want you forever." He paused and his words were so overwhelming she couldn't speak. "I have loved you since the day you slapped my arm in that hall and told me no biker jacket was going to scare you away."

She laughed under her breath at the memory of a girl who had no idea what life had in store for her.

"I loved you the day I left and the day I returned and every day in-between. I love Haylee. When this is done I don't want to go spend another night in the apartment above my bar. I want you and only you and I promise I will never hurt you again. I will never keep a secret from you or lie to try to protect you. I will be straightforward and honest and together we can work through whatever life throws us."

Tears slid down Sydney's face and his thumbs caught them.

"Am I too late?"

She shook her head. "No."

"Do you want me?"

Of course I do!

She nodded and sniffled. "Yes."

"Will you marry me Sydney McAdams?"

Marry him? Marry him! When had he found time to think about marrying her? Why were her legs tingling to jump off the bike and do a marriage dance!

"I feel like we are rushing it." He frowned and she kissed it away. "I am teasing you Jake. We have waited over a decade. I had plenty of time to think about marrying you."

A smile found his lips. "That's not funny."

"You told me to try humor."

"Sexy humor, not mean humor. That was mean," he claimed but there was humor in his eyes.

She kissed him again, and then worked up her most seductive voice. "Walk with me," she said.

They walked across the grass and she let his hand go at the edge of the water.

The moon and stars reflected off the rippling water in tune with her rippling heart.

"Let's go swimming." Sydney slowly pulled her jacket off and tossed it on the sand. She smiled seductively up at him, at least she hoped she looked seductive. She wasn't exactly practiced at this like Abb. Her shoes were next, kicked off, and then she pulled her dress over her head tossing it at Jake who caught it with a slow grin creeping across his face.

"Are you trying to seduce me?"

She frowned, disappointed. "Trying?"

He grinned wider. "Are you planning on going skinny dipping Sydney McAdams?"

She stood in front of him with only her bra and underwear. "I was thinking about it. Are you going to join me?" She turned away from him and unsnapped her bra, pulled her underwear down and dived into the water leaving him fully clothed on the beach.

The water was warm and refreshing after being on the back of a bike for hours.

She surfaced and looked at the shore for Jake. He wasn't there. It wasn't a windy night and the water was calm around her.

Where was Jake?

Just then the water splashed behind her and Jake grabbed for her waist. Sydney laughed, pulling away and splashing him with water.

"Oh, you think so!" he hollered and she could hear some of the stress of his day washing away, so when he swam after her she splashed him more laughing when he sent waves of water in her direction.

Touching the lake's muddy floor, she ran away from him, but he was quick, scooping her in his arms. She screamed and laughed his name as he threatened to throw her in the water. She begged him not to but it was a lost cause and she went flying through the air and back in the water.

"Jake Stow!" she laughed, splashing him again.

LAKESHORE LOVE

Before she knew it, she was crawling through the shallow water hearing Jake splashing behind her. She turned and kicked water at him that only hit his knees and he flew through it landing on his knees and catching her ankle. She didn't try so hard to get away this time as he crawled through the shallow water up her body and his lips crashed against hers.

"This is better sexy humor," he said, lowering her back against the wet sandy beach and settling between her legs.

Sydney laughed. "Practice makes perfect."

"You can practice with me any day."

She liked the sound of that.

***

AFTER THEIR LOVEMAKING skinny-dip swim, they sat on the porch swing, fully clothed and Jake pushed them with one foot.

Sydney was exhausted and felt herself drifting in and out of sleep, while Jake, the night owl, was wide awake, stroking the side of her head.

Snuggled beside him with her feet tucked underneath her, she closed her eyes and listened to nature's songs after he had told her all the stories of his life at the clubhouse. They were worse than Sydney could have imagined and each part he shared, she hoped she was taking some of his grief too. But now, after hours of listening, sleep was invading her.

Jake's cell phone rang and he dug into his pocket and answered it. Hopefully, it was this Jason man giving them some good news. She didn't mind being alone in a secluded cabin with Jake for one second, but she didn't like the fear that accompanied their hiding.

Sydney felt Jake's body stiffen before he sat forward and rubbed his face.

"Don't do anything stupid, Mom. Where are you?" Jake asked, standing up and skipping down the stairs.

Sydney followed.

"Tell me where you are so I can come and get you."

What? No!

Panic arose in Sydney, a familiar horrible panic and there was no taming it back. Now that she knew the truth, the whole truth about these people there was no way she wanted Jake to go searching for his mother when there was a gang searching for him! *Was he crazy?*

"Are you at the club-house? Don't go in that club house Mother!" *She's at the club house!*

"Just stay in your car. I will come get you." *Get her?* It was a day drive, he couldn't go get her. And what if it was a trap? It sure sounded like a trap.

"Then where the hell are you? Stop talking like that." He paused. "Mom...Mom..." There was silence as he was listening to his mother speak and Sydney couldn't hear a word, but from the way his shoulders sunk and his head dropped, she wasn't sure that the conversation was good.

"Mom, I love you too, but stop please. Stop whatever you are thinking. It's not going to help. Yes, alright you love Adalyn, but Mom I don't even know where she is." Another pause. "Call the cops Mom." Another pause.

Sydney's tired body was kicking into overdrive, waking her right up. *What was happening?*

"Yes, they did help last time, but you chose not to let

them. Let them this time. Do not do anything foolish. Mom? Mom? Damn it." He was charging for his bike.

He was going to leave them there. Panic arose inside of her in an uncontrollable panic that consumed her body. He was leaving them to walk into the very people he was hiding them from. He was going to end up dead. He wasn't going to come back. How had this gotten so out of control so quickly and now he was planning on leaving? He was walking away. He was literally walking away.

She had to stop him no matter what the consequences were because he was overtired and not thinking and she loved him and she couldn't stand losing him. Not now. Not when their lives were finally together and they were on the same page in the exact same paragraph, reading the exact same word! She couldn't flip another page of her life without him.

***

JAKE LOST HIS reception, or his phone died. Did his phone die? He was walking toward the edge of the laneway when Sydney chased him down in a panic. "You're going to leave us here? Jake, you can't leave us here."

No, he wasn't going to leave them here. He was going to call Jason and relay what his mother told him. He was also going to try to call her back and try to talk some sense into her. If she could just wait outside the clubhouse or anywhere with his promise to get her, Jason could send men much faster to pick her up. Beth was talking crazy about putting an end to everything and Jake didn't like the sound of that.

"Syd, slow down. She is in trouble. I just have to figure out what is going on and..."

"Call this Jason guy, Jake. Don't go running into

something that could be a trap. Maybe this has something to do with Drake and maybe your mom doesn't know the danger involved. Maybe she's high." Sydney was high on fear and Jake could see it revealing itself over every inch of her panicking body.

"Syd, I am going to call Jason..."

She didn't hear him. "Jake, be reasonable." He was being reasonable, it was Sydney that was going off the edge. "Jason is obviously involved with this so call him. It will take you hours to get to the clubhouse."

He grabbed her shoulders hoping the contact would slow her down. "Sydney..."

It didn't.

"Leaving us here is not the solution. We are alone here when you leave us. Do you need a reason?" She was his reason. He wasn't going to go risk his life when he'd promised it to her. "Do you need a blood reason to make you stay?"

He had three blood relatives in the house but he knew that wasn't what she was talking about. *She wouldn't. Would she?* She had given her word.

"Would that make you stay? Would it? Tell me Jake." Jake had never seen her filled with so much fear. He was regretting the hours of stories he'd just shared, maybe too soon. If he could just get a word in and assure her he was not leaving.

"You are overreacting..."

"I am not!" she yelled at him, cutting him off again and pulling herself out of his grasp.

She was so out of control over her own emotions. "I promise..."

"No, the only promises you keep are to your blood Adalyn and Beth." Jake was going to personally spend the rest of his life digging that specific thought that he himself had planted in her head out until she knew that every promise he made to her he would stand. That family went deeper than blood.

"Sydney, you don't have to be my blood for me to keep my promises to you."

"They're not your only family, Jake." She was hysterical, fearing he would end up like his father. He had to get her settled down because he saw exactly where this conversation was going and it was about to get complicated.

"Sydney, listen to me..."

"Haylee is your family Jake. Haylee is your blood. Haylee is your daughter, Jake."

Jake stopped trying to calm her down and his eyes closed. She'd done it.

"Will you stay now?" she asked, sounding like the fear was leaving her.

He opened his eyes and a new fear had taken over her face.

"Do you think I don't know?" Had she really believed that all these years? "That Haylee was my daughter?"

She wore the surprise she'd been intending for him. "You know?"

"Of course I know. I was with you the night before I left. I can do that math. Do you really think I'm that stupid?"

She stepped back. "You knew? All these years? You knew when you got back? Why didn't you say anything?"

He wasn't mad at her, well he was a little mad at her for going back on their promise at the boat, he'd been very clear, but if he truly believed she would never mention it then he was stupid.

"What was I going to say? I came home and you and Joan already had the word out that she belonged to Kyle. You wanted me to rip her away from her grandmother, who you both needed and step in as the dad that you told everyone had died?"

"You could have spoken up. We could have..."

"Been a family?"

She looked at him hurt. "Yes."

"We are a family."

"You know what I mean."

"You were protecting her and I was protecting her. I was protecting you. I didn't know what my life was going to be after everything that had happened but I saw yours was good. Haylee's was good. You were happy."

"I might have looked happy, but I was miserable on the inside. I wanted you, Jake."

"I wanted you. Now we have each other and I'm not going anywhere. I will tell you every day for the rest of our lives until you stop feeling like I am going to leave you. I don't plan on chasing my mother into the clubhouse, but I have to call Jason and tell him where and what she is planning."

She nodded, stepping back. He caught her and pulled her against his side while he scrolled for Jason's cell number. He hit dial, then looked back at Sydney. "You and I are a team now, together. We will decide together."

"What are we going to tell Haylee?"

With the cell phone still to his ear, he kissed the side of Sydney's forehead. "The truth. She's a smart kid and she loves us both. She will understand...eventually."

She made a pouting noise, which he found adorable. At least they were on the same page.

The phone went to voicemail. He was leaving a message as the rumble of a vehicle coming down the road caught his attention and he stopped mid-sentence. Who was coming down the road at this time of night?

He straightened.

Were they coming here?

He pulled Sydney out of the driveway and into the bush just as the black car pulled in. Jake instinctively put his arm across her middle to protect her from whoever was in that vehicle.

Who was it? Drake? One of his men?

He was devising a plan in his head as he watched a tall, strongly built man emerge from the driver's side. He would recognize that confidence from anywhere.

"It's okay," he whispered to Sydney, who was latched onto him so tight, he would rather turn and take her on the earth's ground then acknowledge the vehicle.

He turned to her. "It's Jason. It's okay."

He felt the weight of her relief against his body.

As they emerged from the bush, the passenger's door opened and the younger version of his mother stepped out. Cautiously checking her surroundings, Adalyn found Jake.

He breathed her name into the heated night.

It was Adalyn. She was alright. She was alive.

Jake stared at his sister, the girl who was now a woman—beautiful, safe and alive. She stared at him and he wondered what she was thinking.

He felt Sydney nudge his side and he looked down at

her.

"Go," she said.

Jake did as she said, meeting Adalyn half way. He hadn't seen her in years and she had aged beautifully.

She looked as unsure as Jake felt. "Hi Jake," she said, her voice was so quiet compared to the days in the clubhouse.

"Hi."

"You look good."

"You look good."

She smiled a shy smile that made her look younger. "I'm a mess," she said. "I have wanted to call you every day."

"I have thought about you every day."

Her smiled widened and Jake's heart melted. He reached over and pulled his sister into his arms noting she was skinny under her yoga pants and sweater.

Her arms gripped him tightly and she spoke into his ear as though she couldn't do it to his face. "Jake, thank you for standing up for me. It was your courage that gave me the strength to walk away from that lifestyle. Your persistence forced me to look past my anger at Dad and see who Mom really was. It was my own pride that kept me away from you all these years."

Pride? Screw pride! "You're my sister. Pride means nothing."

"I know."

"Are you alright?"

She nodded. "I'm okay"

They were finally together.

***

LAKESHORE LOVE

SYDNEY BOILED ANOTHER pot of water for tea before peeking into the living room where Jake, Joan and Adalyn were talking. By the softened looks across their faces, it seemed they were moving in a positive direction, which was fantastic. There was a lot of love between them tumbling around with a lot of secrets and lies that were long past due of being exposed. Sydney loved each of them and hoped for their sakes that they would sort through everything and move forward together, as a family.

Jake glanced over his shoulder as if sensing she was watching him. She didn't shy away and when he saw her, he stood and walked into the kitchen. He didn't say anything, his eyes spoke volumes: happiness, relief, exhaustion, fear. All wrapped up in a crazy late hour.

Jake wrapped his arm around her and walked her backwards and out of view. He didn't let go until her back touched the counter. "I want to get married right away."

"What are you talking about marrying me for when you have all this going on?"

He looked at her. "If we could leave right now, I would take you away and marry you tonight."

That was a sweet thought. "I wouldn't do that to Haylee." She'd already been left out of enough secrets that they would have to re-build.

"We will talk to her together and we will help her to deal with the news together." She loved his sweetness. "Then we are getting married."

"Are you sure you want to marry me? I'm not good at keeping secrets and under stress I've learned I'm not that level headed."

"Yes." He answered so seriously that she laughed.

"Are you sure you want to marry me? I have family baggage and I don't like to talk about my emotions."

"Yes." She matched his seriousness and he kissed her.

"I love you," he said.

She loved hearing him say it. "You what?"

His low deep chuckle sounded almost as wonderful. "I love you."

"I love the sound of that."

He repeated the three words, playfully kissing her neck.

A knock on the front door interrupted them. At the late hour it was alarming, but when Jake opened it Jason walked through looking solemn. He had bad news.

The group shared a knowing look before Jason spoke. "There was a shootout at the clubhouse tonight. I'm coming here unofficially since the bodies haven't been officially identified." He shared looks between Adalyn and Jake. She remembered Jake telling his mother not to go in the clubhouse and from the somber look across Jason's face, Beth hadn't listened.

Sydney felt Jake's squeeze her hand as Jason spoke. "There were casualties. Drake was shot and killed."

It was over. Relief ran through Sydney, but there was more to come.

"Beth was in the clubhouse and she didn't make it out. I'm sorry Jake. Adalyn."

Adalyn made a sound as tears dropped down her face. Joan embraced her shoulder and Sydney knew these two Stow siblings and Joan would work through all their struggles.

"She's dead?" Jake asked as if needing to confirm it.

Jason nodded. "By my understanding, again unofficially, she was responsible for Drake's death."

Sydney felt tears fall from her eyes for Jake and Adalyn's loss.

Jason left shortly after and Joan and Adalyn retired to their rooms. Sydney could see Jake's mind working across his rigid set face. He would need space. She started up the stairs to go crawl into bed with Haylee. In the morning, everything would be better. She was scared and excited to talk to Haylee, but with Jake by her side, she was stronger.

"Where are you going?" Jake called behind her.

She wasn't hurt knowing he would need space to sort through whatever was playing in his mind and she sent him a smile to let him know. She loved him for all of him. "To bed."

He met her at the bottom of the stairs and held his hand out. "My...our...bedroom is on the main level."

Her eyes fell down the hall to the master bedroom. "It's okay if you need some space."

He reached up and grabbed her hand. "I don't need space from you. I need you."

That was all she needed to walk down the stairs and follow him into the master bedroom and snuggle under the sheets beside him.

"I'm sorry about your mom."

"Me too."

"I'm glad Mia never has to meet this man Drake or worry about him finding her. Your mom must have had some Stow blood in her too, to protect all of you the way she did."

His arm squeezed around her. "Thanks."

Sydney couldn't keep her eyes open another second

and fell asleep in the arms of the man she loved.

Chapter Twenty-Nine

SYDNEY GRASPED THE gorgeous bouquet of fresh purple lilacs wrapped in vintage lace from Haylee and inhaled their wonderful aroma. *Lilacs, her favorite.*

"Mom, this is crazy. There are literally hundreds of these flowers everywhere. Along the fenced in area, under the tent, outside the church, inside the church." Haylee inhaled her bouquet and the same smile from the sweet aroma found her lips. "Uncle Jake..." Haylee paused. "...Dad?" She sent Sydney a confused smile. "Do you think he wants me to call him Dad?"

Sydney smiled at Haylee and gently touched the side of her face.

It was all happening so fast, but they had already waited so long to be together.

"Sweetheart, Jake would be honored if you called him Dad. But it doesn't define his love for you or yours for him. He wouldn't be offended if you didn't feel comfortable calling him Dad because he loves you unconditionally no matter what title you choose to use."

Haylee had taken the news just as Jake as said. Understanding...ish. After the initial shock and two days of moping about, sending them glares, Joan had offered to sit down with Haylee. The private words they shared had softened Haylee's outlook. Mid-week on a wonderful evening...every evening spent with Jake seemed wonderful, complete in a way Sydney had never felt before...while Jake and Sydney had been sitting on the back deck discussing the weekend that was only taking place when Haylee was ready, she'd come to finally talk to them.

Sydney almost grinned recalling Haylee standing in front of them, her arms crossed, her weight on one leg and staring down at them with that all too familiar Stow stare. She was still mad at them for lying to her all these years which she made quite clear, but that night under the stars she claimed to understand their reasoning. She forgave them and that was the start of the new bond between the three of them: mother, father and daughter. A family bond that Jake had taught her was strong like no other. Sydney had waited until the next day to bring up the plans she couldn't wait to share with Haylee, who had been ecstatic to be her maid of honor.

"I will think about it," Haylee said.

Haylee, you have your whole life to think about it. Jake's not going anywhere.

"Until then he totally spoiled you with these lilacs. I mean imagine how many flower shops he must have called to find all these or do you think he went knocking on the doors of people with lilac bushes? He doesn't even like lilacs you know."

"What?" Sydney didn't know that.

"He can't stand the smell. Don't you remember that lilac tree you planted beside the entrance at the Cliff House?" Sydney remembered and it was still growing and flowering years later on the edge of the cliff. "He moved it to the cliff so he didn't have to smell it when it is in bloom."

Sydney gasped. "He said it needed direct sunlight to give it full bloom potential."

Haylee laughed. "He didn't want to hurt your feelings since you were in love with it."

"I put lilacs in his office every month they bloom." Thinking back, she thought his flowers always died a little quicker than most, blaming the dark room. She had the growing feeling he might have been pulling them out of the water for an early death.

Haylee shrugged. "Yeah, I guess that backfired on him."

Sydney and Haylee laughed then.

"See what happens when you're not honest," Haylee added, a little snip directed at her and Jake, then she grinned. "He's paying for it now. He's probably standing out there ready to throw every last bouquet out the window."

Sydney could envision that. But instead, she envisioned a man who loved her so much, he suffered through summers of lilacs in his office and a wedding so completely surrounded with them that the air smelled like a wonderful summer day...no matter where you stood or how far away from the purple flowering bunches.

The loud knock on the door was followed by her three sisters piling inside the small room in the basement of the church at Hastings Heritage Museum.

"Oh, Sydney." Kate covered her mouth, taking in the bride. "Gorgeous. Absolutely beautiful." Kate pulled her into a hug, and then touched the vintage lace shoulder of the wedding dress Sydney had purchased at Howard and Audrey's antique warehouse back in Willow Valley. "Only you could pull off this amazing gown and to think you didn't even need alterations. Amazing."

The vintage dress from the fifties was delicate from top to bottom completely covered in antique cream lace and fit her body like it was made for her with a little train at the back.

"Your makeup and hair look amazing," Peyton said next in line. "If I do say so myself." She was biased since she'd styled Sydney's hair to the side with her blonde curls cascading down the front of one of her shoulders. "I kind of always figured you would get married before me and I didn't realize how wonderful marriage with family was." She sighed. "Almost makes me wish I hadn't eloped."

Peyton waited for them to send her *yeah right* looks then sent them a mischievous grin. "I said almost, I definitely wouldn't want to lose my mile high club membership that wouldn't have happened if you had all boarded with us."

Kate slapped Peyton's arm. "Come on. Stop telling us where you two are always doing it."

Abby pulled Sydney into a long, tight hug and she found her sister more quiet than usual not jumping into the playful banter. Possibly ditching her regular black attire for the satin cream knee-length strapless bridesmaid dress that suited the vintage wedding theme had softened her.

"I'm so happy for you and Jake," she said against her hair, her grip not faltering and the sweet smell of a new scented body cream making Sydney curious to what Abby's latest combination was. Its floral smell was enchanting. "And Haylee too. She is so lucky. Jake will take good care of you both." Was it just her or was her younger sister beginning to get soft-hearted? Maybe even, dare she think it, beginning to grow up?

"Abby are you going to cry?" Peyton teased her youngest sister with a pull at her lose blond hair.

Abby pulled away and glared at her sister, straightening her hair. "No," she said defensively.

"What's this?" Peyton reached for the water gathering in Abby's eyes.

Abby swatted her hand and blinked the tears away. "Get lost or I won't help you lose the baby weight after you push those two monsters out of your..."

"Ear muffs!" Haylee screeched, covering her ears. "Seriously, mile high clubs, babies pushing out of...way too much! Way too much!"

Everyone laughed.

Sydney took a deep breath, looking around at her sisters and daughter. It seemed like since the moment the twins returned everything in their lives fit together perfectly. The soap store, Kate reunited with Marc and Rosemary, then Peyton found true love with Colt and now finally, after all these years, Sydney was marrying the only man she ever loved. Her senses today were amplified to the extent that if Abby had started crying, Sydney would have followed suit.

"I love you guys," Sydney said.

Another round of hugs followed before they all took deep breaths and straightened their gowns.

"They're waiting for you," Kate said.

He was waiting for her. Jake. He was all she needed.

"He's waiting for you," Peyton said pinching her arm as she had done only a couple weeks ago when Sydney hadn't known what Peyton had known all along...they were meant for each other.

"Apparently this place is booked solid for weddings,"

Kate was saying as they headed up the stairs. "And I hear Jake paid a couple very well for this date."

Sydney laughed. She had wanted to get married quickly, but it was Jake that had surprised her with the location...only one week after he'd proposed at the cabin.

"If Jake was any other man and had only proposed without even being together a week I would object," Kate continued.

"Thank you for not planning on objecting." Not that it mattered, Sydney was without a doubt certain Jake was the man for her, forever.

"I would have wrestled her skinny ass to the ground for you," Peyton said. "I knew this was meant to be..."

Sydney laughed, cutting her sister off. "Alright already! You were right. Jake and I were destined to be together. We know already!" Sydney wished she had scooped her true love up and listened to her sister sooner.

There was a crowd at the top of the stairs waiting. Sydney was lucky to not only have Rosemary as her flower girl but also had the pleasure of her newest nieces Mia and Lucy as their adorable light purple lace dresses accented the wedding party. Plus, an adorable ring bearer, Benji, who was nuzzled in his momma's arms like he was never letting go again.

Adalyn smiled when she saw Sydney. Adalyn had Jake's mysterious blue eyes and dark hair. The form-fitting dress she wore was loose on her too slim body, the result of not taking care of it for the last half year. Sydney was sad for all she had gone through, even if she was yet to get the details. For the first time, she didn't feel like she needed to know in order to move on. Jake was hers, and he would tell her when he was ready. Adalyn was lucky to have a brother who loved her and looked out for her and even through Adalyn's haunted eyes, Sydney knew things would get better, and easier for her too.

"You look beautiful," Adalyn said. "Jake is a lucky man."

"I'm the lucky one." Sydney hugged her again feeling the tiny stick body under her embrace. "It would have been an honor to have you as one of my bridesmaids," she told her again.

Adalyn smiled, a smile that didn't reach her eyes but appreciative of the offer. "Thank you. But I really want to stand back and watch my brother's happiness."

Sydney suspected there was more to it than that and she couldn't help but glance in the church where Julian was sitting near the front. It had been a happy reunion for the children and Julian when he arrived at Jake's cabin where they were all staying, but Adalyn and Julian themselves weren't having the same happy reunion.

"As long as you're here, happy and safe, your brother will always be happy," Sydney told her.

"I think it's you we have to thank for his happiness."

"How about we agree on family because that's what makes him happy."

"Sydney, you are amazing and I'm glad your minutes away from being a part of my family. I can't thank you enough for watching my children."

Sydney stopped the thank you speech that unfolded every time they were together and reassured her, squeezing her hands a little tighter. "That's what family is for."

Before the music started, Sydney stole a glance at her

soon-to-be husband standing at the front of the church, handsome as always in his tux, hands folded in front. He was chuckling at something Colt and Marc were saying but his eyes kept darting at the door until they caught hers spying. Then his handsome shoulders relaxed, the underlying nervousness only she would notice vanished, but his feet began to move and for a moment she thought he was going to leave his position and walk directly to her. No patience left for a man who had been patient all these years.

Kent touched her arm and Sydney cast a loving smile at her father. He looked so handsome in his black suit and purple tie. "Hi, Daddy."

"Are you ready Sydney?"

Sydney nodded and kissed her dads cheek, not wanting to break her connection with Jake but knowing only minutes from now they would be connected for life.

Her heart belonged to Jake Stow forever.

***

AS THE MUSIC began, Jake straightened his nervous self and watched as his beautiful bride made her way up the aisle. She stole his breath away. The lace dress trailing behind her clung, dipped and swayed with her every curve with each step she took. His body had never been more anxious about anything and he'd been through scary times, but nothing compared to waiting for Sydney to walk down the aisle. To him.

Catching her loving smile through the double wood doors that eased his racing heart knowing she was about to unite with him was nothing in comparison to when Kent gave her hands to Jake. Gave her to Jake to love, protect and cherish for the rest of their lives. He had never been more ready for anything in his life.

"Hey," she said and the word nearly caused him to scoop her into his arms and run away with her all to himself. He didn't...they had their whole lives together.

"Hey."

Her smile widened and shared that private moment back at her house when those two words were traveling down a road of lust.

Jake couldn't take his eyes off her as their vows were read and when he bent down to kiss her, he knew he was the luckiest man alive.

The church of only close family and friends cheered them right outside into the gorgeous summer day.

Jake went through the formalities of shaking hands with the gents and hugging the ladies, but he was anxious to have a moment with his bride.

When he was able to find a free moment to hug Haylee he whispered, "I love you kid."

"I love you too, Dad."

Jake's heart almost burst through his chest as those two tiny words he'd never heard before had the impact of a shaken bottle of wine. He had his wife on one side and his daughter on the other.

"Dad, you're squeezing hard," Haylee giggled and Jake loosened his grip, but didn't let go. She let him hold her for a second longer before patting his back and saying, "I love you and everything, but you're kind of embarrassing me in front of..."

Damien.

Jake let her go and she rubbed his arm supportively before shaking her head and walking to her friend. *Male friend. Damien.* He quickly overlooked the kid again. He was tall, skinny, scrawny, a little nerdy, just like Haylee, which relieved the protective side of Jake...a little.

"They're only thirteen," Sydney whispered to him, catching him analyzing the kid.

"We were only sixteen."

"That's three years away," she blew it off with a wave of the hand.

"You know what else happens in three years..." He was referring to the big license.

Sydney slapped his chest. "Alright, stand here and terrify the poor kid with your stare."

"Thank you."

Sydney laughed and when Adalyn stopped in front of them, she moved onto a conversation with her sisters to give them privacy. His wife was amazing. *Wife.* It sounded perfect.

"Come here." Jake pulled her into a hug. She was so tiny in comparison to her healthy self when he had left all those years ago. "How are you?" he asked, when he let her go.

She smiled but it was so forced it hurt Jake. She was suffering and she wouldn't talk about it, not with him, not with Joan and he was under the impression she was definitely not talking to Julian. Jake knew what it was like to keep things inside and he would be there for his sister when she was ready to talk.

"Good. The kids are happy. They have their Mom and Dad. Mia is none the wiser and will never have to know about Drake." She frowned. "Thanks to Mom."

Jake nodded his head understanding. "She saved Mia

from him."

Jake nodded. "That was the best thing Mom has ever done for any of us." They both looked over at Mia, who since her mother's return, smiled brighter like Lucy and Benji.

"Julian loves Mia like his own blood daughter and as far as Mia knows he's her Dad. He asked to keep it that way."

Jake liked Julian. He didn't know much about him, but his first impression was he was a man of his word and a man who loved family. He hoped Adalyn and Julian would work through the difficulties that lie ahead.

"You should get back to your wife." Wife, yeah he sure did like the sound of that.

Jake hugged Adalyn again and kissed her head before interrupting Sydney, Joan and her new friend, Chester.

Joan grabbed Jake's side and patted his chest. "Doesn't he just clean up so handsome?" Jake, Joan and Adalyn had sat down and had a conversation that bettered all their relationships and even though it wasn't said, he knew Joan hadn't been in the dark about Haylee either, even if she wouldn't come right out and say it.

Joan moved on to laugh and giggle with her date, Chester. *Chester.* He seemed like a nice guy, but if he hurt Joan that man would have to deal with Jake.

"Jake?" Sydney said, as just the two of them climbed in the horse drawn carriage.

"Yes my wife."

She laughed. "You're being cheesy."

"I can't get enough of you, my wife." She laughed again. "You were saying?"

Her bottom lip caught between her teeth and with the flicker of tantalizing in her eyes, he knew that her mind was going down a naughty road. "Now that we're married there's something I've been wanting to do."

Jake kissed the side of her head, ready to do everything with his wife. "Anything for you."

That flicker lit and she lowered her voice in a seductive bedroom tone he didn't know she possessed. "I want to know all the surprises you hide in your closet."

It was his turn to laugh at her forwardness. He liked this new side of her, the provocative side of Sydney.

"I guess after our honeymoon we can make a quick stop there before we head home." *Home to her house, home to their house.* He never wanted to spend another night away from Sydney.

"I kind of always wanted to make love in your bed too."

He laughed again, her boldness was turning his body on fire and they were supposed to be heading to the reception, not the honeymoon suite. "I think we can arrange that."

"Also in your office."

Another rumble of laughter. The effort she'd put into their love making locations thrilled him into wanting to skip the reception and head straight to the honeymoon suite. He had to admit, making love with Sydney in his office had gone through his head a couple of times. It was hard not to, when they used to eat most their lunches together in that small area.

"Anywhere else?"

She nodded. "The shower in Joan's boat."

Here he had believed his wife didn't enjoy risqué plays of words...he was learning something new about her every day. "That was a most recent one of mine as well."

LAKESHORE LOVE

"Do you think they would leave us with the boat and take the hotel?"

"I think it's worth a try. But, Wifey, we have to stop talking about this when I can't have you for the next four hours during the reception."

She smiled that provocative smile and he felt her hands touch his leg. He jumped at the hot contact and she laughed.

"Your bike is right over there. It will take us anywhere."

Jake called up to the driver to head toward his bike before he caught her mouth with his.

"Wifey, you are full of surprises," he said against her lips.

"Wait until you see what's in my closet."

Jake laughed at her boldness and kissed his wife again.

His wife. As cheesy as she thought the title was it was what he'd always wanted, Sydney as his wife, and he was planning on spending the rest of his life loving her like she deserved.

The End

SHANNYN LEAH

Next in the Series:
Lakeshore Candy
The McAdams Sisters
Book Three, Abby McAdams
By The Lake Series
Shannyn Leah

LAKESHORE LOVE

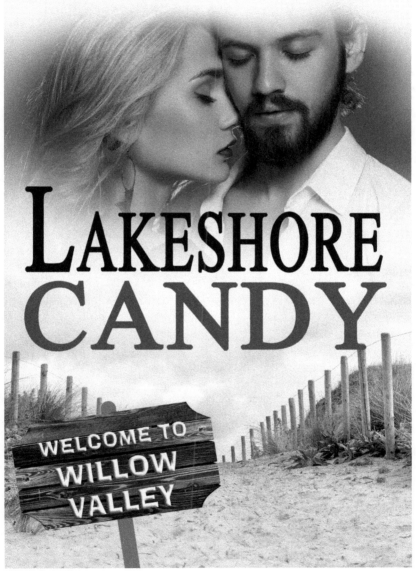

SHANNYN LEAH

By The Lake Series

The McAdams Sisters:
Lakeshore Secrets (Book One)
Lakeshore Legend (Book Two)
Lakeshore Love (Book Three)
Lakeshore Candy (Book Four)
Lakeshore Lyrics (Book Five)

The Caliendo Series:
Sunset Thunder (Book One)
Sunset Rivalry (Book Two)
Sunset Sail (Book Three)
Sunset Flare (Book Four)
Sunset Shelter (Book Five)

SHANNYN LEAH

Contemporary romance author Shannyn Leah loves olives, lip gloss and reading (and writing) romance novels. Her love of words started at an early age and soon grew until, during her teenage years, she'd started writing her own novels. When her mom pushed to finally publish some of the stories, she quickly amassed two complete romance series (By The Lake and Caliendo Resort series) and, in 2016, released her first Fantasy Romance entitled The Gatekeepers (Part One of the Winters Rising series).

When she's not writing contemporary romance books into the early hours of the morning, Shannyn can be found antiquing with her two favorite people, her momma and sister, in their picturesque London, Ontario hometown.

Shannyn would love to get to know her readers as you get to know her (just don't send her any carrots!)Join her mailing list to be notified when new books are released, exclusive excerpts and prizes: www.shannynleah.com/contact.php

Connect with Her

Visit her webpage for extras:
www.shannynleah.com

Please join Shannyn Leah on her facebook page if you enjoy her books here:
www.facebook.com/pages/Shannyn-Leah/418700801622719

If you wish to get in contact with Shannyn, please email her at Shannynleah@gmail.com